F CABOT, M.   EXT
Cabot, Meg
No words : a novel

Praise for Meg Cabot

"There is a school of thought that says reading should be entertaining, and this is exactly what Meg Cabot produces for us: fun."

—Molly Jong-Fast, *Publishers Weekly*

"Through her books and heroines, Cabot offered escapism and empowerment right when I needed it most."

—CNN

"Meg Cabot is best known for her books for younger readers, but her adult fiction is a total delight."

—PopSugar

"Meg Cabot is a fabulous author."

—*USA Today*

"I'd read a cereal box if it was written by Meg Cabot."

—Julia Quinn, author of the Bridgerton series

No Words

Also by Meg Cabot

Little Bridge Island series
The Princess Diaries series
The Mediator series
The Boy series
Heather Wells series
Insatiable series
Ransom My Heart (with Mia Thermopolis)
Queen of Babble series
She Went All the Way
The 1-800-Where-R-You series
All-American Girl series
Nicola and the Viscount
Victoria and the Rogue
Jinx
Pants on Fire
How to Be Popular
Avalon High series
Airhead series
Abandon series
Allie Finkle's Rules for Girls series
From the Notebooks of a Middle School Princess series

MEG CABOT

No Words

A Novel

WILLIAM MORROW
wm *An Imprint of* HarperCollins*Publishers*

P.S.™ is a trademark of HarperCollins Publishers.

HarperCollins books may be purchased for educational, business, or sales promotional use. For information, please email the Special Markets Department at SPsales@harpercollins.com.

FIRST EDITION

Designed by Diahann Sturge

Beach scene illustration © Victor_Vision/Shutterstock, Inc.
Computer illustration © Rauf Aliyev/Shutterstock, Inc.
Stack of books illustration © Robert Kneschke/Shutterstock, Inc.

Library of Congress Cataloging-in-Publication Data has been applied for.

ISBN 978-0-06-289009-2
ISBN 978-0-06-308225-0 (hardcover library edition)

21 22 23 24 25 LSC 10 9 8 7 6 5 4 3 2 1

This novel is dedicated to book lovers everywhere

CONTENT WARNING

Please be aware that although this book is a romantic comedy, it does contain depictions of and discussions about sexual harassment, past (off the page) parental death and depression, a brief disappearance at sea, and both threatened and on-the-page violence (in a book characters are reading within this book).

Little Bridge Book Festival
"Building Bridges Between Authors and Readers"
Norman J. Tifton Public Library
Little Bridge Island, FL

Dear Ms. Wright,

Greetings from beautiful Little Bridge Island, Florida!

My name is Molly Hartwell and I'm the children's librarian at the Norman J. Tifton Public Library. As a longtime fan of your middle-grade series, Kitty Katz, Kitten Sitter, I'm writing to invite you to our library's first-ever book festival. I think you would bring in an enormous and well-deserved children's audience.

Although this is our library's first book festival, the planning for this three-day event—starting next year on Friday, January 3, and concluding the afternoon of Sunday, January 5—has been in the works for some time. This past year we have received our nonprofit status, as well as tremendous financial support from donors who cherish literature like yours.

That's how we're able to offer you first-class airfare to Little Bridge Island, a luxury suite at the Lazy Parrot Inn, and a $10,000 stipend in exchange for you being a panelist. We'd love for you to do a signing, as well!

Please let me know your thoughts. I'd be delighted to answer any questions you may have, and encourage you to visit our website for details about the festival, as well.

It would mean so much to me personally, Ms. Wright, if you would consider attending Little Bridge's first-ever book festival. I know we're a small town and don't necessarily have the kind of amenities that a lot of the larger festivals you attend might, but we plan to make up for that with wonderful weather and good, old-fashioned charm!

Best,
Molly Hartwell
Children's Librarian
Norman J. Tifton Public Library
Molly.Hartwell@lbilibrary.org

CHAPTER ONE

Jo Wright: I just got offered 10 grand to speak and sign at a book festival on Little Bridge Island. Should I go?

Rosie Tate: Are you in a financial position right now where you can afford to turn down $10,000?

Jo Wright: You're my agent, you tell me. When's my next check coming?

Rosie Tate: Not until you hand in *Kitty Katz #27*.

Jo Wright: I'd hand in *Kitty Katz #27* if I could think of something new for Kitty to do. But she's already done it all.

Rosie Tate: Kitty hasn't done it all. She hasn't gone to space.

Jo Wright: How is a teenaged cat going to get to space?

Rosie Tate: You're the writer. Make something up.

Jo Wright: I'm having a little difficulty in that area at the moment.

Rosie Tate: I've noticed. You've missed your extended-extended deadline. Again.

Jo Wright: So basically you're saying I better accept this gig or I'll be broke.

Rosie Tate: How can you be broke? Kitty has made millions of dollars over the past seven years, and I just sent you a royalty check.

Jo Wright: I know, but I had to buy Justin out for his half of the apartment when he decided to move to LA to pursue his dream of being a screenwriter. By which I mean, play video games all day on the West Coast instead of in my living room.

Rosie Tate: I'm glad you kicked the mooch out.

Jo Wright: Whatever. At least I got the apartment. And I still have plenty of savings. But they're all in retirement accounts I can't touch until I'm 59½. That's 27 years from now. So I really need some cash if I'm going to get my dad moved someplace warm. He can't spend another winter here in NY. He broke his wrist twice on the ice last year. And since he isn't old enough yet to qualify for Medicaid and has the worst insurance, I had to pay cash both times for his treatment!

Rosie Tate: Then I think you'd better say yes to the book festival.

Jo Wright: I know, right? But I can't accept the gig, because this book festival is on Little Bridge Island.

Rosie Tate: What's wrong with Little Bridge Island? I've heard it's lovely. One of my other authors went there and said the tropical breeze was so inspiring, she wrote two whole chapters a day the entire time she was there.

Jo Wright: Well, good for her. But don't you know who lives on Little Bridge Island?

Rosie Tate: No, should I?

Jo Wright: *1 Attachment*

Famous Author Buys Private Island in Florida Keys

One of the Florida Keys' most notable—and expensive—estates has finally sold for a cool $6,000,000. Located just offshore Little Bridge, this unique private island features an opulent eight-bedroom, nine-bath mansion with its own boat dock, white sand beach, and pool, and is now the home of bestselling author William Price. Price, known as much for his reclusiveness as for his internationally bestselling novels of tragic love and loss, had been home-shopping in the area for some time before snapping up the island.

All seven of Price's novels have been adapted into films grossing into the hundreds of millions. The author was not available for comment.

Rosie Tate: Oh, HIM. Jo, that was ages ago. No one even remembers it.

Jo Wright: It was at Novel Con last year. Everyone in the publishing industry remembers it.

Rosie Tate: Well, he's an ass. But of course you should go. You probably won't even see him.

Jo Wright: Have you ever even been to a book festival? OF COURSE I'm going to see him. I'll probably have to sit right next to him on some dumb panel.

Rosie Tate: I don't see how. You write delightful little stories for children about a teenaged cat who has exciting adventures while babysitting adorable kittens. He writes horrible books about heartbroken women who fall in love with arrogant dullards who then thankfully die.

Jo Wright: You know at these book festivals they make all the authors go to dinner and cocktail parties with the donors, right? So I'm sure I'll see him at one of those.

Rosie Tate: Oh. Well, just say you aren't feeling well and sit on your hotel balcony and write in the lovely tropical breeze! Only come out to give your speech, do your signing, and collect your check.

Jo Wright: No. I don't want to risk it. Can you just contact the organizers before I say yes and see if he's going to be there?

Rosie Tate: Of course. You have my word: YOU WILL NEVER SEE WILL PRICE AGAIN.

SIX MONTHS LATER

From Will Price, the #1 internationally bestselling author of *When the Heart Dies* and *The Betrayal*, comes a timeless, deeply personal tale of love and loss:

The Moment

It only took a moment for Johnny Kane to realize that Melanie West was the most beautiful woman he had ever seen—and also that he could never have her.

Because in the next moment, Johnny betrayed her.

Now he has to make a choice: admit the wrong he's committed, and live with the sorrow of knowing she could never be his . . . or rewrite both their destinies, and change that moment forever.

Praise for *The Moment*

"An instant classic." —*USA Today*

"At once brilliantly gripping and tragically complex, *The Moment* is Will Price's most important— and intimate—work yet." —*Kirkus Reviews*

"Utterly compelling and emotionally
intense." —*People* magazine

"In this, his seventh novel, Will Price has
written a profoundly affecting work of stunning
moral complexity." —*Publishers Weekly*

"Perfect." —Reese Witherspoon

FRIDAY, JANUARY 3

CHAPTER TWO

E xcuse me."

I lifted my sleep mask to see three teenaged girls standing in the aisle beside my seat. "Yes?"

"Sorry to wake you," said the girl with the lip ring and nearly waist-length braids. "But aren't you Jo Wright?"

I wondered how she knew. Especially since I'd scraped my hair into a ponytail—hair that, in my author photo, was loose, sexily mussed, and honey blond.

But that photo had been taken before Will Price had destroyed my life, and I'd adopted my current regimen of heavy black eyeliner, all black clothes, and matching black hair dye.

"Uh." I lifted the glass from the end of my seat rest. "Yes. Why?"

"I told you it was her, you guys." The girl exchanged excited looks with her companions before turning back toward me. "You're going to the book festival on Little Bridge Island, Florida, this weekend, aren't you? I saw your name on the website."

"Oh." I was disappointed to note that my glass contained

mostly only melted ice. "Yes, I'll be doing a couple panels and signings there."

I glimpsed a flight attendant at the end of the aisle observing my interaction with the girls with amusement. I looked meaningfully down at the melted ice in my otherwise empty glass.

The flight attendant nodded and slipped into the galley as one of the other girls—this one in exaggeratedly large horn-rimmed glasses—squealed, "I can't believe it! I can't believe it's *Jo Wright*! I used to love your books!"

"Oh," I said again.

I've always wondered how I'm supposed to respond to someone who says that they "used to" enjoy my books. Truthfully, it kind of hurt a little to be told by someone that they "used to" enjoy my work. It was nice that they *used to*, but painful to hear that they no longer did.

Was this how the cast of *Friends* felt every time someone came up to them and told them how much they "used to" enjoy their show? That had to suck.

Although not as much as it sucked to be me, because *Friends* earns a lot more in residuals than the animated *Kitty Katz* television series based on my books ever did.

"Thanks," I settled for saying, and was relieved when the flight attendant slipped me a brand-new glass of vodka and orange juice, and took away the empty one. "It's great to meet you. See you when we land!"

Then I took a long sip of my drink—number two, and just as delicious as number one!—and attempted to slide the eye mask back over my face to continue my nap.

"We're going, too," said the third girl, this one wearing a

leather vest with fringe that reached almost to her knees. "We're flying all the way from Manitoba just to be at the festival!"

I slid the eye mask all the way back up. Things were getting interesting.

"Wow," I said. These girls' parents had to be loaded. Flights from Canada to the Florida Keys in January weren't cheap. My own, from New York City, had set the festival back almost two thousand dollars. I'd seen the amount on my ticket. "Manitoba. That's impressive."

"You know, the Kitty Katz series completely saved my life in grade six," the girl in the glasses said. "Obviously I know your characters are only cats, but they were *so much more* than cats to me."

"Lauren loves cats," the girl with the braids assured me.

It was at this point that I noticed that the guy sitting in the window seat next to me had paused the movie he'd been watching on his phone and was now listening to our exchange. Not to sound like a snob, but he was a bit scruffy-looking for first class—cargo shorts, a Batman T-shirt (*Dark Knight*, not *Lego*, which in my opinion is the best Batman movie, but there's no accounting for taste), with pale feet shod in flip-flops, along with a goatee.

Goatees are not my favorite, but my friend Bernadette says I've got to stop judging men who wear them just because my ex Justin did and he turned out to be a loser.

And of course, we *were* on a flight to the Florida Keys. My seatmate's scruffiness could be forgiven. Everyone goes to the Florida Keys for pleasure, not business.

Everyone except for me.

"Jasmine's right," Lauren gushed. "I totally love cats. And reading. The Kitty Katz series was so inspiring to me that I decided I wanted to become a writer myself!"

I raised my eyebrows. "Really? That's great."

"Thanks! In fact, I'm writing my own book."

"She totally is!" Jasmine nodded emphatically enough to send her braids swinging.

"Great," I said, taking another sip of my drink. My *free* drink!

"Girls." The flight attendant approached. "We're going to be making our descent into Little Bridge in a few minutes, so I'm sorry, but I need you to return to your seats."

"Awwww!" The girls were not happy, especially Lauren. "I was going to ask for a selfie."

"Well, you can get one with me at the book festival," I said. "Wouldn't that be better than one here on the plane? The lighting here is not exactly optimal."

"I guess." Lauren continued to look crushed—or about as crushed as a twelve-year-old with perfectly clear skin and rich parents could.

But if Kitty Katz had been her favorite series way back in grade six, Lauren had to be older than twelve. It was so hard to tell how old girls were these days. With all the makeup tutorials out there on YouTube, showing them how to expertly blend bronzer into those hard-to-reach crevices, most of them looked old enough to be in college, or even graduate school.

I felt a prickle of guilt over Lauren's disappointment. She

may only have "used to" like my books, but at least she'd liked them once, and she'd recognized me without my festival badge, the one I'd been urged repeatedly to wear in every communication from the library staff, so that I "could be identified as soon as possible" by the festival's volunteers, whom I'd been told would be waiting for me at baggage claim.

"We can do a selfie now if you really want," I said, in spite of all the glares I was getting from my fellow first-class passengers. They didn't like having their sacred space invaded by teenagers from coach.

All of them except Dark Knight, my seatmate. He, I noted, was grinning.

"If you make it quick," I added, for the sake of the unhappy travelers around me.

Lauren gasped with delight and quickly hunched down beside my seat. "Say Kitty Katz," she cried, holding her phone high above both our heads.

"Kitty Katz." I smiled up at her phone. She'd decorated the case with stickers of a Korean boy band. These girls really were adorable.

CLICK.

"All right, girls," the flight attendant said, clapping his hands. "That's *enough*. It's time to go back to—"

But the girls weren't ready to go anywhere.

"Are you doing a panel with Will Price?" Jasmine asked.

I almost choked on the refreshing mouthful of screwdriver I'd just taken. "I'm sorry, *what?*"

"Will Price," Jasmine said. "You know, Will Price, who

wrote *When the Heart Dies?* He's going to be at the festival, too."

"Um, no." I shook my head with enough force to cause the end of my ponytail to swat Dark Knight in the shoulder. "Sorry," I said to him, because of my hair.

"No problem." Dark Knight was still smiling, watching my exchange with the girls like it was a lot more entertaining than his movie.

To the girls, I said, "No. I mean, no, I'm not doing a panel with Will Price because Will writes adult novels and I write children's novels. And also, Will isn't coming to the festival."

Jasmine blinked at me with her perfectly made-up eyes. "Yes, he is."

"No, he's not." I smiled at her to show that I meant her no ill will. I don't usually argue with children—I'm actually rarely around them, except for my super's daughter, Gabriella, who takes care of my cat, Miss Kitty, for me when I'm away. But I had been assured multiple times by my agent on this point, and Rosie was never wrong. "Will Price isn't attending this festival. I know he owns a house on Little Bridge Island, but he's in Croatia right now, on the set of the film of his latest book."

His latest piece of sentimental garbage was what I wanted to say, but I didn't, because it's rude to bad-mouth a fellow writer's work (out loud), something Will Price had evidently never been taught, since he'd felt free to bad-mouth my work to one of the most highly circulating newspapers in the world.

"No." Jasmine was holding firm. "Will does have a house

on Little Bridge. Well, technically, a *mansion* on a *private island* off the coast of Little Bridge. And he *was* in Croatia filming the movie version of his latest book, *The Moment*—"

"Oh my God." The girl in the vest looked like she was about to have an out-of-body experience right there on the plane. "You guys. *The Moment* is my favorite Will Price book of all time. When Johnny finally tells Mel the truth—that he's loved her from the moment he first saw her—and that the reason they can never be together is because he's the one who—"

Lauren punched her friend in the arm. "Cassidy, stop. God, spoiler alert! Some of these people may not have read it yet!"

Most of the people in the first-class cabin looked as if they had no interest in reading anything by Will Price. Most of them looked much more interested in their alcoholic beverages, and in the girls returning to their seats so that they could finish those drinks in peace before we began preparations for landing and the flight attendant took them away.

"But I guess Will is back, or, like, on his way back," Jasmine went on, "because he posted to his fans this morning that he wouldn't miss the island's first book festival for *anything.*"

What?

I closed my eyes. No. This was *not* happening.

Except that it was.

Great. Freaking fantastic. So Will Price was going to be at this book festival. Despite Rosie's promise, I was going to have to see him—not only see him, but probably be in a room with him, and even have to talk to him.

Kill me. Please kill me now.

"I. Am. So. Excited!" Cassidy's out-of-body experience was turning into divine ecstasy along the lines of Saint Teresa's. "Now I can get my copy of *The Moment* signed! And maybe ask Will to sign my chest. You know he's hetero, right? And single."

"Ugh, gross, Cassidy." Lauren looked offended on behalf of her friend. "He's, like, old."

Cassidy grinned. "Not too old for me."

Great. How super for her.

I, however, was going to drown myself. As soon as the plane landed, I was going to walk out of the airport and fill my pockets with stones and then wade into the ocean and drown myself like Virginia Woolf.

A stern male voice rang out, startling all of us and causing me to fling open my eyes.

"Okay, girls. That is *it*." The flight attendant had had enough.

Ignoring the girls' cries of protest, he shooed them back to their seats, then returned and firmly closed the curtain separating the first-class cabin from coach.

"I'm so sorry about that, Miss Wright," he said to me, sounding like he meant it.

"Oh, please. It's fine." I gave him an It-happens-all-the-time smile and wave.

But of course, it didn't happen all the time. It *used to* happen all the time, but not anymore. Not since so many readers of Kitty Katz, Kitten Sitter—which at one time had been the number one bestselling book series for tweens, an animated television series (on cable), and even a feature film (straight to streaming and DVD)—had grown up and started flocking to Will Price's stupid, depressing books and even stupider, more depressing movies.

I downed the rest of my drink then lowered my eye mask, leaning back against my headrest. What was I worrying about, anyway? I wasn't going to have to see Will Price. Rosie was right: All I had to do was give my speech, do my signing, maybe take a dip or two in the hotel pool—hey, it was January and below freezing in New York; it was seventy-five and sunny on Little Bridge Island—collect my ten thousand dollars, and go home.

And maybe . . . just maybe . . . I might even try out this famous Little Bridge tropical breeze I'd heard so much about, and see if it gave me the inspiration to write *Kitty Katz #27*.

Everything was going to be fine. Just fine. All I needed to do was have a pawsitive attitude. That's what Kitty Katz would do. With the right attitude, Kitty always says, everything will be purr-fect!

Right?

CHAPTER THREE

Wrong.

Little Bridge Island was so small that it didn't have a proper airport, with Jetways that stretched from the arrivals terminal to meet incoming planes so that passengers could disembark.

Instead, we were supposed to climb down a steep flight of metal stairs that airport personnel had shoved up against the door, then walk out onto an active runway.

This would have been charming and even fun, like something from *Kitty Katz #12, Kitty Goes Hawaiian*, when Kitty and her friends went to Meowuai, if I'd checked a bag.

But after years and years of work-related travel, I'd learned never to check a bag, because it so often got lost right before a super-important Kitty-related event. I'd once been forced to speak before a thousand Barnes & Noble booksellers in jeans and a Stay Puft Marshmallow Man T-shirt because that's what I'd been wearing on the plane and my bag was nowhere to be found.

So I always packed everything I needed into a carry-on,

and as a consequence, my carry-on weighed a ton. How was I going to lug it down a rickety, narrow flight of metal steps while wearing stacked heels (because of course I had on my most fashionable pair of winter boots, as it had been snowing when I'd left New York)?

Then, as I stood at the top of the stairs, squinting in the sudden blast of heat and bright sunlight, cursing my impulse to bring a thousand promotional bookmarks for the next installment in the Kitty Katz series (which I hadn't even written yet, so the bookmarks simply said *Don't Fur-get: KK#27, Coming Soon!*), a miracle happened.

"Here, let me help you with that."

Dark Knight tugged my suitcase from my hand.

"Oh, no!" I was shocked. "You don't—"

But before I could stop him, Dark Knight was moving quickly down the steps with my suitcase dangling from one hand as lightly as if it contained only catnip.

"Thank you so much." I hurried down the stairs to join him on the tarmac, where painted yellow lines directed us toward the tiny arrivals terminal. "You really didn't have to do that."

"Well, it's not every day I get to meet a celebrity."

"I'm not a celebrity." Blushing, I took the suitcase from him, yanking on the handle to extend it so I could move it from the path of the passengers disembarking behind us. "I'm just—"

"I know." He jerked what appeared to be a fishing pole and also the case for a ukulele from a luggage cart onto which airport personnel had begun unloading bags that had been gate-checked. "You're just Jo Wright, author of the Kitty Katz series, and you're here for the Little Bridge Book Festival."

"Yes." I knew he'd been eavesdropping. Well, it had worked out well for me. I nodded at the pole in his hand. "And you're here for a little fishing?"

"Among other things. I'm Garrett, by the way."

"Hi, Garrett."

Garrett and I fell into step with the other passengers along the pathway leading to the arrivals terminal, me wheeling my suitcase behind me. Everywhere I looked, I saw palm trees, and even—yes, there it was, past the private jets parked at the far end of the tarmac—the ocean, smooth and blue and stretching as far as I could see.

I didn't feel like walking into it anymore, though, Virginia Woolf style. Things were starting to look up. Not because of Garrett—although he was pretty easy on the eyes, despite the goatee and the flip-flops.

No. It was because after the cold, stale air of the plane—not to mention the icy winds of Manhattan—the heat and humidity of Little Bridge was a welcome change. I could feel my hair beginning to rise up at the roots in delighted surprise. This was it: the tropical breeze Rosie had mentioned, the one that had inspired that author of hers to write two whole chapters in a day.

And even though the sun was glaring and I was starting to sweat already beneath my leather jacket, that tropical breeze caressing my face, and the scent of seaweed and brine coming from the ocean felt almost . . .

Well, as if I were coming home.

Which was ridiculous, of course. I'm a born-and-bred New Yorker, used to the darkened bowels of the subway and the frigid wind whistling between the skyscrapers. The tropics and I were *not* friends.

As if he were reading my mind, Garrett asked, "First time?"

I had to raise my voice to be heard over the sound of all the airplane propellers that were spinning around us.

"In Little Bridge? Yes. But I've been to Florida before. I've been coming down here a lot recently, looking at senior living communities."

Garrett raised his eyebrows. "Little soon for that, don't you think?"

I laughed. "For my dad. He hasn't been handling winters back home too well lately. I've got to find him a new place before—"

My voice died in my throat. Not because I was envisioning my father's imminent passing, but because we'd arrived at the doorway to the arrivals terminal, just inside of which stood a small, dark-haired woman holding up a whiteboard with my name on it.

Except mine wasn't the only name on it.

I'd been expecting to see the name Bernadette Zhang, a fellow author and friend of mine who'd texted long ago that she'd also been invited to the festival. We'd promised to spend every free moment we had in Little Bridge together, drinking, taking in the sun, and having highly un-literary discussions about other authors we both disliked.

But instead I saw an entirely different name below mine.

WILL PRICE

No. It couldn't be.

"Hey," Garrett said, because I was standing frozen in front of him, blocking the entrance to the terminal. "Everything okay?"

"Yeah." I shook myself. "Sure. Sorry. I'm fine."

"You don't look fine."

"Yeah, I know." I was suddenly way, way too hot in my leather jacket. "I'm probably going to have to kill someone, is all."

Garrett glanced in the direction I was staring, but of course didn't see what I was seeing. "Anyone in particular?"

I shook my head. "Not in the immediate vicinity."

"Well, that's a relief." He laughed.

I wasn't feeling so amused, though. Rosie had promised—*promised*—me that Will Price wasn't going to be at the festival. Sworn on her soul that she'd checked and *double-checked* with the festival staff.

I'd even scoured the website myself before writing to commit to the event. But there'd been nothing: no sign of Will Price anywhere on the Little Bridge Island Book Festival page. Zilch.

So what had happened?

Behind me, I heard Garrett murmur, "Um, well, I checked a bag, so, uh, I better go see if I can find it. I'll see you later?"

"Yeah," I murmured back. "Sure. See you later."

I knew I was being rude—the guy had carried my suitcase for me, after all, and been sweet about Lauren and her friends and my ponytail swatting him—but I had bigger problems to worry about. What was I going to do about having to share a car with Will Price? Was I actually going to have to *talk* to him? What was I going to say?

Honestly, this was really just too much to ask. It was one thing to have to be at a festival with him. But *ride in a car with him*? No.

Should I just turn around? Maybe I could find the departures terminal and buy a ticket back to New York.

But then I'd lose my ten grand, and I really needed that money. Who knew when Dad was going to fall down again and I was going to get saddled with another gigantic hospital bill?

Oh, whiskers, as Kitty would say. I was just going to have to suck it up.

Once again deeply regretting many of my life decisions, especially the one to come to Little Bridge, I wheeled my suitcase toward the woman with the whiteboard. I had to dart and weave between dozens of tourists, all wearing winter coats like me, and all crowded into the tiny arrivals terminal, either trying to rent a car from the single car rental agency or grab their bags from the single loudly cranking baggage carousel.

"Hi." I'd reached the woman holding up the whiteboard. I pointed to my name. "That's me."

"Oh, Ms. Wright!" The woman's face broke into a rapturous smile. "Welcome to Little Bridge! I'm Molly Hartwell, the children's librarian. Thank you so much for coming."

The woman's greeting was so charming that I almost forgot my hatred of Will Price (almost, but not quite).

"Hi. Please call me Jo. Thanks for having me. It's really great to be here. I hope you weren't waiting for me long."

"Oh, no," Molly replied. "Not at all."

But I couldn't help noticing that she was shifting her weight from foot to foot, and also that she was clearly pregnant. To my untrained eye (except for many hours of watching *Call the Midwife*), she looked ready to pop.

"I'll be taking you to your hotel." Molly's tone was as bright as her dark eyes. "Do you have any other bags to pick up from baggage claim?"

"No. Everything I need, I have right here." I nodded proudly down at my carry-on. If they gave prizes to authors for packing instead of literary content, I would definitely have won them all.

"Oh." Molly looked slightly disappointed, and continued to shift her weight from one foot to another. "I hope you don't mind, but there are two other authors arriving any minute that I thought we could pick up at the same time. It would keep me from having to make three trips back and forth to the hotel. And you know, we are trying to be eco-conscious here on Little Bridge. The authors should be coming through those doors any second—"

Because of my expert packing, I'd been in this situation before. Enough times that I reached out, took the whiteboard from Molly's hands, and said, in response to her surprised expression, "No problem. I'll wait for them. I know you've been here awhile and could probably use a bathroom break."

Molly's cheeks went red. "Oh, no, Ms. Wright! I'm fine! I don't want you to—"

"It's Jo. And I'm fine with this. Will and I go way back. I'll take good care of him while you're gone."

That's what I said out loud. Inside in my head, I was saying, *Will and I go way back, and if he shows up while you're gone, I'm going to murder him, and when you return from the bathroom, all that will be left of him is a puddle of his own blood, but no one will be able to prove I'm his killer, because I will have so skillfully disposed of his body and gotten rid of all the evidence.*

But of course I wouldn't actually do that, because I'm a Wright: I'd inherited from my very British father's side of the family an almost pathological fear of confrontation. It was because of this fear of confrontation that my father had saved no money for his retirement, and had instead given everything he had to his best friends and fellow bandmates every time they needed to be bailed out of a jam (which was frequently). His generosity was completely admirable, except that now he needed me—or, more accurately, Kitty Katz, to support him (although, again to his credit, he'd never asked me to do so. He'd have sooner withered away from starvation than ask anyone for help).

Always at odds with this, however, was what I'd inherited from my mother's very Italian side of the family: a hot-blooded thirst for revenge.

Molly's face crumpled with grateful relief. "Oh, *thank you.* If you really don't mind—I've been dying to go. The baby seems to be sitting right on my bladder. I'll only be a minute—"

"Take your time." I hoisted up the whiteboard so that

anyone coming through the doors from the tarmac would be sure to see it.

At least, that's what I did until Molly turned her back and waddled off in the direction of the ladies' room. Then I lowered the sign and wondered what would happen if I spat on Will's name and wiped it away with my sleeve.

But no. I couldn't do that. I'd only get Molly in trouble, and she seemed like a nice person. She was the one who'd written me the kind letter, offering me the ten grand and gushing over her love of Kitty Katz. I would never do something like that to a fan.

Although it would certainly serve Will Price right if someone, *anyone* out there showed him that he wasn't as universally beloved as he thought he was, and that books about teenaged cats were *just as* important (to some people) as books about whatever his books were about, which I still didn't actually know, because I'd never read one—at least not all the way through. Of course I'd glanced through one or two that I'd happened to spot in airport bookstores during layovers. I'd read enough to see that his prose was accessible. He wasn't *talentless*.

But those endings! My God.

Will insisted in interviews—not that I'd read any of them. Well, all right, I might have skimmed one or two—that his books were tragic love stories. But not romance novels. Oh, no. Definitely not that! Because he was a man, and most male authors of adult books would slit their own throats before admitting they'd written a romance or women's fiction or even a family drama. Everything they wrote, many of them insisted, was *literary fiction* (unless of course it was sci-fi, horror, or mystery).

So nauseating.

I'd tried to watch *When the Heart Dies* once when I'd been channel-surfing and it had turned up on HBO, but it had been so depressing—the hero died at the end (all of Will's heroes in all of Will's books died at the end)—that I'd had to switch to a *Great British Bake Off* marathon to cheer myself up.

Why did Will Price need a ride from the airport anyway? He lived on Little Bridge. Where was he even coming from? Were Lauren and her friends right? Had he really left the set of his latest movie to come to this book festival? Was he so controlling that he couldn't allow a book festival in his own town to take place without him being there?

And if so, why couldn't he take an Uber or a taxi or a limo or whatever entirely too highly paid authors like himself rode around in? Why did he need one of the book festival volunteers to drive him in the author bus or van (which, in my experience, was undoubtedly what would be transporting us)? Why couldn't he—

BOOM.

The automatic doors to the tarmac parted and there he was, like some kind of god, the sun casting a golden halo all around him. Will Price, in the flesh.

BAM! My heart ricocheted off the back of my ribs.

Really? The mere sight of him caused my heart to skip a beat? Why? WHY? I didn't even like him. He was just a man, a stupid man who wrote even stupider books.

The only reason my heart did the dumb *BAM* thing was because this was the first time I was seeing him (in person, as opposed to the million photos of him that I could not seem to escape, that appeared all over social media and the copies of *People* my dentist kept scattered around her office and in-flight magazines and even, unfortunately, *Library Journal*, since less discerning librarians were bonkers for him, too) since The Incident.

Unfortunately, he looked just as good now as he had then.

It was easy to spot him in the crowd, not only because of the golden light that seemed to encircle him, but because of the way the crowd appeared to part for him, too, as if everyone sensed they were in the presence of greatness. This might have been because Will stood about a head taller than most of the other passengers, and that wasn't even counting his mass of thick, curly, dark hair, which was looking more unruly than usual. Wherever he'd been, he had apparently not had easy access to a barber, much less a razor, since he was sprouting four or five days' growth of dark facial hair.

He was peering down at his cell-phone screen as he walked, a large backpack slung over one of his ridiculously broad shoulders. He did not, I had to admit, look like either a multimillionaire or a backstabbing bestselling author, in his gray T-shirt, jeans, and Timberlands.

What he looked like was a god, and every woman—and even some of the men, probably—in that terminal knew it.

That was the thing about Will Price, though: those good looks of his were deceptive. They'd managed to fool many, many people into thinking he was a sweet guy—a guy like the heroes he wrote about in his books, who lived only to adore and worship women . . . until he killed them off in some tragic freak accident, leaving the heroine brokenhearted but "stronger for having known what real love was."

Barf.

And now Will's good looks were fooling Lauren and her friends. I could see the girls clustered around the single baggage carousel with all the other passengers, waiting for their luggage to arrive.

But the second Will walked by, Lauren's head popped up from her phone's screen as if she had some kind of hot-male-celebrity-author radar. I saw her eyes widen, then her thin shoulder blades raise as she sucked in her breath.

"*Will!*"

The next thing I knew, all three girls were swarming him, Cassidy—the one who wanted her chest signed—shrieking the loudest of all.

"Will, Will," she cried. "Oh, Will, I'm your biggest fan! Can I get a selfie with you?"

"Uh." Will looked up from his phone screen. Now he stood—those dark eyes shaded by lashes that were wasted on a man—looking confused and startled, as the teens jumped around him. "Um—"

"We're here for the book festival," Lauren declared. "We're going to go to every single one of your events!"

Will seemed about as thrilled as if she'd just informed him that she was an oral surgeon about to give him a dental bone graft.

"Oh," he said. "That's . . . brilliant."

And of course he said *brilliant* instead of *great*. Because, as if Will weren't hot enough looks-wise, he was also from some small, picturesque village in England somewhere, and had an accent I'd heard more than a few women (and men) swoon over as "the sexiest author voice ever."

"Such a shame," someone in publishing had once lamented to me, "that Will Price doesn't narrate his own audiobooks! We've asked and asked him, but he won't do it. He says he hates the sound of his own voice. Can you imagine? He's so modest!"

No one had ever asked *me* to narrate my own audiobooks. I had offered many times, feeling pretty confident that I could do a good job, seeing as how kids seemed to love it at school visits when I read *Kitty Katz* out loud. I even did different little voices for all the characters: a high-pitched one for Kitty and a low-pitched one for her boyfriend, Rex Canine, as well as the popular "Kitty Katz claw" hand salute that symbolized pawsitivity. I was *good!*

I had, however, been gently but firmly told by my publisher that it was better to "leave such things to professionals."

Unless you were Will Price, apparently, with a deep, manly voice and a British accent that pronounced *butter* like "buttah," as in "buttah wouldn't melt in his mouth."

Barf again.

"Can we get a selfie?" The girls crowded in around Will, their cell phones raised like battle-axes. "This is so cool!"

Will was wincing those dark, expressive eyes of his as if he were in pain. He was evidently not usually met in airport terminals by throngs of adoring teenaged fans . . . or at least, not his hometown airport terminal.

And poor Will! There was no publicist nearby to stop the assault. Certainly this hadn't occurred to the girls' mothers—who I assumed were the attractive, well-dressed women standing nearby, their own phones raised in amusement to film their daughters leaping around their favorite author. They weren't doing a thing.

I supposed that if Molly the librarian had been there, she'd have stepped in to intervene. But she was still occupied in the restroom.

Honestly, though, how was what was happening to Will so terrible? No one was telling him that they *used to* love his books. No one was saying that he *used to* be their favorite author. He should have been happy that he even had fans, given how deeply unsatisfying his books were.

But of course he didn't realize this, because he was Will Price.

"I really think we ought to save the selfies for the festival, don't you, girls?" he said in the condescending tone of voice people usually reserved for toddlers or golden retrievers.

"Noooo." The girls kept snapping away with their phones. "Just one more?"

He looked so uncomfortable and dismayed that I couldn't help laughing out loud. This was almost as good as if I'd wiped his name off the whiteboard.

Unfortunately, laughing was a mistake. Because somehow he'd heard me—don't ask me how, considering the din in the terminal, with the clanking of the baggage carousel and the excited buzz of the rest of the passengers snagging the keys to their rental cars—and looked my way.

That's how I was able to witness the exact moment that Will Price recognized me—despite my hair color, which I'd changed so dramatically since the last time we'd met.

And that's how I saw those dark eyes go wide as his gaze went from my face to the whiteboard and then back again.

That's when his skin, beneath the days' old beard, went pale, and the heavy backpack he'd been carrying slid off his shoulder like he'd lost all muscle control. It landed with a solid *thunk* on the terminal floor.

Wow.

Well, I'd expected him to feel *something* upon seeing me again. A little embarrassment, maybe (if he actually had any feelings, which, after what he'd done to me, I'd always doubted).

But *this*? He looked like he'd seen a ghost.

"Er," I heard him say, his gaze still riveted to my face. "Listen, girls. I don't have time to chat right now. I have to—"

Go? Do you have to go now, Will? Oh, why is that? Because the woman whose work you maligned to the *New York Times* is standing in front of you holding a sign with your name on it and you're too much of a coward to go up to her and say you're sorry? Is that why? How purr-fectly claw-ful for you.

But to my surprise, he didn't head for the exit. Instead, he took a step toward me—

"Will? Oh, Will, *there* you are!"

I raised my eyebrows as a lithe blonde tore through the crowd, then launched herself at Will. Dressed in a barely there white bikini over which she'd thrown a pair of cutoffs and a gauzy red beach cover-up, she hit Will like a rocket.

"Will!" she gushed as she wrapped her sun-bronzed arms around his neck and her endlessly long legs around his waist. "I'm *so* sorry I'm late!" Surprisingly, she had a British accent, too. "I've got the car parked right outside. Are you ready? You didn't check any bags, did you?"

"Uh, no. No, Chloe, I didn't." He attempted to peel the girl off him, looking, oddly enough, kind of irritated to see her. Which was weird, since most men I know don't mind when beautiful blond girls wearing very little show up at airports to throw their arms around them.

"Great!" Chloe, her sandaled feet back on the ground, reached for the gigantic backpack he'd let fall to the terminal floor. It so figured that Will Price would let a tiny slip of a girl like that carry his bag. What was she, anyway, his assistant? Girlfriend? I guess Cassidy was wrong, and while hetero, Will wasn't single after all.

Although I noted with cynical interest that they did not kiss hello, even though he'd been away long enough to grow a partial beard. He'd probably been warned by his media consultants not to kiss any of his romantic partners in front of fans. It would spoil their dreams that he was available.

"Come on," Chloe said, tugging on his arm. "I'm double-parked. We've got to go."

"Oh." He threw me one last look. "Er, thanks." To the girls, who were already raking Chloe curiously with their gazes, wondering who she was and why she was taking their darling Will away from them, he said, "Sorry, that's got to be it for now. My ride's here. I'll see you at the festival, though, right?"

The girls cried, "Awwwww," in disappointment, but quickly recovered and began waving enthusiastically at their literary idol. "Bye, Will!" "See you tomorrow!" "I'm going to buy tons of copies of *The Moment* for you to sign for all my friends!"

Then a very uncomfortable-looking Will was swept from the terminal by the sweet, lovely Chloe.

What was *that* about? Why was *he* feeling uncomfortable? He hadn't felt uncomfortable bad-mouthing my writing. Why should he feel uncomfortable now, seeing me in an airport holding a whiteboard with his name on it?

"Was that him?"

I turned and saw a familiar figure at my side.

"Oh, hi, Garrett." In addition to his fishing pole and ukulele, Garrett was carrying a giant duffel bag. Unlike me, he didn't seem to suffer from lost-checked-bag syndrome. "Was that who?"

"Will Price. I didn't think *he'd* be riding on the author bus with us."

I turned to stare at him. "What do you mean *us*?"

He pointed to the name beneath Will's on the whiteboard I was holding—the name I hadn't noticed because I'd been too wrapped up in my loathing of Will Price. "That's me."

CHAPTER FOUR

His full name was Garrett Newcombe.

"I write and illustrate graphic novels for young adults," he said. "*Dark Magic School*? You've probably never heard of it. Or me."

Of course I'd heard of him. *Dark Magic School* was at the top of the children's bestseller list every week. Gabriella, my super's daughter, was bonkers for it. I couldn't believe I hadn't recognized Garrett from the author photo on the backs of her books.

In my own defense, however, the goatee had thrown me. It was new.

"Oh, sure," I said, like I'd known all along who he was. "Nice to meet you."

"Same. Oh, hold on. You've got a little something in your—" He reached out as if to touch my ear. I ducked instinctively since I've never been a fan of strange men touching me. But it was too late.

"Ah, got it." Smiling, Garrett held up a shiny silver coin that he'd pretended to pull out of my ear.

Oh, yuck. He wrote books about magic *and* he was a magician? No, thank you. I may have written books about talking cats, but that didn't mean I believed in, much less liked, magic. Cats actually *can* communicate. My own, Miss Kitty, tells me exactly what she wants on a regular basis, quite vocally, usually at seven in the morning.

Magic, however much we might want to believe in it, is completely made up. Miracles don't happen. People get sick and often die, and the only thing that can stop that is science. Look at what had happened to my mom.

But since I was going to be stuck with this guy for the weekend, I forced a smile. "Ha-ha."

"Here." He shoved the coin at me. "You can keep it."

"No, thanks."

"No, really. It's a *Dark Magic School* number eleven commemorative guild piece."

"That's okay. Save it for one of your fans."

"Oh, I shipped two thousand ahead to the hotel to give out to the fans. Really, you can have it."

"Great." Reluctantly, I pocketed the "guild piece." I could give it to Gabriella, anyway. She'd love it.

"So why are you holding that?" He pointed at the whiteboard.

"Oh, the librarian from the festival had to run to the bathroom." I made a hand motion to illustrate a swollen belly and mouthed the word *pregnant*. "I said I'd fill in for her."

"Oh, that's so nice of you. Really great." Garrett was gushing like I'd single-handedly saved a child from drowning. "So what's the deal with Will Price taking off like that with that girl? Is he too good for the author bus or something?"

I shrugged. "He lives here. She came to pick him up."

He raised his eyebrows. "I didn't know Will Price had a girlfriend. Everyone always talks about how he's a commitment-phobe or something. She looked kinda young."

"Maybe she's his sister." Of course I didn't believe she was his sister. Why was I coming to his defense? The man was my nemesis.

Garrett laughed. It wasn't a very pleasant laugh. "None of my sisters ever greeted me like that at the airport. Hey, didn't I hear about some big dustup between you two a while ago?"

"Between Will Price and me? I don't know." I did not want to get into what had happened between Will Price and me. Not in the middle of the world's tiniest airport with a bestselling magician slash graphic novelist, anyway. I looked around for Molly. What was taking her so long? "Did you?"

"Yeah, I did. Wait—I remember now." Garrett looked at me and snapped his fingers. "Somebody plagiarized the two of you. That's it. It was all over the news."

I took a deep breath. Great. "Yes. Nicole Woods."

"That's right!" Garrett actually slapped his knee, he was enjoying himself so much. "Oh my God, that was huge, a bestselling author like her caught plagiarizing? But it was also kind of hilarious, since you and Will couldn't write more different books."

"Hilarious. Yeah." Hurry up, Molly!

"And didn't Price say something about that? Something not too flattering—like if Woods was going to copy from somebody, at least she could have chosen to copy from somebody who actually writes good books?"

I cut him off before he could say it. "Yes, that's right. Wow, you have a good memory." What was wrong with this guy? Why was he bringing up something he had to know had been a pretty unpleasant time for me?

But that was the thing about writers—not all of them, but quite a few. They spent all their time behind computer screens, and very little engaging with actual human beings, which meant that they had no idea how to interact with them. Case in point, Justin, my ex. And now, apparently, Garrett Newcombe.

"But fortunately they destroyed all the copies of Nicole's book," I went on brightly. "And she got the help she needed for the addiction that she said caused her to resort to plagiarism in the first place." Sure. Sure, Nicole. Sleeping pills. That's why you had to steal large chunks of my hard work from me. I took sleeping pills for a while after my mom died, and I managed never to steal anything from anyone. So I'm not sure that excuse of yours holds up. "So it's all water under the bridge now."

"Oh." Garrett looked disappointed that I wasn't more upset. He'd evidently been hoping to hear some dishy author drama. "Really? And Price apologized?"

"There was no need for him to apologize. Unlike Nicole, Will didn't do anything wrong."

"Didn't do anything wrong? He said your books weren't—"

I guess Garrett was better at reading human emotion than I'd thought, since he seemed to notice my frown and abruptly reversed course. "Not that I agree with him. I think your books are great. Really great. I've read them all to my nieces. They can't get enough of Kitty Katz. When's the next one coming out, anyway?"

"I don't have a pub date yet."

"But even so," Garrett went on. He never shut up, this guy. "You must have really wanted to let that guy have a piece of your mind. You know, afterward, when you heard what Price said about your books not being good enough to be worth copying. I personally can't stand authors like that, ones who are so dismissive of children's books and think literary novels are the only ones worth reading."

Ha! Like Will Price's books were literary.

"If it had been me," he blathered on, "I'd have called the bastard out—on social media, anyway—and demanded an apology."

I shrugged. "I didn't think it was worth it."

"Not *worth it*?"

"Isn't it classier to shake it off? That's what I always have Kitty do in my books. I like her to set a good example for readers by rising above the haters."

I didn't want to admit the real reason I'd never responded to what Will had said: that the Wright way was to seethe silently while inwardly plotting revenge.

Except now it looked as if I might actually have an opportunity to get it.

Only how? My mom had been the best at getting back at people. She was Sicilian, and in Sicily they—

Fortunately, that's when Molly the librarian came racing back from the ladies' room, her cheeks flushed.

"Oh, *thank you*! I feel so much better now." She took the whiteboard from my hands and smiled brightly at Mr. Dark Magic. "Hi! You must be Garrett Newcombe. We're so honored to have you."

"I'm honored to be here." Garrett smiled what I'd now begun to think of as his weasel-faced smile, even though there really wasn't anything weasel-faced about him. I was just in a bad mood due to his reminding me that I'd still never gotten my revenge on Will Price. "So, is this it? Can we go to the hotel now? Because I for one am ready for my first official Florida Keys margarita."

Molly looked crestfallen. "Oh, I'm so sorry, Garrett. Not quite yet. We have to wait for one more author. His flight should be in already, I don't know what's taking so long—"

I put on my most innocent expression. "Oh, do you mean Will Price?"

Molly brightened. "Yes! Do you know him?"

"Just a little." I ignored Garrett, who was smirking. "He actually came through here while you were in the bathroom. Someone picked him up—a blond girl?"

Molly's happy smile didn't waver. "Oh, was it Chloe?"

I shrugged, trying to keep my own expression carefully neutral. "I don't know. He didn't introduce her. It could have been someone named Chloe."

"Well, great then! He's all set." Molly reached for my carry-on. "Let's go!"

"Whoa, whoa, whoa." I snatched my bag back. "I can carry my own luggage, Molly. And I certainly don't let pregnant women carry it."

Molly laughed. "This weekend isn't about me. It's about celebrating all of you lovely authors. Now if you'll follow me, your carriage awaits!"

"Well, I don't know about you," Garrett said to me as he trailed after Molly through the terminal's automatic doors and out into the bright sunlight of the parking lot, "but I'm ready to be celebrated."

"Me, too."

Before I exited, I turned to wave to Lauren and the rest of the Will Price fangirls, who were still waiting at the baggage carousel for their luggage. "See you at the festival, ladies!"

But they didn't hear me, because they were too busy staring down at their phones, coming up with captions for their photos with their idol.

CHAPTER FIVE

hy? *Why* did I start reading his stupid book?

It wasn't my fault, though. Will's publisher had supplied the organizers of this book festival with enough complimentary copies of *The Moment* to slip into every attendee's swag bag. I'd found mine waiting on the bed when I checked into my room.

How could I resist thumbing casually through it?

Really, it was impossible not to, with its ridiculous cover showing—like all of Will's books—an outrageously attractive pair of white people (a man and a woman, of course), almost but not quite kissing.

I didn't *want* to start reading it. But I purposefully hadn't brought any other books with me. Rosie's words about her other author—the one who'd come to Little Bridge and written two whole chapters a day—kept haunting me. If I didn't have anything to do, maybe I'd be tempted to write.

But then, right in my complimentary swag bag, I'd found a book by my nemesis. How could I resist?

And the Lazy Parrot Inn was the perfect setting in which

to read a book about "one man's journey to redemption." It had been hard to tell from the photos on the website exactly what the hotel was going to be like. It had certainly *looked* nice (especially since I wasn't paying for it), but people and places almost always look better online than they do in real life.

But I'd been delighted to discover upon our arrival that the Lazy Parrott was exactly as advertised. A lovely Victorian mansion with gingerbread trim, idly spinning ceiling fans, and deep, comfortable porch chairs, it screamed "relaxing oasis" in all the best ways. Brightly colored paper-umbrella-festooned drinks could be ordered from a tiki bar near the large, kidney-shaped pool in the center of the inn's lush garden courtyard—a pool which was not only heated (not that it needed to be, given the island's warm winter temperature), but also boasted a waterfall and an adjoining hot tub.

I knew the minute I saw it that the Lazy Parrot's pool was where I was going to be spending all my free time during the festival. Not that my room wasn't incredibly luxurious— room 202, a second-floor suite that looked out over the rooftops of downtown Little Bridge, all the way to the ocean, with a huge four-poster bed and its own Jacuzzi tub and kitchenette (plus a fully stocked minibar that included both peanut and plain M&M's, my author snack of choice).

But the pool! The pool and the hot tub! I was going to be in them until my fingers and toes pruned.

And not because I was hiding from Will Price. No way. I was most definitely going to face him. Not only face him, but get revenge on him for what he'd done . . . or at least say something appropriately cutting to him.

Just not yet. Because I needed this break. I deserved it. I'd been working hard, not only at trying to come up with a plot for *Kitty Katz #27*, but at getting Dad to agree he was better off spending the winter months somewhere warm, like this place.

So it was fine for me to take some time off and float on a raft in this beautiful pool with a margarita and read Will's incredibly crappy new book. No one could judge me for that.

And no one was, since I seemed to be the only person staying at the Parrot who'd had the common sense to think of relaxing in the pool. Garrett had disappeared into his room—102, just below mine and facing the courtyard, so I knew it had nothing like my amazing view—as soon as we'd arrived to "get some work done."

Sure. Whatever, dude. You get right on that. I'll be in the pool, reading *The Moment*.

I didn't tell him this, of course, out of fear he might try to join me. Instead, I sunnily answered, "Of course!" when he asked if I'd meet him later in the lobby in time to catch the author bus to the festival's first event—a cocktail meet-and-greet, followed by a sit-down dinner with donors.

But even as I'd assured him I'd be there, I hadn't been sure I'd have the guts to actually show. And now, floating in the sun, I was even more certain. Grateful as I was even to be invited to such events—the author everyone *used to* love—I couldn't help dreading them, even when they didn't include

Will Price. I, like so many writers, was horrible at making small talk, and even worse at eating and drinking while doing so.

I was hoping an hour or two of floating in the sun would help trigger what Rosie had mentioned had happened to her other author: a sudden rush of artistic inspiration, so I'd actually come up with an idea for *Kitty Katz #27* that felt exciting enough to write down. Two chapters a day? I would take that in a hot New York minute.

What was happening instead was that I was getting sucked into Will Price's insipid, highly readable prose.

Meeeeee-OW!

Unfortunately, I'd already failed rule number one of relaxing while in the tropics: leaving my phone behind. I realized this when I heard its official *Kitty Katz* mobile ringtone blare from the towel on which I'd left it at the side of the pool.

Meeeeee-OW!

Because of the book I was holding—the cover carefully bent back so no one would see it was Will Price's latest—I had to paddle one-handed to reach my phone. It took me quite some time to get there.

Meeeeee-OW!

Oh, no. I'd missed a call from my dad. I quickly called him back.

"Hi, Dad, it's me. Is everything okay?"

Dad's voice, rough from years of singing with his folk-rock group (that had never become popular enough to earn any money, but had a large enough cult following that he remained hopeful), said calmly, "Of course everything's okay. You're the one who never called when you got in. I thought we had a deal? You're always supposed to call."

"Of course." I winced guiltily. "Sorry, Dad. I got in okay. Guess where I am right now?"

"Hmmm, let me see. Boise, Idaho."

Laughing, I said, "No, Dad, I told you before I left. At a book festival in the Florida Keys. But guess where I am right this minute."

"Since it's the Florida Keys, I'm going to guess a bar. Green Parrot in Key West? You know the boys and I once played there. Sonny got so drunk, he—"

"No. Floating on a raft in the hotel pool on Little Bridge Island, drinking a margarita."

"Sounds terrible. Get out of there!"

"Dad, stop it." I was still laughing. As much as my dad frustrated me sometimes, he could always make me laugh. "You know this could be your life if you'd just take my advice. Did you manage to watch the virtual tour of that place in Mount Dora?"

"Oh, I saw it."

He did not sound pleased. Still, I barreled on, keeping my voice chipper.

"And? What did you think? It's a nice place, right? Better than the last one."

"Not exactly."

"What do you mean, not exactly? This one has everything you've been asking for: all on one level, with a nice yard and even a detached garage for you to practice in."

"Yeah," my father said, "but did you look at the neighbors' garbage cans?"

"What do you mean, the neighbors' garbage cans?"

"After the tour, I used that Google Maps thing you showed me to zoom in on the house, and I could see the neighbors' garbage cans," he said. "And right there, I saw it: a Dead Head sticker."

Oh, no. "Dad."

"The neighbors have *Grateful Dead* stickers on their garbage cans! You *know* how I feel about jam bands."

"Dad." I sighed. Suddenly my nice, relaxing time in the sun didn't seem so relaxing. "I'm sure those Google Map photos are really old. The people who own those garbage cans probably don't even live there anymore. Mount Dora is a lovely town, I've been there. They have tons of arts and folk music festivals there, and the average seasonal temperature is seventy-five degrees. It's a very charming—"

"No, I don't think so. I think I'll just stay in New York." Dad started to cough, which unfortunately he'd begun doing all too often lately as soon as the temperature in the city neared the freezing mark. "It's cold, but I know all my neighbors, and they respect *serious* music. And there are festivals here in New York, too, you know."

"Dad, are you sure it's the stickers, or the fact that you're too stubborn to let your daughter buy a house for you? Because you know what Mom would say about that."

"Oh, she'd kick my rear end for being a chauvinist pig!" Dad chuckled. "So of course it isn't that. But I really do think you should save your money, sweetheart."

"Dad, I have plenty of money. I want to spend some of it on you. Nothing would make me happier."

"But that's silly. You need to save it for when you get married and have kids of your own."

Like that was happening anytime soon. At this point I was about as likely to get married and have kids as Melanie West, whose husband Johnny "Ace" Kane had (accidentally? Or on purpose?) run over and killed while smuggling moonshine in the first chapter of *The Moment*. The first chapter! Will seemed to like to get his trauma into his books early.

"What if I don't want to get married and have kids?" I asked. "You know, Dad, for a musician, you really are awfully closed-minded. Has it ever occurred to you that the millions of people who love the Grateful Dead might actually be—"

"Um, sorry to interrupt."

I looked up to see a petite Asian woman with short, purple hair standing by the edge of the pool. She was wearing a pretty pink dress coupled with a necklace made of very lethal-looking—but plastic—daggers.

"It's almost time for the author bus to dinner," she said, pointing at the face of her smart watch (which of course I was too far away to see). "Are you going to get out of there and get ready, or are you going to wear your swimsuit to the party?"

"Bern!" I nearly fell off my raft in my haste to paddle to the side. "Dad, I gotta go."

"I'll talk to you later, kid. Let me know how the rest of your festival goes." He hung up.

"Bernadette!" I held out my arms for a welcome hug. "I'm so glad to see you!"

"I'm glad to see you, too, but not *that* glad." Bernadette took a quick few steps away. "You're going to get me all wet, too, and I'm in my dress-up clothes."

I laughed. For Bernadette, anything that wasn't yoga pants and a T-shirt was "dress-up clothes." I felt the same way, for the most part.

I'd known whip-smart and tougher-than-she-looked Bernadette for ages. Though we lived on opposite sides of the country, we texted nearly every day and saw each other several times a year at various book festivals. The author of multiple extremely popular young-adult series, Bernadette's most recent featured a teenaged female assassin who lived in a far-off galaxy. Ergo, the knife necklace.

"When did you get here?" she asked.

"A few hours ago. You?"

"Early this morning. I took the red-eye to Miami from SFO, then a little puddle jumper from Miami to here. I've already had a trolley tour of the town, a tasting at the rum distillery, and bought a beautiful painting from a pink-haired artist named Bree in some gallery down the street. This is the best day off I've had in ages."

"Really?"

"Yes, are you kidding? I just handed in my latest revision, May's finally getting the hang of potty training, Sophie started kindergarten, *and* we're finally refinishing the wood floors. Everything has just been *drama, drama, drama.*"

I grinned. Sophie was my goddaughter, and even though

we weren't related by blood, she seemed to have taken after me. Everything with Sophie was either brilliant or a disaster.

"I love that house and both my girls to bits, but God! I'm glad to let Jen be in charge for the weekend." Bernadette's anesthesiologist spouse, Jen, was my dream partner. Unfailingly supportive and cheerful, Jen earned a steady income and could also cook and write emergency prescriptions. "It's so good to see you."

"You, too. How long has it been? Decatur Book Festival?"

"That's it. God, that was a blast. I thought for sure we were going to get kicked out of that hotel. Anyway, what are you still doing in the pool? I know how you hate itineraries, but the meet-and-greet is in half an hour. You're going to be late for the author bus."

I shrugged, feeling another twinge of guilt. I never looked at festival itineraries if I didn't have to. I enjoyed living life on the edge when I wasn't at home, bound by my normal routine of waking-writing-eating-sleeping (or not-writing, as the case may be).

Besides, I knew if Bernadette was going to be around, I didn't have to. She was such a take-charge kind of person, she'd tell me everything I needed to know—and what I didn't, too.

"Yeah, I don't think I'm going to make it to the meet-and-greet," I said.

"What?" Bernadette stared down at me in shock. "What do you mean? You *have* to go to the meet-and-greet, Jo."

"Yeah." I watched as the hotel's resident cat, a gray tabby just out of kittenhood, found a small brown lizard and pounced on it, only to have it dart easily away to safety. "It's just that Rosie said she knows an author who came here and got really inspired to write. So I'm waiting for that to kick in."

"But there'll be free alcohol. You and I always go to the events where they're serving free alcohol!"

"I know. But it's not *mandatory* that we attend."

"Of course it's not *mandatory*. But it's free booze! And they flew us here first-class, didn't they?" Bernadette had on her Mom Face—the one she always wore when Jen called to say that one of their kids was acting up. I realized I was about to be schooled. "They're putting us up in this amazing hotel. They're paying us a really generous stipend for what, a few hours of work? There's a panel and signing tomorrow and then another one on Sunday. It's hardly *labor* intensive. And the meet-and-greet is at some rich donor's mansion. Don't you want to see inside some rich donor's super-fancy mansion? There'll probably be some gross catered food we can make fun of. You know how much you love making fun of gross catered food."

"Yeah. I know. It's just that . . ."

"It's just that what?"

"It's just that Will Price is here."

"*Here?*" Bernadette gasped and glanced around the hotel's pool area in horror as if Will Price might come leaping out of the bushes at any moment.

"No, not *here*. I meant here on the island. He's coming to the festival."

Bernadette's eyes widened. She knew how I felt about

Will—and she knew why I felt that way, too. She'd been at the con where he'd said the thing that he'd said.

"No." She shook her head in disbelief. "No *way*. I thought your agent checked and said he was going to be in—"

"Well, Rosie was wrong." I stared glumly down at my margarita. The plastic cup was now empty. "I just saw him at the airport."

"Oh, well, that doesn't mean anything. He lives here, doesn't he? Maybe he was—"

"No, I checked. His name's been added to the festival website. He's definitely going to be at all the events. And did you look in your swag bag? There's a free copy of *The Moment* in it."

"Oh, God." Bernadette looked appropriately skeeved out. "What are you going to do?"

I pointed at the raft I was floating on. "Doing it. Going to stay right here, where it's safe, except for when I have to do a panel or signing." I did not add that I'd be reading *The Moment* to find out if Johnny ever fessed up to Melanie about offing her husband. I actually didn't care about that. Very much.

Bernadette pressed her lips together. This was always a clear sign that she was entering full mommy mode.

"No," she said, shaking her head until her purple bangs swayed. "No way. You are *not* doing this. You are not hiding from some *man*."

Oh, jeez. Here came the not-so-fun part of Bernadette's otherwise great personality. She always got this way whenever I refused to confront someone. My steak was a little too underdone, but I didn't want to send it back? Bernadette would fuss until I did. Water glasses on the table not getting refilled quickly enough, but it was clear the waitstaff was in the weeds? Bernadette was always ready to call the manager, whereas I, who'd paid my way through college waitressing, felt that was unfair.

Now she was going full-on ballistic with my plan to avoid Will Price all weekend.

"Especially some man who dissed you!" she cried. "Not just you, but the entirety of children's literature. You are climbing out of that water and getting dressed and coming to this meet-and-greet with me if I have to *drag* you out of there."

"Okay, okay," I said, already starting to paddle to the pool's steps. "Fine. But I'm not going to talk to him."

"Of course you are." Bernadette glared as I wrapped myself in a towel. "You're also going to look gorgeous and unobtainable and make him regret every single one of his life choices, while mentioning to everyone who'll listen that the reason your books have been selling so successfully for so many years in so many countries is because they inspire hope while also offering comfort with their gentle life lessons and happy endings, something Will Price's books decidedly do *not* do. Now go get changed before you make us late for the author bus."

"Fine," I said. "Okay."

But the truth was, in that moment *I* was the one who was regretting many of my life choices . . . especially the one where I'd agreed to come to Little Bridge Island in the first place.

The Moment by Will Price

Never in my life had I seen a woman more beautiful. I'm not talking about the conventional kind of beauty. She was no movie starlet, starving herself to fit into the fashion of the day. Her beauty was the kind that came from the inside, shining through those blue eyes with wit and intelligence. The warmth of her smile could light up a cityscape. The fact that she smiled often, and in my direction, was enough to make me realize how lucky I was . . . until I remembered what I'd done.

When she found out, she would never smile again . . . at least not at me.

CHAPTER SIX

We weren't late for the author bus, mainly because instead of drying my hair, I opted for pulling it back into another ponytail, not caring whether anyone noticed if it was wet. Then I raced down to meet Bernadette.

"Now, that's what I'm talking about." Her gaze traveled approvingly up and down my black palazzo pants and matching black top. "I don't think anyone will be able to tell you've spent the past year suffering from crippling anxiety, depression, and low self-esteem."

"You forgot writer's block."

"Wait, *what*? You're not writing *anything*?"

I shrugged. "Not anything I'm getting paid for. *Kitty Katz number twenty-seven* was due last year and all I can seem to write instead is either an apocalyptic *Sense and Sensibility* or a book about a girl whose mother dies of cancer, leaving her to be raised alone at age fourteen by her scatterbrained musician father who never managed to save a dime for his retirement."

"Okay," Bernadette said. "Kinda bleak, but I'd read both."

"Thanks, but no one else seems to want to. Rosie's been sending them out, and they've gotten rejected everywhere. They're not *Jo Wright* enough, apparently."

"How can something written by Jo Wright not be Jo Wright enough?"

"Oh, you know. Upbeat."

Bernadette burst out laughing. "People think *you're* up-beat?"

"Well, people who only know Jo Wright, author of *Kitty Katz, Kitten Sitter,* not Jo Wright, the person."

"Oh, I get it. Once you're known for writing a certain thing, it's hard to market you if you write something totally different."

"Exactly. I guess I kind of understand what they mean. The *Kitty Katz* books are known for cheering readers up. I wouldn't want to write something that bums people out." Like the drivel that came out of Will Price's way-too-handsome head.

"I don't think you could possibly write something that bums people out."

"Oh, I don't know. I've been in a pretty dark place lately." Thinking of ways to murder Will Price, for instance.

"You could try getting those other books published under a different name," Bernadette suggested.

"Yeah, but then I'd have to build a whole new social media following under that name."

"And create a whole new website," Bernadette said with a sigh.

"And get new author photos."

"Which you need." Bernadette tugged on my black pony-tail. "But I get it. So much effort."

"Right. I might as well just stick to Kitty, even though the well seems to have gone dry." Unless Little Bridge Island worked its magic.

Too bad there was no such thing as magic.

We began heading toward the hotel's foyer, where we could see through the open French doors that other authors were gathering to wait for the bus that would take us to the event.

"Do you think your writer's block is because of what's going on with your dad—the fact that he isn't doing so well but refuses to accept help—or because of what that idiot Price said about your writing?" Bernadette asked.

I gave her the stink eye. "Are you trying to psychoanalyze me? Because I think you should know that as a lifelong Man-hattanite, I already have a therapist."

"Of course you do. I was just wondering."

"Who knows? I hope it's because of what's going on with my dad. If it's because of what Will Price said, then what kind of professional does that make me, that I could be so easily thrown off my game?"

"That kind of thing would throw anyone off their game. He said it about you to the *New York Times*, for crying out loud."

I kicked at a fallen leaf on the pathway. "Well, I've always prided myself on my professionalism."

"You *are* a professional. *He's* the one who—"

"Let's drop it. Look, I'm getting better. I've stopped main-lining M&M's. I'm not eating cookie dough for breakfast any-more. I even managed to get off the couch and get a pedicure before I left the city. See?" I lifted the hem of my palazzos to show her my toenails twinkling out from a pair of black platform slides.

"Black polish." Bernadette laughed wryly. "Of course."

"I know, right?" I gave her an evil grin. "To contrast with my upbeat personality."

"There they are!"

As soon as we entered the lobby, an older white man dressed all in black, just like me, rushed toward us. I recog-nized him immediately as a globally popular horror writer with whom I'd attended numerous events before.

"We were looking all over for you!" Saul Coleman (not the name under which he wrote) appeared anxious. "Where have you been? The author bus just pulled up!"

"Oh, stop fussing, Saul." Saul's wife, Frannie, a petite brunette who looked as elegant as if she'd stepped from the pages of *Vogue*, came over to kiss us both on the cheek. "Jo, Bernadette, it's so good to see you both."

"It's wonderful to see you, too." I squeezed Frannie's ex-pensively ringed fingers. "You look great." To Saul, I said, "Sorry we're late. I took a dip and had to change."

"A *dip*?" Saul's eyes widened, as did those of his wife. "You went in the *pool*?"

Frannie tightened her grip on my hand, drawing me closer and then dropping her voice to a whisper. "I can't believe you went in the water, Jo. Haven't you heard about the flesh-eating viruses you can get in Florida?"

"I'm pretty sure those are only in lakes," Bernadette whispered back. "But I'll double-check with Jen if you want me to."

"Would you?" Frannie glanced suspiciously at the woman working behind the front desk, who'd been extremely sweet and helpful to me when I'd checked in. "You can just never be too sure in the tropics. Even the *bugs* can kill you. Dengue, Zika, West Nile—it never ends!"

Bernadette and I exchanged knowing grins. Like me, Frannie was a lifelong New Yorker, but the Hamptons were about as far as she'd willingly go out of the city.

But because Saul adored her and always wanted her by his side, she bravely accompanied him to all of his book events. Their marriage was, like Bernadette's, one I envied.

After my disastrous five-year relationship with Justin, however, I wasn't jumping back into the dating pool anytime soon—only real pools, with plenty of chlorine, and of course a tiki bar nearby.

"I wonder what kind of food we're going to get at this thing tonight," Frannie fretted. "I mean, they don't even have a bagel shop on this island. No bagels! Can you believe it? Not that the bagels would be any good if they *did* have them. You can only make good bagels with New York City tap water. Everyone knows our tap water is the safest and best-tasting in the entire—"

"Fran, will you stop?" Saul rolled his eyes in loving frustration at his wife. "I'm sure the food will be perfectly fine."

"I don't know, you might be right, Mrs. Coleman." Bernadette always enjoyed baiting Frannie. "Since this place is an island, I suspect they serve a lot of fresh fish here. But who knows what's in the water. Given all the cruise ships, there might be—"

Frannie looked pale. "Oh, God. I'm sticking to chicken. Oh, no, wait, I saw some chickens running around loose on the street! Why do they have chickens roaming around loose on the streets here? What kind of place allows chickens to run around loose on the streets?"

"Well," Bernadette began to explain, "on the tour I took earlier today, they said it's because when grocery stores with refrigeration finally moved to the island, the residents released the chickens they used to keep in coops in their backyards for eggs and Sunday dinner, and since then, those chickens have—"

"Stop." Frannie held out a hand. "I don't want to know any more."

"Hey, everybody." Garrett Newcombe strolled into the lobby. He'd changed out of the Batman shirt and cargo shorts he'd been wearing at the airport into khaki pants and a blue button-down, which was a step up.

But he was still wearing flip-flops, and also clutching the swag bag we'd all received in our hotel rooms.

"Hi, I'm Garrett Newcombe," he said unnecessarily, since he had on his author badge. We were all wearing them, as we'd been directed to by the festival staff. "Of the Dark Magic School series?"

"Oh, Garrett!" Frannie beamed. "Our grandson loves your books! I'm Frannie Coleman, and this is my husband, Saul. You might know him better as the author Clive Dean."

Garrett's jaw dropped, his gaze laser-focusing on Saul. The name Clive Dean had a tendency to do that to men (and some women) of a certain age. "Oh, Mr. Dean. This is truly an honor. Your books are what inspired me to become a writer, sir."

Saul beamed and reached out to shake the hand Garrett had extended. "Oh, isn't that great? That's always nice to hear."

I had to give Garrett credit for that one. He couldn't have said anything more perfect to Saul.

But then he ruined it by adding, "Maybe your grandson would like this."

Then he reached out and drew a coin from Frannie's ear. He didn't seem to notice that as his hand neared her face, Frannie ducked instinctively, as I had, leaning away from him.

"Ta-da!" he cried, presenting the coin to her. "An official *Dark Magic School* number eleven commemorative guild piece! I'm sure your grandson will love it."

"I'm sure," Frannie deadpanned as she dropped the "guild piece" into her purse. Frannie disliked being touched by strange men as much as I did, even strange men who claimed to love her husband's books.

Her husband, however, was delighted. "Hey, that's really neat, Garrett!" Saul cried. "Show me how you did that."

"Aw, I can't, Mr. Dean." Garrett winked at the rest of us.

"A good magician never reveals his secrets. But stay tuned. I'm going to perform a trick at tomorrow night's dinner that's going to knock everybody's socks off."

Saul chuckled. "Neat!"

I made a mental note to stay as far away as possible from tomorrow night's dinner. I'd had about as much "magic" as I could take in a twenty-four-hour period.

Frannie appeared to be thinking the same thing, since she sidled up to Bernadette and me to whisper, "What is wrong with this guy?"

"Hmmm-hmmm." Bernadette pretended to fuss with a strand of her purple hair. "From what I hear, quite a lot."

I pretended to fuss with my own hair. "Like what?"

"People say he's a player."

Frannie and I glanced at each other, then at Garrett, then burst out laughing.

"For real," Bernadette insisted. "The rumors were all over Novel Con last year. A bestselling male author was hitting on female fans."

That caused both of us to quit laughing. *"What?"*

"It's true. Whoever the guy was, he apparently had a real way with the ladies."

I stared at Garrett as he pulled a coin from Saul's ear, giving him a slow-motion demonstration of his trick. "Well, it couldn't have been Garrett. Look at him. He's wearing *flip-flops* to a donor dinner."

"True. But you could see how to an inexperienced, impressionable young woman, he might seem . . . impressive."

I still couldn't believe it. If there was one rule in the publishing business—besides not to plagiarize—it was that you never, *ever* slept with fans.

Oh, it was all right to *socialize* with them, as long as you kept things on a strictly professional basis. I'd had many lunches and even a few dinners with *Kitty Katz* fans, sometimes because they'd won a meal with me at a charity auction or occasionally because they or their parents had reached out in some way—a reader who was ill or depressed or simply needed a dose of Kitty love or advice, something I was always happy to give. Even at my lowest points this past year and a half, I was able to throw on some lip gloss and get in a cab or online and try to make one of my adorable Kitty Klub members feel better.

But there was never any physical contact except maybe the briefest of hugs, especially if they were underage. That was Professional Writer 101.

"How did I not hear anything about this?" I demanded. "I was at Novel Con last year, and no one said a word about it to me."

"No, you weren't," Bernadette said. "You were at Novel Con *the year before last*. You skipped it this year, remember? And you wouldn't have heard about what happened there because lately you've had your own drama to deal with."

I nodded, unoffended. Nothing she was saying was untrue. The Nicole Woods scandal and subsequent fallout with Will had kept me off anything except my own social media pages for months. I hadn't wanted to read anything publishing related. And following quickly on the heels of that had been my breakup with Justin and all of Dad's medical drama.

"But *I* was at Novel Con this past year with Saul," Frannie said, "and I didn't hear a word about any of this."

"It was mostly on Twitter," Bernadette said.

"Oh, *Twitter.*" Frannie rolled her eyes. "No wonder we didn't see it. Our son handles all of Saul's social media for him. But are you sure it was *him?*" She glanced at Garrett distastefully. "He's hardly Chris Hemsworth or Evans or whoever that Chris is all you girls always seem to be talking about."

Bernadette—who had no interest in any of the Chrises—shook her head. "No, I'm not sure. But it's not about looks, Fran. To a naive fan, someone like Garrett might seem glamorous. He could promise them things—a meeting with his editor, a role in his next film. The rumors were that it was a number one *New York Times* bestselling author who had a new movie coming out—"

I gasped. "But that could be anyone. That could be *Will Price.*"

"It wasn't Will Price," Bernadette said. "I know you hate him, Jo, but the rumors all said it was an author of *young-adult* books."

"A lot of young adults read Will's books. There were some teenagers on my plane who were Will Price superfans."

At least, they'd looked and acted like teenagers. I still wasn't entirely sure how old Lauren and her friends had been.

Frannie was gasping, too, but for a different reason. "There's going to be a *Dark Magic School* movie? Oh, my grandson will be thrilled."

Bernadette ignored us both. "Look, whoever it was, what he did was total sexual harassment. But because none of the women came forward, nothing ever came of it. It was all just rumors."

"So how do we even know any of it's true?" I asked.

"That's the thing. We *don't*."

All three of us stared at Garrett as he pulled another coin (without asking) from the ear of the woman behind the front desk. Granted, she wasn't young—judging from the deep creases in the tanned skin of her décolletage, she could have been anywhere from fifty to seventy-five.

But she giggled, loving the attention.

"I guess we'll just have to keep an eye on him, then, won't we?" Frannie said.

"Oh, we most certainly will," Bernadette agreed.

And an eye on Will Price, I thought to myself darkly, thinking of Johnny Kane's despicable actions in *The Moment*. Johnny was, after all, in love with a girl whose husband he'd killed (however accidentally). What kind of weirdo thought up a story like that?

Then again, what kind of weirdo wrote twenty-six books about a talking teenage cat?

It was right then that a tall, good-looking man in a sheriff's uniform strode into the hotel lobby. He held a clipboard and wore an expression of resignation.

"Are we all here now for the author bus to the book festival meet-and-greet?" he asked.

"Yes!" Frannie perked up and waved. "Here we are."

"Okay, then." The guy in the sheriff's uniform tucked his clipboard under his arm and made a twirling motion in the air with a finger. "Let's move it on out."

Frannie narrowed her eyes as if she thought we were all about to be kidnapped. "Wait. Who are you? Where's the librarian, Molly, who picked us up from the airport?"

The uniformed officer heaved a sigh. "Molly asked me to drive the bus this evening since she's already at the event, helping to set it up. I'm Sheriff John Hartwell, her husband."

The tightness left Frannie's face. I could tell that she was thrilled at the idea of having an armed law enforcement official drive her around. Frannie felt unsafe anywhere that wasn't within one hundred miles of Saks Fifth Avenue . . . and of course Madison Square Garden and her beloved Knicks. "Oh! The *sheriff!* And Molly's *husband! Well.* This is more like it. Let's go, then."

As we climbed aboard the author bus—really just a rented mini-shuttle—me using extra care since the heels on my slides were even higher than the ones on my boots, Saul said to his wife, "Frannie, what do you think is going to happen to us? Look at this place, for Christ's sake. It's like something out of a movie on the Hallmark Channel."

He had a point. Maybe I hadn't noticed it so much on our way from the airport because the sun had been so blindingly bright.

But now, after sunset, I could see that downtown Little Bridge really did look like someplace out of a Christmas rom-com, with its quaint, pastel-colored houses and businesses, mostly little candy and ice-cream shops. Old-fashioned streetlamps weren't the only things twinkling with holiday lights: strands of lights had been wrapped around the trunks of palm trees all along the street, as well, and every so often, we passed a business with a dolphin or Santa-hat-wearing mermaid in the window, made up entirely of twinkling LED displays.

"Well, I don't know," Frannie fussed as she dug inside her purse for her lipstick. "Where *is* everyone? I've hardly seen a single soul."

"If you'd look up for half a minute, you might be surprised."

Making an impatient face, Frannie looked up and out the window, then gawked. Tourists, still enjoying their holiday break from school or work, crowded the sidewalks. As they strolled, they paused to listen to musicians playing in open-air bars and restaurants, or simply to take in the ocean view and warm, balmy breeze.

"Wow." Bernadette, beside me on the bus, was staring out the window, as well, watching the same happy family as they devoured what appeared to be slices of frozen Key Lime pie, dipped in chocolate, on a stick. "I'm starting to feel a little guilty for leaving Jen and the kids behind."

"Seriously. You're the worst mom," I teased her.

"I guess I'm going to have to come back here with them someday."

"Or just Jen," I said, as we passed a couple walking hand in hand, holding real coconuts with the tops cut off and straws sticking out of the openings. "Leave the kids behind with your mother."

"Yeah, that sounds better, actually."

"I come down here quite a lot," Garrett volunteered. "I scuba, you know. And the fishing is really great, too. You've probably seen on the itinerary for tomorrow that Will Price is taking us all out for a picnic lunch on his cat after our panels."

I stared. "His *what?*"

"His catamaran." Garrett looked at me pityingly. "It's a type of boat."

I tried to hide my disappointment that it wasn't a real cat, though obviously I'd been uncertain how we were going to have lunch on one. Still, you never knew. Florida was weird. "Oh."

"From what I hear, Will's is a real beauty, a sixty footer, brand-new. Probably set him back a couple million. But don't worry." Garrett, apparently mistaking our stunned silence—two million dollars? For a boat?—for fear of deep water, went on, "We won't head out too far. We'll probably stick close to the mangroves, so if you'd prefer to do some snorkeling or something, that'd be fine. I could help if you want to learn to scuba. I'm certified for open water."

"Gee," I said. "That's so sweet. I think I'll stay at the hotel and try to write." Or finish Will's terrible book.

"I'm going!" Saul was guileless enough that he didn't realize Garrett's invitation hadn't been extended to him. "I'd love to scuba!"

To his credit, Garrett looked surprised but didn't withdraw his invitation just because Saul was of the male persuasion.

"That'd be great," he said. "I'd love to teach you, Saul. You, too, Mrs. Coleman."

But Frannie was having none of it. "Saul, you are *not* going scuba diving off some boat tomorrow! Do you even watch the news? Don't you see all the people who fall overboard and get caught in riptides and drown or get eaten by sharks every year in Florida?"

"Actually, we've yet to lose a single citizen to sharks," Sheriff Hartwell said mildly from the driver's seat. He'd put on the brake. "We have nurse sharks around here, but they never attack anyone unless provoked. They're more scared of you than you should be of them. Anyway, we're here. Will Price's house."

CHAPTER SEVEN

LITTLE BRIDGE BOOK FESTIVAL ITINERARY FOR:
JO WRIGHT

Friday, January 3, 6:00 p.m.–9:00 p.m.

- Welcome Cocktail Meet-and-Greet and Dinner -

The board of the Little Bridge Book Festival welcomes you to Little Bridge in the home of one of our most prestigious donors.

What?

"Wait," I said. "*Where* are we?"

"Will Price's house." Garrett gathered up his tote bag and began to scramble from his seat, eager as the teacher's pet on the first day of school. "You didn't know that's where we were going for dinner tonight?"

"No." I tried to tamp down the panic I felt rising. "I thought we were going to a donor's house."

"We are. You didn't know the largest donor to the Little Bridge Book Festival is Will Price?"

"But—but . . ." I was confused. "I read that Will lives on an island."

Garrett smiled at me condescendingly. "This *is* an island, Jo."

"Not *Little Bridge* Island. A different island." All I could see through the bus windows was a high stucco wall, presumably surrounding a house, but I was certain the bus hadn't boarded a ferry. "This looks like the exact same island we were just on."

"We crossed a bridge," Garrett informed me, as patiently as if he were speaking to a very small child. "Will's island is only accessible via boat or a bridge with a private gate. Did you not notice us going across the long bridge with the private security?"

"Um." I threw a panicky glance at Bernadette, who was staring, goggle-eyed, out the window, exactly as I was doing. She obviously had no idea what was going on, either. "No."

"Saul!" Frannie had realized that her husband had fallen asleep. She began to shake him. "Saul. Wake up! We're here."

"Wha—? What? Oh." Saul roused himself. "Well, what do you expect? You made me get up at *five* this morning to get to the airport—"

"Sure. It's all my fault." Frannie rolled her eyes at us. "It's always my fault. Come on, lover boy, it's showtime."

Saul rose and followed his wife from the bus. "I wasn't really asleep," he assured me and Bernadette as he passed our row. "I was only resting my eyes."

"Crap," Bernadette said, when we were alone on the bus. "I'm so sorry about this, Jo. I had no idea. What do you want to do?"

"What *can* we do?" A glance at the driver's seat revealed that the sheriff had already disembarked along with the others, and disappeared with them through a wooden gate in the stucco wall. "I'm pretty sure the sheriff's not going to drive us back to the hotel."

Bernadette, ever a good friend, leaned over and placed a hand on my bare arm. "Do you want to walk back?" she asked. "I don't think it's really that far. Or we could call an Uber or a taxi—if they'll let one past the private gate."

"Don't be silly." I gave her a dazzling—and completely fake—smile. "We're here. Might as well go in and make Will Price regret his life choices, right?"

"I guess so." Bernadette chewed her lower lip uncertainly. "If you really think—"

"It'll be fine."

I had no confidence whatsoever that it was going to be fine, but what choice did I have?

Besides, Kitty Katz would never have let a thing like this bother her. She'd comb her whiskers and strut straight ahead, tail held high.

So I followed Bernadette through the tall, Spanish-style wooden gate into . . .

Jurassic Park.

That's what it looked like at first glance, anyway. Flaming tiki torches lit a flagstone path through towering lush tropical trees and plants.

Only instead of alarms going off to warn us of our impending doom at the mouth of a Tyrannosaurus rex, I could hear what sounded like a small live band—including a female singer—playing jazz vocal standards.

And instead of velociraptors, there were young women standing along the path every few feet in red-and-white cheerleading uniforms with the letter *S* emblazoned on the chest, holding trays of canapés.

"Hi," said the first cheerleader I encountered. "Welcome to Little Bridge Island. Would you like some fish dip?"

"Uh, no," I said. What in the whiskers? Then I added, "Thank you," so I wouldn't seem rude.

"Oh, no problem," the perky brunette said, still smiling. "Just so you know, though, the dip is made from completely organic, locally sourced ingredients, and the crackers are gluten-free."

"Oh," I said. "Great."

What. Was. Happening?

Further down the flagstone path that twisted through what appeared to be Pleistocene-era-jungle plant growth, it was so tall and dark and primeval, I began to catch glimpses of a sprawling mid-century modern single-level ranch-style house.

Made entirely of glass, steel, and stone—Will Price did not, evidently, ascribe to the Victorian-era aesthetic favored by the rest of Little Bridge Island—every room in the house was warmly lit, and I could see other people moving around inside as well as outside.

So we were not, evidently, about to fall into the mouth of

a volcano or be buried beneath a landslide (both fates met by heroes at the ends of Will Price books).

Still, I wasn't touching any of the food or drink we were being offered. What if we were about to be drugged and offered up as a human sacrifice?

Then, toward the end of the path, I saw the sheriff who'd driven our bus having an in-depth conversation with another one of the cheerleaders, this one holding a tray of what appeared to be grilled shrimp skewers. Both the sheriff and the cheerleader were laughing, perhaps a more disturbing sight than any I'd seen on Little Bridge thus far: this was the first time all night that I'd seen the sheriff smile.

I grabbed Bernadette by the elbow. "What is going on here?" I whispered. "Why does that sheriff look so happy? And what's with all the cheerleaders?"

Unlike me, Bernadette had said yes to every canapé she'd been offered. Now, her mouth full of mozzarella ball and tomato, she said, "Uh, I don't know. I think they're volunteering to raise money for their school. I saw a sign next to a tip jar on a table back there. You didn't bring any cash with you, did you? I left all mine back at the hotel. We should give them five bucks."

I shook my head. "No. And what are you doing, eating all that?"

"What do you mean?"

"Didn't you hear a thing Frannie said?"

Bernadette swallowed and laughed. "Oh, come on. You know Frannie. She's a worrywart. But this stuff is good. You should have some. And the kid said it was all organic."

"That's what they want us to believe! The reality is, we've just stepped off the bus into some kind of weird sex cult being run by Will Price on his private island."

"Um," Bernadette said, licking her fingers, "I don't think that's it. I'm pretty sure that one over there is the sheriff's daughter."

"What? Why would you think that?"

"Because I just heard her call him 'Daddy.'"

"Oh, sweet kittens." I rolled my eyes at her naïveté. "No wonder Will Price lives here. This place is Hell, and he's the Devil. Come on, let's go." I pulled on her arm, trying to drag her back to the gate.

"Wait, hold on." Bernadette put on the brakes. "Yes, Will Price is a pretentious jerk. But let's at least have a couple drinks before we leave, since we came all this way, and he's paying for them. That's the best way to get back at the patriarchy— by making them spend their money on us."

Before I could stop her, she marched straight up to one of the cheerleaders—this one a pretty Black girl holding a tray of champagne flutes—and said, "Hi, I'm Bernadette Zhang. What's your name?"

"Oh. My. God!" The girl's eyes widened. "Bernadette Zhang! You write the Crown of Stars and Bone series!"

"Yes, I do." Bernadette lifted one of the champagne flutes. "Thanks for reading."

"It's so cool to meet you! I love your books! I'm Sharmaine."

"Hi, Sharmaine. Thanks for the champagne. What's with the cheerleading getups?"

"Oh, we're not cheerleaders. We're the Snappettes, the high school dance team. And that's not—"

Bernadette was already making a face as she tasted the liquid in the glass. "Gah!"

"Sorry, I meant to tell you." Sharmaine looked apologetic. "That's not champagne, it's sparkling apple juice."

"Ugh." Bernadette put the glass back on the tray. "That's what my kids drink. They can't get enough of the stuff. I personally can't stand it. Too sweet."

"Yeah, sorry about that," Sharmaine said. "We're not allowed to serve alcohol since we're under twenty-one. They've set up a bar right around the corner there, though, if you—"

"Thank you so much." I hurried over to once again grab Bernadette by the arm. "It was nice to meet you."

"Wait." Sharmaine stared at me—well, at the badge dangling around my neck, the plastic laminate casing around it gleaming in the tiki-torch light. "Are you *the* Jo Wright, the author of *Kitty Katz, Kitten Sitter?*"

Naturally, I couldn't go running back to the bus after that. "Yes," I said. "It's nice to meet you, Sharmaine."

"Oh! My! God!" Sharmaine stooped to place the tray of sparkling apple juice on the side of the path. "I'm so sorry, but would you both mind? I just *have* to get a selfie with the two of you. You don't even understand. *Kitty Katz* was, like, my favorite series of *all time* when I was a kid. And the Crown of Stars and Bone series is, like, my life now."

"No problem," Bernadette said, and wrapped her arm around my waist while Sharmaine swept a cell phone from the waistband of her shorts, held it high, and leaned in for a quick, expert selfie, smiling like the Instagram star she undoubtedly was.

"Seriously," she said a second later. "My friends are going to *die*. You don't even *know*." Then, as she tucked her phone away again and stooped to pick up the tray, she whispered furtively, "Only, can you not mention that I got a photo with the two of you? Because they were really firm with us that we aren't supposed to be doing that. Mr. Price donated like twenty-five grand to the dance team in exchange for us helping out with the festival this weekend, and I really wouldn't want to let him down."

Bernadette elbowed me in the ribs before I had a chance to blurt out what I wanted to, which was *Wait, Will Price? Will Price donated money to your dance team? Are you sure? Because Will Price is Satan and would never do something nice.*

Unless of course it was to somehow take advantage of a nice young girl like Sharmaine. *That* I would believe.

"Absolutely," Bernadette said to Sharmaine. "We totally understand. Come on, Jo. Let's go find that bar."

Then Bernadette was dragging me down the path toward the house and the sound of the jazz ensemble.

"B-but," I stammered. "Did you hear her?"

"Yes, I heard her." The path had widened, and we'd left the jungle overgrowth for a wide-open area, a sort of courtyard leading up to the house, in the middle of which a large group of well-dressed, mostly older white people were gathered, laughing and chattering over the sound of the band, a bassist, drummer, and gorgeously curvaceous Latina female vocalist. "Let it go."

"I'm not going to let that go. You expect me to believe that *Will Price* supports female athletes? Or artists? Or whatever high school dance team members are? No way. He just wants teenaged girls in short shorts serving him at the party he's throwing on his private island."

"Do you think that maybe you're letting your antipathy toward him cloud your judgment a little?" Bernadette snagged a cheese tartlet from the tray of a passing Snappette.

"No. I saw who picked him up from the airport. She was age inappropriate."

"I'm not saying you're wrong. I'm just saying we should gather more information before we make a final decision. And by gather more information, I mean hit the bar for free booze, okay?"

"No. Not okay. Have you even—"

"Have I even what?"

I'd been about to ask her if she'd even read *The Moment*, then realized what I'd be admitting: that I'd read it (or had started reading it, anyway).

And that was far too humiliating a confession to make out loud. So instead I ground my teeth—something I'd been doing so much lately, my dentist had recommended that I wear a mouth guard at night to combat TMJ—and glared at all the happy partygoers around me. Most of them I didn't recognize, but I was able to pick out Saul and Frannie exactly where I most expected to find them—standing in line for the bar—and Garrett where I wasn't surprised to see him—pulling a "guild piece" from the ear of a well-dressed older woman who could only be a donor, and who of course screamed in delighted surprise at the "trick."

There was Molly consulting with an older man in a white chef's jacket and black pants—the caterer, since they were both in Will Price's perfect-looking, chrome-and-stainless-steel-appliance kitchen, which I could easily look into since his house was made almost entirely of sliding glass doors and none of the curtains had been drawn. That's how I was able to see that each room was exquisitely decorated in masculine tones of beige and taupe and gray, not a thing out of place, even in the bedrooms, where each bed—king-sized, of course—was tightly made, the pillows piled high and all facing a wall on which hung an expertly executed piece of modern art. No flat-screen televisions in Will's house (I had one in every room, of course, and kept them blaring all day long unless I was working, which lately was never).

But where was our host? How was I going to make him regret all of his life choices if I couldn't even find him?

"Jo! Bernadette!"

We looked over as a lanky Black man detached himself from the crowd by the bar and approached us. It was Jerome Jarvis, this year's national poet laureate, holding a beer in his hand.

"I was wondering when you two were going to get here," he said, smiling.

"I could say the same thing about you." Bernadette stood on tiptoe to give him a quick hello peck on the cheek. "Why weren't you on the author bus?"

"I walked here from the hotel. It was a long plane ride from Iowa. No direct flights. I needed to stretch my legs a little. Unfortunately, I wasn't the only one who had that idea—"

A piercing shriek split the air. "Bern! Jo!"

An attractive blond woman I recognized only too well from previous events separated herself from another crowd of people and lunged toward us. It was Kellyjean Murphy, whose witch-werewolf romance novels (written under the pen name Victoria Maynard) were all the rage.

"Oh my gosh," Kellyjean cried, stumbling a little—not because she was drunk. Kellyjean, a mother of four and aromapath from Texas, didn't consume alcohol or any other "unnatural substances." No, she stumbled because she wasn't used to the high-heeled gold sandals she had on. "Can you believe this place? Will Price must be making a fortune! I mean, I know his movies make a lot of money, but what kind of advances do you think he's pulling in? Have you seen his pool? That waterfall? And the beach? All white sand. I hear he has it flown in from the Bahamas. I think I might start killing off some of my characters if this is the kind of money you can make from it. Ha-ha, I'm kidding, of course!"

Jerome looked at Bernadette and me tiredly. "Yeah," he said. "Kellyjean is here. She walked over with me." The look of pain on Jerome's face illustrated what a long journey that must have been.

"Oh my gosh." Kellyjean, once she got started, was like a faucet that couldn't be turned off. She just gushed and gushed. Her broad Texas accent made the gushing all the more entertaining—or unbearable, depending on your perspective. "Jerome and I did walk here! And, boy, was that a mistake. I didn't think it was going to be that far, but golly, halfway across that bridge, my toes started killing me." She rubbed one of her tired feet. "But the view was *spectacular!* So, are any of you takin' Will up on his offer of a boat ride tomorrow? I sure am. The water here is *amazing*, so crystal clear, you could probably see mermaids through it if you got out far enough from the shore."

Kellyjean was an adult woman who believed not only in witches and werewolves, but also mermaids. I knew this from having been at previous events with her. There was a Netflix series based on her books that was rumored to be one of the top-rated shows on the streaming service.

Kellyjean wasn't stupid, though—no one with a career as successful as hers could be. She was simply a wide-eyed believer in all things mystical.

"How unfortunate," Jerome said, after another quick slug of beer. "I think I have a panel tomorrow afternoon."

"No, you don't!" Kellyjean dropped her foot and playfully slapped his shoulder. "None of us have any panels tomorrow afternoon. They're all in the morning."

"Oh." Jerome looked disappointed that his excuse hadn't worked. This wasn't his first rodeo with Kellyjean, either.

Kellyjean looked at Bernadette and me expectantly. "What about you two? Although you're probably going to be sick of Will by tomorrow, Jo, since you're sitting next to him tonight."

I stared at her, unsure whether this was another one of Kellyjean's flights of fancy or an actual fact. With her, it was often hard to tell. "What do you mean?"

"Haven't you checked out the tables for tonight?" Kellyjean was doing some yoga stretches even though we were at what was essentially a public event and she was wearing a maxi dress. But it was a maxi dress with a floaty skirt, in keeping with her identity as the author of romantic supernatural lore. "They're over on the beach, behind the pool with the sparkly waterfall. I always check where I'm going to be sitting first thing when I'm going to a dinner to make sure the caterer has me down for a vegetarian plate, and I saw your place card when I was looking for mine. Yours is at the Ernest Hemingway table, place of honor, right next to Will Price."

CHAPTER EIGHT

Sitting next to Will Price was the furthest thing from an honor to me.

But Kellyjean didn't know that.

And obviously whoever had done the seating chart for the welcome dinner didn't know it, either.

"Uh," I said, throwing a quick glance toward the pool. Long and rectangular, it took up most of the far side of the yard, sending wavy turquoise reflections splashing across the white terra-cotta flagstones as well as the lush canopy of green palm fronds above. A six-foot wall ran along the entire back of it, covered in bougainvillea and bright swirls of iridescent green tile. A steady stream of water flowed from the top of this wall to tumble into the pool below.

It was behind this wall that Kellyjean had indicated that the dinner tables were arranged.

"Would you guys excuse me for a minute?" I asked. "I'm just going to go look for the restroom."

Bernadette stared daggers at me. She knew exactly where I was going and that it wasn't the restroom.

"Oh, sure," Kellyjean said. "It's over there." She pointed in the general direction of Will's house. "Wait till you see it. Will has the most amazing soap. It's from Provence, France, and it's made from all organic ingredients—pure lavender, which as you probably know soothes sadness and also helps ward off mosquitos."

"Great," I said, and ditched the three of them. I had a mission to complete.

This mission was going to be more difficult to accomplish than I'd thought, however, because I had my name badge dangling from my neck.

So for every two feet of progress I made toward the dining area—where I intended to swap my place card for someone else's—I lost another foot being greeted by an enthusiastic reader—just not necessarily of my books.

"Jo Wright!" The older woman I'd seen chatting with Garrett seized my elbow. She was holding a fluffy miniature poodle and was dressed in Floridian high style: an extremely sparkly caftan, flowy white trousers, and jeweled sandals. "I've heard such lovely things about you. It's so wonderful that you were able to come!"

"Thank you," I said, politely shaking the hand she offered. Her badge said that her name was Dorothy Tifton and that she was a Gold Patron, which probably meant that she was high up there in donor status. Was she responsible for my ten-thousand-dollar stipend? "It was so nice of you to invite me."

"Oh, that was all Will," the woman said with a modest wave of her hand. "To be honest, I'd never heard of you until he mentioned you and said we simply had to invite you. I only read mysteries—and romance, of course. Is there mystery and romance in your books?"

Will? Will was the one who'd invited me?

Was I being punked? Maybe they were starting a new version of that show, only for authors. But who would watch that?

"Um," I said. "Yes, my books have mystery and romance. But they're for children." Which made it all the more strange that Will was the person who'd invited me. He'd made it clear that children's books were so beneath his notice that he didn't even consider them literature. "And they're about talking cats."

"Oh, well, then I *certainly* won't read them." Mrs. Tifton laughed cheerfully. "As you can see, I'm a dog person! Say hello to Daisy."

"Hello, Daisy," I said vaguely to the dog in her arms.

"Oh, look!" Mrs. Tifton bounced the dog up and down. The dog panted and wagged her tail. "She likes you!"

"Great. I like you, too, Daisy." Had I stepped off the plane into an alternate reality? Now I was talking to a dog.

"Well, have a wonderful night," Mrs. Tifton said. "Daisy and I look forward to seeing you at your events tomorrow."

"Thank you," I said, and when Mrs. Tifton waved her dog's paw at me as I moved past her, I waved back.

Sure. That was completely normal. A completely normal conversation on Little Bridge Island, which was a completely normal place.

No. No, this place was *nuts*. I needed a drink, and right away.

Except that there was still a mad crush at the bar, and Garrett was there, too, pulling more guild coins than ever out of people's ears.

No. Abort, abort—return to original mission. At least I was able to see that what Sharmaine had assured me was the truth: there were no underage cheerleaders—sorry, dance team members—serving or being served alcohol.

So I steeled myself and rounded the side of the pool to where Kellyjean had said dinner was going to be served.

It was a different world. After the noise and heat of the party—the chatter and music—it was like stepping from a hot, crowded nightclub into a beachside hideaway straight out of Bali.

Small, gentle waves lapped softly at a sandy white beach. Warmly lit party globes hung on strands from thick, tall palm trees, beneath which sat a half-dozen large round tables, each covered in a long white tablecloth and surrounded by ten or twelve chairs. Wineglasses and silverware marked each place setting, and glinted faintly in the half-moon that could just be seen sliding up behind the tops of the palm fronds.

I had to admit that the effect was beautiful. In the center of each table sat an old-fashioned glass hurricane lantern lit by a single dancing flame, and beside the lantern, a pile of leather-bound books. Guests determined which table they were assigned to by checking a sign at the entrance to the dining area, where a seating chart was hanging from a small palm tree. Each table was named after the author whose books adorned it—mostly dead authors with some affiliation to Florida, such as Tennessee Williams, Wallace Stevens, and Zora Neale Hurston.

Thanks to Kellyjean I already knew I'd been assigned to the Ernest Hemingway table. It didn't take me long to find it—nor did it take long for me to discover that Kellyjean had been telling the truth. Someone had seated me right next to Will Price. Great.

I'd already checked the seating chart and seen that Bernadette was at the Elizabeth Bishop table. I plucked up someone's place card from beside Bernadette's (Drew Hartwell. No idea who she was. Possible relation to the sheriff? Was everyone on this island related to one another?) and was moving back toward the Ernest Hemingway table with the intention of swapping it with my own when a voice caused me to freeze.

"Hello?"

I swung around to see one of the dance team members, a tray of salads balanced carefully in her hands.

"Um," I said. "Hi."

That's when I realized, to my horror, that this wasn't just any dance team member, but Chloe, the little blonde from the airport who'd hurled herself at Will Price.

Chloe? *Chloe* was in *high school?* Will Price was dating a *high school student?*

So I'd been right all along about him. Wait until I told Bernadette . . . and then everyone in the entire world. My revenge would be complete!

"What *are* you doing?" she asked, her British accent quite pronounced. She didn't ask it in a particularly hostile way. She sounded more curious than anything.

"Um," I said, feeling the place cards in my hand begin to dampen with sweat. No. No, no, no, no. "I'm—"

Fortunately, at that moment, another Snappette appeared from nowhere, also carrying a tray of salads. This was the brunette I recognized from earlier, the one Bernadette had said she'd heard call the sheriff "Daddy." She, too, froze in her tracks, her eyes widening when she saw me.

"Oh . . . my . . . God."

Chloe threw her a quizzical look. "What?"

"Chloe," the brunette breathed. "That's *her*."

Chloe's blond head whipped back around to look at me. "No. Way."

"No, really. It is." The brunette shifted her tray of salads onto her hip. "You're Jo Wright, author of the Kitty Katz series, aren't you?"

Never in my life had I been more glad to be who I was. Because I was pretty sure that this time, it was going to get me out of an awkward jam.

"Yes," I said. "Yes, I am. And you are?"

"I'm Katie Hartwell," she said. She couldn't reach out to shake my hand thanks to the salad tray, but she looked as if she wanted to. "And this is my friend Chloe Price, and we. Are. Your. Biggest. Fans. Seriously. Except maybe for our friend Sharmaine—"

"It's true." Chloe looked as if she were torn between

screaming and crying. She could barely hold on to her tray. "Kitty Katz is my favorite series of all time. I've read every single one of her adventures a hundred times at *least*."

I couldn't help noticing that neither of them had employed the words *used to*. I also couldn't help noticing something else.

"Chloe *Price?*" I asked. "Are you related to Will Price?"

"Oh, yes." Chloe brightened. "He's my brother. He's a writer, too. Do you know him?"

So the blonde I'd been so sure was Will Price's girlfriend really was his little sister?

There was absolutely nothing about Will having siblings in any of his bios. Not that I'd read them all. Okay, I'd read them all, searching for some hint as to what had happened to him in his past to make him such a bitter and entitled person. I'd found nothing. He'd had every privilege in the world: grown up in some sheepy area of England that looked incredibly idyllic to me (having only been to England a few times on tour, and mainly only to large cities, I had no idea, but it looked idyllic in photos); went to great universities (in England, of course); got his first book published (after a seven-figure auction), which then went on to become an international bestseller.

Why he was constantly writing super-angsty books, often set in America instead of his own country, I had no idea. But come on. The guy was basically hashtag blessed.

"I know Will a little," I lied. "I didn't know he had a sister, though."

"Oh, no one knows about Chloe. Will's very protective," Katie assured me. "He's super rich, and he's afraid she might get kidnapped. Although no one around here would do something like that."

"Katie." Chloe looked embarrassed.

"Well, it's true." Katie was evidently one of those people who thought that if something was true, it was all right to blurt it out. "My dad's the sheriff, and he wouldn't let it. But have you checked out Will's net worth?"

"Um, no," I said, though of course I had, many times. His net worth was the same as my own, except that I'd written nearly four times as many books as he had (though admittedly mine were a lot shorter, since they were for kids) and I'd tucked all my money safely away in defined benefit plans I couldn't touch until I was older than my dad was now. I hadn't gone around throwing my royalties away willy-nilly on stupid things such as *mansions* on *private islands* and *boats*.

"Well, right, then," Katie went on. "So you know he's loaded. He's practically paying for this entire book festival. Well, him and Mrs. Tifton."

"Katie!" Chloe looked horrified.

"Well, it's true."

"Yeah, but it's rude to talk about things like that."

"But—"

"It's okay." I interrupted, not only because I didn't want to see the girls get into an argument, but because I couldn't quite believe what I was hearing. Will Price was paying for this book festival?

Obviously I knew he'd loaned the use of his house and

apparently his boat for tomorrow's author outing, and also given a hefty donation to the girls' dance team.

But donated actual money to promote books—*children's* books, which he'd quite publicly claimed weren't even "real" literature?

Why? What was Will up to?

"Sorry." Katie was looking at me apologetically. "Chloe's right. I shouldn't have said anything."

"No." Chloe looked furious with her friend. "You shouldn't have, Katie. My brother is very private. Not just about me, but about . . . well, *everything.*"

Oh, this was interesting. What did Will have to be so private about? I'd never read a word about him having a wife or kids—every article referred to him as too "busy and dedicated to his career" to share his life "with a partner," as he called it.

But I could understand that. I'd tried living "with a partner," too, and it hadn't gone too well. My "partner" had always been nagging me to go out and do things with him (on my dime) when all I'd wanted to do was stay home and write about funny kitten-sitting adventures.

And Justin had then had the audacity to accuse *me* of being the weird one in our relationship!

I shook my head. "No, don't worry about it," I said. "It's fine. It's very . . . nice of your brother, Chloe, to have included me." The words stuck in my throat. But she seemed like a genuinely sweet girl, so I had to say something kind about her brother, as much as it pained me.

"Are you serious?" Chloe shot me an incredulous look. "Of

course he included you. You're my favorite author! You don't even know—your books helped me through one of the worst times in my entire *life*."

Wow.

Suddenly I knew I couldn't do what I'd been thinking a moment earlier, which was to put Drew's place card back where I'd found it, then sneak off the island and into an Uber back to the hotel.

And not just because I was sure that by now all the ink had washed off the hand-calligraphed card and onto my sweaty palm, but because when someone says something like that, you have to stick around.

Plus, it was too late. People from the meet-and-greet—which was apparently over—were starting to file in to grab their seats for dinner.

And leading the pack—standing a head taller than everyone else, and looking cool and relaxed despite the heat—was none other than the man of the hour himself, Will Price.

CHAPTER NINE

Everything was fine. Everything was going to be great.

I just had to be normal and act like I didn't know that my mortal enemy, Will Price, had paid for me and my friends to be here.

Wait. Was he paying our stipends, too?

What in the name of sweet kitty heaven was going on here?

Never mind. It didn't matter. I could do this. I could totally do this.

Fortunately there was wine. Members of the catering team—they were the ones in white shirts and black trousers—were walking around the tables with bottles, asking the guests who were filing into their seats which they preferred, red or white.

Perfect. Wine would help. Straight vodka would be better, but wine would work.

Letting the crumpled place card I was holding fall to the sand—it was nothing but a sweat-stained swatch of cardboard now, but completely biodegradable—I snatched up a glass from a table I was passing on my way back to the one I'd been assigned, then held it out to the closest server.

"Red or white?" she asked with a bright smile. "Tonight we have a lovely Pinot Noir and a Sauvignon Blanc."

"Either," I said. "Both. I don't care."

The server smiled and poured a generous serving of red wine into my glass, half of which I managed to down in almost a single gulp just as a smiling Molly approached.

This would have been fine—I could have handled a conversation with a children's librarian just then—if I hadn't spied Will Price strolling behind her, looking casually princely in the glow of the lamps and moonlight.

All right, I told myself. This was it. Our showdown. I was going to find out exactly what in the whiskers was going on, then let him have it. He wouldn't be feeling so princely once I was through with him. That's right, buddy, I've got your number. You better have an apology and some explanations ready about what's going on around here or *you're* the one who's going to get kicked back to the author bus.

"Oh, Ms. Wright, there you are," Molly said brightly. "I've been looking for you everywhere. Have you met Will Price? He's one of our festival's board members, and a writer, as well."

Wait. Will Price was a donor *and* a member of the festival's board?

And she really thought I hadn't heard of him? Was she unaware of the plagiarism scandal that had linked Will's name with mine forever, much to my everlasting chagrin? Did she not know we'd all received a copy of *The Moment* in our swag bags, and that some of us were reading every word?

Then again, Molly was a librarian living in the Florida Keys on a small island that felt a million miles from the rest of the world. And judging by that sheriff's smile and how close she seemed to giving birth, she'd obviously been keeping herself busy doing other things.

"We've met," I said, and boldly stretched my inky right hand toward Will while plastering the smile across my face that Rosie had nicknamed "Fake Jo." Make him regret his life choices, remember? "How are you, Will?"

"I'm well, thank you." He took my hand in his. His skin felt warm but dry, unlike my own, since I was sweating up a storm. Stupid Florida humidity.

He'd changed since I'd seen him at the airport that morning. He'd been unable to do anything about his hair—it still fell in unruly dark curls around his handsome, angular face—but he'd made an effort to get rid of some of the five-day stubble, at least. He'd ditched the jeans and Timbs for a white cotton button-down, the sleeves rolled up at the elbow to reveal muscular, tanned forearms, and pale blue linen trousers. He looked cool, calm, and collected.

It wasn't fair. He had the home-court advantage and knew it.

But I wasn't going to let him win, any more than Kitty Katz ever let her mortal enemy, Raul Wolf, win when they competed against each other during school debates and spelling bees.

"I'm so glad you were able to come," Will said to me in that deep voice that fans of his audiobooks loved so much.

"Thanks for inviting me. You have a lovely home." How I longed to throw stones through those glass windows of his. "I met your sister, Chloe, just now."

Will's dark eyebrows lifted, registering surprise. But before he could say anything, Molly cried, "Oh, Chloe! Isn't she sweet? She and my stepdaughter, Katie, have become inseparable since Will and Chloe moved here. We're so lucky to have them both on the island. Will's become such an asset to the literary community, and Chloe is—well, Chloe is Chloe!"

I couldn't help it: I smirked. *Will Price, an asset to the literary community? More like an ass.*

I know. Real mature. But I can't help it, I write for kids.

Unfortunately, Will seemed to notice my little smirk, since I saw those dark eyes narrow at me.

"Sure," I said, wiping the smile off my face. I should never have touched the wine. "I can imagine."

"Anyway, if you'll both excuse me," Molly said, "I have to go help everyone find their seats. Ms. Wright, you're at the Hemingway table over—"

"Oh, yes, I know. And I told you, it's Jo, please."

"Right! Jo!" Molly twinkled at us, then waddled over to where Kellyjean was causing a huge clog in the flow of traffic, not because she didn't know where her seat was, but because her sandals had finally become too much for her, and she'd sat down in the middle of the beach and begun undoing them.

That left Will Price and me alone with each other for the first time since we'd been in that green room together at Novel Con a year and a half ago.

Well, as alone as two people could be at a dinner party with over fifty other people milling around them.

We hadn't really been alone in that green room, either. People had kept coming in and out.

But I, at least, had thought we'd gotten along so well. Besides bonding over the terrible coffee, we'd chatted about how difficult it was, getting up so early to give a speech to so many people. (Novel Con was one of the largest annual fan conventions in the publishing industry, and there was no greater honor than giving the breakfast speech on day one of the convention, but it wasn't glamorous. It required being in the green room by six A.M., while the audience of five thousand filed in to find their seats at their tables in the auditorium by eight.)

Will had even complimented my dress. I'd splurged for once and hired a stylist who'd assured me that the "springtime green" designer wrap dress she'd chosen and I'd purchased (for an exorbitant amount of money, or at least what seemed like it to a girl who was used to picking up bargains at factory outlets) would bring out the blue of my eyes and what were then the honey-blond highlights in my hair.

It seemed to have worked, too. I'd caught Will surreptitiously checking me out.

And I hadn't minded, because I'd been admiring the broadness of his shoulders in his dark blue sports coat, the way the corners of his mouth turned up at the sides, and, yes, God help me, the slight but perfectly noticeable bulge in the front of his oh-so-perfectly form-fitting jeans.

But why shouldn't we have checked each other out? We were around the same age, and in the same line of work. And of course we'd both been plagiarized by the same person. We'd even bonded over that (or so I'd thought) as we'd waited to be called to give our speeches, describing how each of us had found out (he'd been told by his publisher, I'd been tweeted by a fan) and what a weirdo Nicole was for thinking she'd get away with it.

I'd honestly thought that despite his terrible books (simply not my taste, given that I'd experienced the death of a loved one firsthand, and didn't care to relive that trauma through fiction), Will Price seemed like a nice person.

What a pity, I'd thought at the time, *that I'm saddled with Justin, who claims to be a writer but never actually writes anything and then complains that we never go out because I'm too busy writing all the time. I could maybe see myself with a guy like Will. Or maybe even Will himself.*

It wasn't until the next week, when the *Times* story hit, that I learned what a mistake *that* line of thinking had been.

I sipped my wine—the server had come around again to refill my glass—and decided Will should be the one to speak next. Also that what he said had better be an apology or I wasn't going to say another word to him all night, which would be awkward, considering I was sitting beside him.

He did speak next, but he didn't apologize. Instead, he said, "Chloe told you, didn't she?"

This was so unexpected that I forgot all about not speaking to him until he apologized. "Told me what?"

He studied my face for a moment, his brown eyes—as dark as the shadows beyond the festively lit tables—seeming to rake my face, looking for some clue that I knew . . . what?

Then, apparently deciding I didn't know whatever it was, and that he was in the clear, he reached in relief for one of the wineglasses that had been poured on the table nearest us, even though it wasn't his assigned seat, and took a hearty swig.

"Never mind," he said.

Now I forgot all about not speaking until I got an apology. He thought I didn't know what his lovely sister had told me—that she was a fan of my books! After all the nasty things he'd said about me and my writing (well, all right, it was only one nasty thing, but one was enough), it turned out that his own kin adored me and my creation!

"As a matter of fact, she did tell me," I said, feeling a rush of exultation. "She told me *everything*."

This couldn't have had a more satisfying effect. Those deliciously dark eyes of his widened, and the normally up-turned corners of that pouty mouth—what was such a small mouth doing on so large a man, anyway?—sloped downward.

"She *did*?"

"Oh, yes." I was loving this. My mother's ancestors were so right. Revenge delayed was the very best kind. "Absolutely. And I can't say I'm surprised."

He seemed to have forgotten the wineglass in his hand. It

sank so low that the little remaining liquid in it was spilling out, splashing onto the sand.

"You're . . . you're not?"

"Of course not." I was really impressed with how assertive I was being. Bernadette would have been proud. "I have fans her age all over the world . . . some from much farther away than England. And your sister is hardly the first to tell me that my books got her through a difficult time—the worst time in her entire life, I think, is how she put it. Which makes me wonder if things got a little awkward for you around your house after she found out how you threw me under the bus to the *Times* the last time we met."

The wineglass in his hand righted itself, and his head came up. It had been sinking, along with his shoulders, the entire time I'd been talking, until he'd begun to resemble one of those saints paying penance in all those paintings at the Metropolitan Museum of Art—a totally hot saint. But a saint nonetheless.

But now he straightened and asked in a tone of surprise, his dark eyes narrowing, "Wait . . . *that's* what Chloe told you? That she's a fan of your books?"

"Yes, of course." What was wrong with him? "What did you think she said?"

"Nothing." He set the now empty wineglass down on the nearby table and seemed to exhale—in relief.

"Why?" I demanded sharply. "Are you going to try to tell me it's not true? Because I was standing right over there when she said it. She and her friend the sheriff's daughter and their other friend, Sharmaine, all said—"

"Oh, no." He toed some of the wine-damp sand. "It's true."

Then why on earth was he looking so relieved? He should have been looking ashamed—ashamed for being such a judgmental hater of literature for girls (and some boys, and of course non-binary children as well).

"So what happened?" I asked. "Did you think neither of us were going to notice when you decided to talk smack about Kitty Katz to the press? Because I can assure you that I did. My own *father* wrote to let me know. He has a Google alert on my name. Do you have any idea what it feels like to be called by your dad and told that internationally bestselling author Will Price—who I *thought* was a friend of mine—was going around saying that Nicole Woods should have had better taste than to copy me? How do you think that made me feel?"

Finally he looked up. And this time when he did, I could see that there was heat in those dark eyes of his. What kind of heat—shame, anger, humiliation, all three—I couldn't tell. But something was flaring there, deep inside the darkness.

"I'm sorry," he said in a voice that was so low, I could barely hear it above the excited chatter of the other dinner guests, the squeaking of wooden chairs as they sat, and the clink of silverware as they hungrily attacked their salads. "I'm so sorry that happened to you. It shouldn't have."

Wait. What was going on? Was he *apologizing?*

"I was going through a difficult personal time." He was still talking, that deep voice so quiet, it was almost a purr. "I wasn't as selective of my words as I ought to have been. But I realize that's no excuse."

"Wait," I said, confused.

I realized I must have been gaping at him, but none of this was going to plan. He wasn't supposed to apologize, or make excuses. He was supposed to haughtily ignore me or maybe call for his butler to haul me from his grand tropical estate.

He wasn't supposed to say he was *sorry*.

I had no idea how to react except to keep going, saying all the things I'd rehearsed saying to him a thousand times in my head . . . although of course I'd never imagined him *apologizing*, so nothing I'd planned made sense anymore . . . especially since it was getting all garbled in my head with what he'd said.

"You were going through *a difficult time?* You completely dissed me and basically the entirety of children's literature because you were *going through a difficult time?* I've gone through difficult times, Will, and I've managed to keep my feelings about other people's books to myself. And believe me, my feelings about *your* books aren't particularly positive."

I wasn't going to mention that I couldn't put down *The Moment.* That was beside the point. Especially now that I'd noticed that Bernadette, over at the Elizabeth Bishop table, was watching my interaction with Will intently, making questioning faces and mouthing something that looked like *Are you all right?*

Meanwhile Garrett, over at the Tennessee Williams table, was giving me a mock golf clap for finally standing up to the great Will Price. Neither of them were close enough to hear what I was saying, but apparently my body language was giving me away.

I was on a roll. This was my big chance to finally tell Will Price what I thought of him.

Except none of it felt as good as I'd imagined it would feel.

Still, I kept going. I had to. For all of womankind and children's literature and my mother and Sicily and, of course, cats.

"Were you on *drugs* or something?" I demanded. "Are you trying to tell me that *sleeping pills made you do it*, like Nicole? Because I've taken sleeping pills and they've never made me say really mean things about other writers' work to journalists before."

"No, I was not on drugs."

Now Will's deep voice really was a growl. And it wasn't hard at all to tell what he was feeling. The heat in his eyes had disappeared. His gaze had turned as cold as the steel and concrete his house was made of.

He didn't resemble a penitent saint anymore, either. He looked a lot more like the coal-eyed devil I'd always known him to be. His lean jaw was set so firmly that there was a muscle leaping beneath it, like a spring that was about to come flying loose.

"Look," he whispered. He had to whisper because Kellyjean was coming over, tripping barefoot across the sand toward us with a questioning look on her face. Knowing Kellyjean, she was probably going to ask Will if there were water sprites living in his pool or something because she'd just seen one. "I really am sorry about what I said. I ought to have apologized a lot sooner, but I—well, I've never been very good with words—"

"Hold up. Never been very good with words? *Will, you're one of the bestselling writers in the world.*"

"Even so." The muscle in his jaw was jumping all over the place. His eyes were like twin embers. "Sometimes I find it difficult to express myself. And I—"

"Sorry to interrupt." Kellyjean floated up to us in her bare feet and shimmery maxi dress. "But aren't you Will Price?"

Of course Will was one of the few people not wearing his name badge. Why would he? He was Will Price, easily recognizable from having his books in every spinner rack in every bookstore in every airport and grocery store in the world. Sometimes there were even life-sized cardboard cutouts of him standing beside the displays of his books—cutouts that I longed to punch, but never had the guts to.

Kitty Katz, of course, would have.

"I just wanted to introduce myself," Kellyjean went on, apparently oblivious to the animosity crackling in the air between Will and me, even though Kellyjean insisted she was very much in touch with people's auras. "You probably recognize me as Victoria Maynard, the author of the Salem Prairie series, but my real name is Kellyjean Murphy. I'm sure you've heard of my books—there's a Netflix show based on them."

"Hello, Kellyjean." Will's voice sounded strained, though he smiled as warmly as someone who might actually have heard of and enjoyed the Salem Prairie series, which I highly doubted he had, since it performed best with female readers/viewers ages 18–54 and heavily featured CGI shape-shifting wolf sex. I'd never missed an episode. "Pleasure to meet you."

"Oh, likewise! Thank you so much for hosting us tonight, and for inviting me. Your home is so lovely. I just can't get over the pool. It's all I can do not to rip off my dress and jump in right now."

"Well, feel free." He kept up the fake smile while I watched the muscle in his jaw continue to leap around like Miss Kitty on catnip. "I want all of my guests to enjoy themselves."

Kellyjean tittered as Will laid a hand on one of my bare arms.

Will Price was touching me. Why was Will Price touching me? Why was I *enjoying* the fact that Will Price was touching me?

"If you don't mind," he said to Kellyjean, "we need to take our seats. I know the caterer's anxious that we get through the salad course so they can begin serving the main while it's hot."

"Oh, of course!" Kellyjean began to back away. "But I'm going to take you up on that invitation for a swim!"

"Sure," Will said. "Anytime."

Then he began steering me toward our table, speaking to me in that same low, intense voice he'd used before.

"Look," he said. "I know I'm not in much of a position to ask favors from you. But I'm going to ask one of you anyway: accept my apology. If you can't, I'll totally understand, but please at least try to pretend to get along with me for this weekend, which I and many others have worked hard to make as enjoyable as possible for you. If you can't do it for me, do it for my sister's sake. She's been through a lot—more than you can imagine—and she loves you and your books so much."

I stared straight ahead as these last few words sunk in.

What the whiskers? What had just happened? Will Price had apologized, and I'd let him? I'd actually let him, just because his sister had had a bad time (and so had he) and, also, she liked my books?

Apparently, I had.

Because now I was letting him take me to our table, and pull out my chair for me, and sit down next to me, and hand me my napkin, and make polite small talk with the other people at our table, who turned out to be Molly and her sheriff husband, Mrs. Tifton and her dog, some friends of Mrs. Tifton's, and Saul and Frannie.

And now I was letting him pour more wine into my glass, and ask if I'd prefer vinaigrette or blue cheese dressing on my salad (there were small serving pitchers of both on the table).

"Uh, vinaigrette is fine," I heard myself murmur.

Then he *poured the vinaigrette on my salad*. Like he was my waiter!

And I sat there with my fork in my hand, thinking, Should I just go ahead and start eating? Or grab my bag and run for my life?

Because this was not the natural order of things. Will Price turning out to be a kind person who actually cared about my feelings—or anyone else's—was not something I'd ever considered remotely possible.

There seemed to be only one reasonable course of action under the circumstances, and that was to drink as much wine as possible.

The Moment by Will Price

I finally convinced her to let me take her out for a meal. But as the waiter set course after course down in front of me, I tasted none of it. She was my meal. My eyes feasted on her whenever I thought she wouldn't catch me looking.

What was even more amazing was that she seemed to like me, too. She laughed at my jokes, her smile radiating across the table like a second sun. Even when she wasn't laughing, her face was still alive with animation, her every mood flickering across those lovely blue eyes like goldfish in a pool.

I wasn't the only one looking at her. Every head in the place turned to admire her as I helped her into her coat, male as well as female. I thought I might burst with pride at the fact that she was there with me.

The only problem was how—and when—to tell her how I felt.

CHAPTER TEN

The wine was a bad idea.

I managed to keep it together through the salad course and the "mains"—a choice of grilled vegetables, yellowtail, or beef tenderloin. (Saul and I had the yellowtail, Frannie the tenderloin.)

I kept silent while Will stood up and welcomed all of us and thanked us for being there. I maintained an appropriate level of dignity during dessert (key lime pie), not asking everyone at the table who didn't eat theirs if I could have their slices.

I even made it onto the author bus (this time it wasn't the sheriff or Molly who drove, but a male librarian named Henry) without falling over or otherwise disgracing myself.

But when we got to the hotel and Saul insisted we all have a nightcap (his favorite: Baileys on ice), I lost it.

"Okay, everyone take out your phones," I said as we sat down with our cool, deliciously creamy drinks and dipped our bare feet into the pool. "You're all great writers and incredible researchers. So I need you to help me research what horrible tragedy happened to Will Price and his sister approximately a year and a half to two years ago."

Saul had already passed out on one of the chaise lounges, his drink untouched in his hand, and Garrett had retired to his room with the excuse that he needed to get more work done—not on his book, it turned out, but on the big magic trick he was planning to perform on Saturday night, the one I had absolutely no intention of watching.

But Kellyjean was sitting with us, even though she didn't drink. She said she'd wanted to stay up to watch a meteor shower one of her sons had told her was supposed to be visible in the Florida Keys this weekend.

The moment she heard what I wanted her to look up on her phone, however, she turned her head away from the night sky. "What makes you think something tragic happened to Will Price and his sister?"

"Because he said so. Both he and his sister said something about it. My books apparently helped her through one of the worst times in her life, and around the same time, Will said he was going through such a difficult period that he lost his head and bad-mouthed me to the *New York Times*."

"I don't understand," Kellyjean said. "Why not just ask Will?"

"I did," I said. "He doesn't want to talk about it. Apparently he's very protective of his privacy."

"Well, there you go, then." Kellyjean turned her gaze back toward the stars. "You shouldn't pry. Everyone deserves their privacy."

"Um, excuse me." I really should have stopped at one glass

of wine after all the screwdrivers I'd had on the plane, and then the margarita in the pool, and of course I should have said no to the Baileys now. But I had not. I had had two or three—or four—glasses of California's finest Pinot Noir, and it had all gone straight to my head. "But are you saying I don't deserve an explanation for why Will Price dragged my good name through the mud?"

"He told you," Kellyjean said. "Something so deeply tragic happened to him that he doesn't want to talk about it, and it made him behave badly."

"If it were only his sister we were talking about, I would fully respect her right to privacy. But it isn't. I have the right to know why Will said what he did."

"Did he say he was sorry?"

"Well, yes. But I still need to know."

"For heaven's sakes, why?"

"*Because*, Kellyjean, I'm a *writer*! I'm curious about people and what motivates them."

"Well, I'm a writer, too, and I say butt out."

"Maybe because it wasn't *your* good name that he trashed."

"I think there's more to it than that," Kellyjean said primly.

"Oh, really? Like what?"

"Like you're in love with him."

"*I'm in love with him?*" I started laughing. "Kellyjean, what on earth would make you think I'm in love with Will Price?"

"I've got eyes in my head, don't I? I've seen the way you look at him. When you two were talking when I came up to you on the beach before dinner, you could have cut the sexual tension with a knife."

"That was hatred, Kellyjean. That was pure, unadulterated hatred."

Kellyjean shook her head. "I don't think so. I'm a romance writer, Jo, don't forget. I'm an expert in these things."

Astonished, I looked over at Bernadette for help. "Are you hearing this?"

"Uh, Kellyjean," Bernadette said. "I have to agree with Jo here. This isn't one of your paranormal romances. No one is going to shape-shift into a wolf. I can assure you, Jo hates Will's guts."

I did hate his guts. I absolutely did.

Although I had to admit that some of the parts outside his guts were pretty appealing. Sitting next to him all night, I'd been all too conscious of his hands—big, strong-looking hands for a man who apparently did nothing all day but type.

And those wide shoulders I'd first admired back in that green room hadn't gotten any less irresistible, either. Neither had his night-dark eyes.

Ew, yuck, what was I doing, describing Will Price's eyes as night-dark? That was like something straight out of a Will Price book . . . both a cliché and not true. Will's eyes were brown. Just plain brown.

Not that I didn't think of those eyes, and often. Occasionally, when I came across photographs of Will in airline magazines (he was forever getting interviewed in them, and I was forever coming across those interviews as I flew to and from book events), I blacked out those brown eyes and even his teeth with whatever pen I had handy, then left the periodical for the next passenger to discover. *Who hated bestselling author Will Price so much that they'd do something like this?* I often imagined the passenger wondering to themselves when they came across the defaced photo of him. *What did he ever do to them?*

Ha! Plenty!

Ugh, I needed to drink some water. But Baileys tasted so much better.

"I think it's good for Jo to find out what Will's hiding," Frannie was saying when I tuned back into the conversation. "Supposing it turns out he secretly ran over her husband?"

"Happens." Jerome shook his head. "Happens all the time. White people are crazy."

Kellyjean looked confused. "Jo, are you *married?*"

I grinned. "No, Kellyjean. They're talking about Will's new book, *The Moment.*"

"Oh. Well, I don't think this is a joking matter," Kellyjean said. "If Will doesn't want you to know what happened to him and his sister, you shouldn't be trying to look it up. It's an invasion of his privacy, and it's wrong."

Frannie sighed. "Loathe as I am to admit it, Kellyjean is right, but not for the reasons she thinks. It's wrong because it's futile. I see Will Price's name in the news every week, practically, for donating to charity or coming out with a new movie or being nominated as one of *People* magazine's sexiest men alive. If something bad had happened to him, we'd know already."

"Hey," Jerome said. "*People* magazine nominated *me* as one of the sexiest men alive, and all of you missed it."

"Funny, Jerome," I said. "Very funny."

Bernadette had her cell phone out. "The only negative thing I can find online that happened to Will is the plagiarism thing."

"If he's so protective of his privacy," I said, "it wouldn't necessarily be something the press would know."

"I'm protective of my privacy, too," Jerome said. "So protective that when *People* magazine tried to name me one of their sexiest men alive, I turned them down."

Frannie laughed. "That's because your wife wouldn't share you, Jer."

"Well, yes, that is true."

Kellyjean looked confused. "Wait, I can't tell if y'all are serious or playing with me."

Bernadette was still scrolling through her phone. "They're playing with you, Kellyjean. Jerome wasn't named one of *People* magazine's sexiest men alive. And I can't find a single piece of dirt on Will Price aside from the Nicole Woods thing, Jo. He's never dated anyone, never had a job outside of publishing. It's like he graduated from college and went straight into bestseller-dom. His very first book, published when he was twenty-three, was a smash hit. A lot like yours, Jo."

"Uh, not at all like mine. Kitty Katz got rejected a hundred times before she became a smash hit." I leaned back and gazed up through the palm fronds swaying in the breeze. I didn't see any meteors, but frogs croaked all around us, the only sound, besides that of the waterfall over by the Jacuzzi and our own voices, in the hotel courtyard. "Never mind, it's okay. I have a message in to my agent. You know agents get all the best dirt. I'm sure she'll have something for me by morning."

"I still don't understand why you have to go poking into that poor man's business," Kellyjean said. "What all happened over at the Hemingway table tonight, anyway?"

"Nothing," I said.

I meant it, too. My evening had been completely uneventful once Will had asked me to drop what had happened at Novel Con. The conversation at the table had been light— Saul sharing hilarious stories from the horror-writing business, Molly and Sheriff Hartwell sharing how they'd met, and Dorothy Tifton sharing a bizarre but entertaining story about how she'd helped catch a local thief.

Aside from his welcome speech, Will had hardly uttered a sound, except to laugh in all the right places at the others' stories, and ask if I liked my food, or if I needed anything. It had been almost like sitting next to a very attentive butler. A very good-looking butler from England, who'd spent a good deal of his time worriedly watching his younger sister every time she flitted past with a tray or dish.

But when Chloe hadn't dropped a single thing or otherwise embarrassed herself in any way, I'd noticed him relax a little. He'd even taken off his shoes beneath the table, and rubbed his feet in the sand. I don't think he thought anyone would notice, but then, he probably didn't think anyone was paying that much attention to him.

But I was. I couldn't help it, much as I might have wished differently. Any more than I could help noticing that he had very sexy feet. God, what was wrong with me?

"I don't understand any of this," Kellyjean declared. "I think y'all are being very mean to poor Will, especially considering the fact that he's invited us to his house and this festival and offered us those very generous stipends."

I snorted. "Oh, please. If Will thinks he can make me forget what he did to me by paying me off with a ten-thousand-dollar stipend, you're crazy."

There was silence around the pool. The frogs suddenly sounded extremely loud, as did the splashing of the waterfall over by the Jacuzzi.

I realized then that I'd said something very, very wrong.

"Wait a minute." Bernadette's voice sounded unlike her usual flippantly casual tone. "You're getting a *ten-thousand-dollar* stipend to be here?"

"Um." I looked around at the stunned faces of my friends and fellow authors and felt my stomach lurch. Uh-oh. "Yes. Aren't you?"

"Heck, no!" Saul suddenly sat straight up. If he'd ever been asleep at all, he was certainly awake now. "I'm only getting *fifteen hundred*!"

Frannie patted her husband on the knee. "Now, now, dear. Fifteen hundred dollars is nothing to sneeze at. And we're getting a lovely, all-expense paid, first-class vacation out of it. And think how many books you'll sell at your signing tomorrow and Sunday."

"I'm only getting fifteen hundred, too." Bernadette looked at Jerome. "You?"

He nodded. "Same. How about you, Kellyjean?"

Kellyjean was staring up at the stars again. "I don't know.

My agent arranges all of that. But I don't think it's anywhere close to ten thousand." She looked back at us. "Why would Will Price pay Jo so much more than the rest of us? No offense, Jo, you know I love you. But I have a Netflix series, and you don't."

I shook my head, my throat suddenly dry. I had no idea why . . . and didn't want to venture a theory, since every one I could think of sounded absurd.

"*I know why.*" A new, masculine voice rang out from the darkness. I gasped in alarm, thinking for a moment that Will Price had driven over from his mansion to join us for a nightcap and overheard everything we'd said.

But it was only Garrett who stepped from the shadows, wearing the complimentary robe the hotel had supplied over a pair of ridiculously bright yellow board shorts. Apparently he'd decided to take a break from rehearsing his magic trick to go for an evening dip in the pool.

"Isn't it obvious?" Garrett sounded indignant. "He wanted to make sure she'd show up, of course."

Kellyjean gasped as she whipped her head around, long blond hair flying, to look at me. "Of course! Jo isn't in love with Will. *Will is in love with her!*"

"Oh, come *on*," I said.

"Really, Kellyjean," Frannie scolded. "Now you're just being silly."

"How is that silly?" Garrett dropped the towel he'd brought with him onto a nearby chaise lounge and then sank down onto it. "I'm not the romance writer here, but it's a pretty good explanation, isn't it?"

"Honestly, Garrett," I said. "You're wrong. Will's made it pretty clear that he hates my guts as much as I hate his. And we've only met one time before this, and that was almost two years ago for approximately an hour, after which he dogged me to a reporter. Does that sound like the act of a man in love?"

"That doesn't mean anything." Saul shook his head. "I carried a torch for Frannie for years after meeting her only once, but she wouldn't even consider going out with me because I told her I thought the Knicks stank. I had to swear allegiance to a basketball team I don't like to get her to even consider a date."

Frannie patted him on the hand. "And you've never regretted it, have you, dear?"

"Will probably only paid me such a huge stipend to make sure I showed up here so he could clear his conscious," I insisted. "He told me he thought about apologizing before, but wanted to do it to my face." I didn't mention how Will had said he hadn't been able to find the words. No one would have believed me.

"Well," Jerome said. "That is one expensive apology."

"If anyone deserves it, it's Jo," Bernadette said warmly. "I mean, Jo's had terrible writer's block ever since Will said all those nasty things about her books."

I sent Bernadette a warning look. I appreciated the sympathy, but enough of my private business had been shared with the group.

It was too late, though.

"Oh, no!" Garrett exclaimed. "Is that why there hasn't been a new *Kitty Katz* book this year, Jo?"

"Yeah, I was wondering the same thing." Jerome looked concerned. "They're Aesha's favorite. She asks me when there's going to be a new one all the time."

I didn't think things could get worse from there, but they did. Kellyjean scrambled to her feet and ran over to throw her arms around me.

"Oh, you poor thing." Kellyjean hugged me. "I had no idea you were blocked. Do you want to use some of my essential oils? I have some sourced from the *Rosa damascena* plant that should open you up to inspiration and joy. Did you bring a diffuser?"

I was already enveloped in whatever essential oil or perfume Kellyjean habitually wore, and the scent was so strong, it was making my eyes water, not opening me up to joy. "Uh . . ."

"Never mind," Kellyjean said. "You can borrow mine. Remind me when we get upstairs to bring it around to your room."

"No, really, it's okay—"

"I *insist*." Mercifully, Kellyjean released me, but still held on to one of my hands, which she squeezed. "We're *artists*, Jo. We have to *help* one another in our hours of need, not tear each other down."

Great. Now I felt terrible for having asked them all for help snooping into Will's personal life.

I felt even worse for letting slip how much more I was being paid to be at the book festival than they were. But how was I supposed to have known they weren't receiving an equal (or greater) stipend? Male authors in the book industry often received higher advances and speaking fees than their female counterparts. It was odd that it was the opposite way around this time.

"So are we all reading that book of Price's, the one that came in our swag bag?" Jerome asked out of the blue.

I kept my mouth shut. The real trick to being a writer, I'd learned long ago, was to keep quiet and observe.

"Saul is." Frannie twinkled at her husband. "Saul loves it."

Saul shrugged. "So sue me. The guy spins an entertaining yarn."

"That female love interest, Melanie, remind you of any-one?" Jerome asked.

"Melanie?" Saul thought about it. "Not really. Is she sup-posed to?"

"I think she is." Jerome looked at me. "You reading it, Jo?"

I shrugged uneasily. "I skimmed it a little." I was such a liar. I was up to Chapter Ten and devouring every word.

"Melanie doesn't remind you of anyone?" he asked. "Physi-cally, I mean."

"Not really. She's such an idiot. The fact that she can't figure out that Johnny killed her husband? That's so unre-alistic!"

"Oh, I don't think Johnny did it," Jerome said.

"Of *course* Johnny did it," I said. "He *says* right in the book that he did it!"

"Johnny *thinks* he did it."

"What is that supposed to mean?"

"I think Johnny's going to turn out to be innocent. You wait and see."

"Wait—did you skip to the end? Jerome! Spoiler alert!"

"And on that note," Frannie said, rising to her feet, "Saul, I think you and I should go to bed."

"You're right." He slipped an arm around his wife's waist. "I have a big day tomorrow, a panel and a signing, plus that tour of historical Little Bridge, since you won't let me go out on Will's boat."

"I'm always looking out for you, honey." Frannie kissed him on the cheek. Those two were such relationship goals. It was so cute.

"Don't forget the author bus leaves early tomorrow morning," Bernadette reminded all of us. She'd gathered up her bag and climbed to her feet as well. "No stragglers." Of course she looked directly at me as she said the last part.

"I'm looking forward to hearing all of you speak tomorrow," Garrett said. He was getting up to leave for his room as well. I guess he'd decided against the midnight swim. "I think your panels will be highly informative."

God, could he be a bigger suck-up?

Then I realized *everyone* was leaving.

"Wait." I blinked at all of them as they filed past me. "That's it? The night is over?"

"You and I have the first panel, Jo," Bernadette warned me from the outdoor steps to her room. "Right after the welcome speech. You should go to bed. You know what you're like if you don't get enough sleep."

I loved Bernadette, but sometimes she seemed to forget I wasn't one of her kids. I waved at her. "Thanks! But I'll be fine. I'll meet you in the lobby by eight."

"Sure you will." Bernadette rolled her eyes as she pulled the key to her room from her bag.

"I *will!*"

Kellyjean squeezed my hand again while smiling at me kindly. "I'll make sure you're up by then if you want, Jo. I'm always up at dawn so I can watch the sunrise. And if you want I can bring my diffuser to your room now and show you how it works. I promise my oils will get you writing again."

I smiled back at her, though the thought of having a diffuser in my room pumping out her strong-smelling oils was completely unappealing. "Thanks anyway, Kellyjean. But I'm afraid it's a lost cause. I don't think tincture of rose oil or whatever is going to make any—"

"Look!" Kellyjean gasped, and then her arm shot past my face as she pointed toward the night sky. "A meteor! Do you see it?"

I followed the direction of her index finger and was shocked to see not one, but two bright stars dive across the dark, velvety heavens and disappear amid the palm fronds above our heads.

"I saw two of them." I gripped Kellyjean's hand with excitement. "Two!"

"I saw three!" she cried. "Oh, Barnabas is going to be so thrilled when I tell him. Now, don't forget to make a wish."

"On a falling meteor?"

"Of course!"

I should have realized she meant it. Kellyjean believed mermaids—and fairies and werewolves—were real. Why wouldn't she believe that a wish made on a falling star (also known as a meteor) would come true, as well?

"You do what you want," she said. "But I'm wishing." She closed her eyes, looking as if she was concentrating very hard, so I did the same. Why not? It wasn't like my luck had been so great lately that I could afford not to. And it certainly couldn't hurt.

Only, what to wish for? I didn't believe in wishes any more than I believed in mermaids or magic, but for over a year, whenever I'd found an eyelash or saw the first evening star, I'd superstitiously wished for the same thing:

Something bad to happen to Will Price.

Not for him to die or anything. Wishes weren't real, of course, but even if they were, I would never wish for anything like that to happen to someone.

But I wouldn't mind seeing something just a *little bit bad* happen to Will Price. Like for him to get the kind of debilitating writer's block that I had.

Or maybe for him to get into a Twitter war with a beloved social icon like Tom Hanks, so that everyone turned on him.

Or possibly for him to get stung by a jellyfish. Just *something*.

But now that he'd apologized—even if his apology had been very stiff and British and come out of nowhere and therefore not been very satisfying—I was surprised to find that I didn't wish him that kind of ill anymore.

Obviously I didn't *like* him, even if he did have a very cool sister who was on a dance team and loved my books.

But I didn't wish him ill.

So I decided to wish for something else. Something positive instead of negative.

Was it possible that the essential oils Kellyjean wore had already rubbed off on me and were making me a better person?

When I opened my eyes, I found her staring at me expectantly.

"Well?" she asked. "What'd you wish for?"

"Kellyjean, you know I can't tell you that. I don't know much about wishing, but I do know that if you tell someone what you wished for, your wish won't come true."

"Oh, that's nonsense. In my family, we always tell each other our wishes, and they still always come true. Here, I'll tell you what I wished for: that while you're here on Little Bridge Island, you'll find whatever it is that you're searching for."

I was touched. Kellyjean could be a ditz sometimes, but she was a genuinely sweet person.

"Oh, Kellyjean," I said, leaning over to give her a hug and this time finding the scent of her oils agreeable. "Thank you. That is so nice. But you didn't have to waste your wish on me. And what makes you think I'm looking for something, anyway?"

"It's never a waste to use a wish on another person," she said, hugging me back. "And of course you're looking for something. That's what's keeping you from writing your next little kitty cat book. And let's be honest, Jo: you're such a mess right now, you need wishes way more than I do."

That sounded more like the Kellyjean I knew. "Thanks a lot," I said with a wry laugh as I released her.

"You're welcome, hon. So go ahead, tell me. Whadja wish for?"

But I shook my head. The wish I'd made was one I intended to keep all to myself . . . at least for now.

The Moment by Will Price

When Melanie raised her head to look at me, her eyes were shining as bright as the moon. I caught my breath, tightening my grip on her shoulders and drawing her close to me.

I don't know how I found the nerve, but somehow, my mouth grazed hers, just once. Then, when she didn't object, again.

A second later her arms slipped around my neck, and I found my hands cradling her head, my fingers tangled in the thickness of her hair. Our open mouths met.

Kissing her was easy. I kissed her lips, her cheeks, her throat, the soft hollows behind her earlobes. My hands explored the territory beneath the fitted green jacket and found that she wore something silky beneath it. Her fingers clung to the back of my neck, and the touch of her lips sent chills up and down the backs of my arms.

She kissed me like she meant it. I wasn't used to that.

SATURDAY, JANUARY 4

CHAPTER ELEVEN

Meeeeeee-OW!

I woke up to the ringtone on my phone jangling in my ear. I struggled to find it in the mountain of fluffy hotel throw pillows I'd passed out against, lulled into unconsciousness by a combination of wine, *The Moment,* and the diffuser Kellyjean had insisted on setting up before returning to her own room.

"To bring you inspiration," she'd said.

What the gentle hissing sound and surprisingly pleasant scent of rose had apparently brought me instead was the deepest sleep I'd had in months.

Meeeeeee-OW!

Blinking groggily, I saw that Bernadette was calling.

"Hello?" I croaked.

"Where are you?" she screeched. "It's eight o'clock and I'm down in the lobby where you said you'd meet me. The festival starts at nine o'clock and we have our first panel right after that and the author bus is coming any minute and *there's no sign of you.*"

Kittens! "I'll be right there."

I leaped from the bed and into the shower, then threw on makeup and whatever clothes I could find that were the least wrinkled, which turned out to be a black sundress topped with a jean jacket, last night's mules, and sunglasses to cover the terrible job I ended up doing on my eyeliner in my haste to apply it.

When I got downstairs, I saw that everyone was in the dining room enjoying what appeared to be a full buffet breakfast, complete with eggs, bacon, waffles, mimosas, and an enormous fruit salad that included fresh mango. I knew this not because I had some, but because Kellyjean, who looked bright as a newly gathered bouquet of wildflowers, called out as soon as she saw me, "Oh, Jo, I'm so sorry I forgot to wake you! But you just have to try the fruit salad. The mango is so fresh!"

In response I could only shake my head—my hair was still wet from my shower; I hadn't had time to dry it and so had again pulled it back in a ponytail—poured coffee into a to-go cup, then grabbed a chocolate croissant from a basket of baked goods, noticing that Frannie had been wrong: they did have bagels on Little Bridge Island, and they looked just as good as bagels from New York.

"There she is," Garrett cried when he saw me. He had on his cargo pants again, along with a T-shirt that read *Dark Magic School Grad*, and Crocs. The man was wearing Crocs to an event at which he was a paid speaker, and he wasn't doing a cooking demonstration. "Good morning, sunshine!"

I wanted to tell him to shut up, but that seemed unnecessarily rude. Instead I added cream and sugar to my coffee and mumbled, "Sorry I'm late," to Bernadette, who looked fabulous as always in a tiger-striped shirtdress along with her dagger necklace and black leather booties, her purple hair standing in carefully gelled spikes.

"It's okay." Bernadette, organized as ever, had a coffee to go in one hand and the book festival guide open in the other. "Although by rights I'm the one who should have had trouble getting up. It's five in the morning in San Francisco right now. But anyway, here's the lowdown. You and I are doing a panel on female empowerment in the children's novel. From *Little Women* to *Teenage Assassins in Space*, How Young-Adult Literature Focused on the Female Point of View Has Developed and Changed Through the Years. Molly is moderating. This should be a breeze. We've done plenty of panels just like this before. How do you feel?"

I assessed myself and was surprised by the answer. "You know, it's weird. I don't feel that bad, actually. Maybe it's the fresh sea air."

"Or the fact that you finally told Will Price where to get off."

"Well, I don't think I'd go that far."

"Wait." Bernadette eyed me. "You *didn't* tell Will to go screw?"

"I mean, kinda. But he basically apologized before I got the chance."

"Oh, right. The 'I was going through a difficult time' apology. Did we figure out what the difficult time was?"

I pulled out my phone. "No. I texted Rosie last night to see if she knew, but she hasn't written back. It's a bit early for her, and also the weekend, so I don't know if—"

"Good morning." Frannie came sailing up behind us looking as if she'd just had her hair and makeup professionally done, wearing all black except for a red scarf tied jauntily around her neck, a to-go cup of what I knew would be jet-black coffee in her hand. "I can't wait to hear you two speak. Saul and I are really looking forward to it."

I smiled at her. Frannie dragged Saul to every author's panel at every book festival or con they attended, even though he was only expected to show up for the ones at which he was a panelist. Frannie was extremely supportive of other authors, and Saul was extremely supportive of Frannie.

"I hope you're going to come to my panel, too." Garrett had crept up with the many things he was carrying with him to the festival, which for some reason included his fishing pole, the festival swag bag, and the ukulele in the case I'd seen him pick up on the airport tarmac. "Kellyjean and I go on right after Bernadette and Jo. We're doing World Building: Making the Magic Happen."

Barf. Magic, again?

"It's going to be so good." Kellyjean drifted over, wearing another floaty maxi dress, but this time with more sensible shoes, having apparently learned her lesson, and carrying an enormous straw beach bag along with an equally enormous straw beach hat. "I can't wait to hear more about the Dark Magic School. But they don't really practice dark magic, do they, Garrett? Because you know children really need to be learning that what they cast out into the universe will come back at them, times three."

Garrett laughed. "That's only in cheesy teen witch movies."

Bernadette and I side-eyed each other. We both knew this was the wrong thing to say to Kellyjean, who took her magic very seriously.

"Of course that's not just in movies," she cried. "I hate to think what kind of negative energy you're out there teaching kids to draw to themselves with your books."

"Oh, wow." Jerome came up behind us, holding a coffee and looking mildly excited. "I see there're already sparks flying between two panelists and the festival hasn't even officially begun. This is going to be some day."

Silently, I agreed with him, but I didn't want to add any more fuel to Garrett and Kellyjean's fire. Instead I took a bite of my croissant, relieved to see that the author bus was pulling up outside. "Oh, look," I said. "Here's our ride. Let's get going."

But my relief turned to another feeling entirely when the doors to the minibus slid open to reveal that the driver this time wasn't Molly or her husband, but someone I recognized instantly by his overlong curls, broad shoulders, too-small mouth, and night-dark eyes.

"Good morning," Will said cheerfully from his perch behind the wheel.

I stood there frozen, my coffee in one hand and croissant in the other, staring up at him. What was happening? Was I still asleep? Was this a nightmare . . . or a dream?

No. Definitely not a dream.

Because even in my dreams I wouldn't have pictured a bus driver who looked as delicious as this. Unlike Molly, Will filled the seat, looking large and absurdly competent for someone I knew perfectly well didn't make a habit of going around driving mini-shuttles in his daily life.

Still, he had the sleeves of the pale gray button-down he was wearing rolled up like he was just some ordinary transit worker, driving his daily route—though those rolled-up cuffs revealed muscular forearms that I knew had become toned from regular workouts in his home gym, not hauling the luggage of passengers.

To my astonishment, he was smiling. Not the fan-friendly smile I'd so often defaced in airplane magazines, but a smaller, less assured smile that seemed to be saying, *Hi. I know this is awkward, but there's nothing I can do about it, so I'm hoping this is all right. Is this all right?*

Um, no. No, it most certainly was not. Especially not after the love scene I'd read in his book last night.

"Wh-what?" I could find no words. "Wh-where's Molly?"

The smile didn't waver.

"Oh, she's at the hospital."

Frannie came squawking up behind me like one of the chickens we'd seen running around loose on the streets the night before. "*What?* Is she all right?"

"I think so," he said. "It's probably a false alarm—she's not due for another two weeks. But, you know—" He shrugged. "Better to be safe than sorry, right?"

Frannie, Bernadette, and Kellyjean exchanged knowing glances. "First baby," they all said in unison, members of a club I was relieved, at that particular moment, not to be a part of.

"Well, is the festival still going to go on?" I was hoping the answer was no—not because I wanted to deprive the people of Little Bridge Island of their first-ever book festival, but because I really didn't want to have to spend any more time with Will than was strictly necessary. Even though I'd lose out on selling a lot of books (probably), I'd be fine with being as far away as possible from those eyes and those arms.

Unfortunately, the answer was not to my liking.

"Of course the festival is still going on." Will was laying it on thick, giving us the hundred-watt smile I recognized from the red carpet photos at his many movie premieres. Not that I'd spent much time poring over them. Okay, maybe I had. "Molly always considered this a possibility since the festival was so close to her due date, so she made a backup plan. And this is it." He gestured broadly at himself, which sadly only drew my attention once again to those wide shoulders and lean waist, which even his oh-so-casually-loose resort wear couldn't hide. "I'm here to give you all a lift."

Never in the history of time had there been such a good-looking—and well-dressed—bus driver.

This was a disaster.

No one else seemed to think so, however.

"Well, all right, then!" Frannie cried. "Saul? Saul, come on. Will's driving."

Then she and Saul climbed onto the bus, followed by Jerome (who at least murmured a polite "Excuse me" to me before he passed by), and then everyone else.

It was only when I was the last author standing on the sidewalk that Will said to me, conversationally, "Since Molly probably won't be back in time, I'll be giving the opening speech just before your panel in order to welcome everyone to the festival."

What? Bernadette and I were going to have to follow an opening act by *Will Price?*

I thought of Lauren and her friends on the plane and how happy they were going to be about this, and felt a little queasy.

"Jo?" Will eyed me. I think he was wondering why I'd been standing for so long with my coffee and croissant held frozen in my hands. I'd stood there so long, in fact, that the hotel's resident cat had walked up, butted its head against my bare leg, got tired of my lack of response, and moved on. When had I ever not leaned down to pet a cat that had head-butted me? Never, that's when. And it was all Will's fault. "Are you all right?"

"Yes." No. No, I was not all right. I was never going to be all right. "Yes, I'm fine."

He smiled again, not quite the hundred watter, but close. "Great! Well, you've already got quite a crowd gathered over at the library, so we better get going."

Perfect. Just perfect.

Things only went downhill from there. The croissant, I soon realized, had been a poor choice, since I noticed after I took my seat that I had croissant flakes all down the front of my black dress.

Yes, I'd been talking to Will Price while covered in pastry crumbs.

Not only that, but the weather outside was so warm and sunny that it had seemingly attracted every tourist from every wintry corner of the globe. And all of them had emerged from their hotels at the exact same moment our bus left for the library, darting out into the street without looking (because apparently they thought downtown Little Bridge was like Main Street in Disney World, and not a real street with actual vehicular traffic that might run them over, so they could just wander out into the middle of it).

So Will kept throwing on the brakes to avoid hitting them, making the milky coffee and not-yet-digested chocolate croissant inside my stomach lurch.

But then, as if all of that wasn't bad enough, for some inexplicable reason Garrett, who was sitting on the seat in front of me, decided to remove his ukulele from its case, turn around, and begin playing (and singing) the song "You Are My Sunshine."

"'You are my sunshine, my only sunshine,'" he sang, directly into my face. "'You make me happy when skies are gray. . . .'"

For a few seconds, everyone on the bus, including me, sat in stunned silence.

Then, just when Garrett got to the part about "please don't take my sunshine away," I lost it.

"Garrett," I snarled. *"Stop it."*

Garrett did not stop.

"What's the matter, sunshine?" he asked, continuing to strum away. "You don't like fun? Hey, everybody: Jo Wright doesn't like fun!"

What was wrong with this guy? I was ready to pour what was left of my coffee over his head.

"I like fun," I snapped.

"Oh, I don't think so," Garrett said.

"I do. I do like fun. Just not someone singing in my face at *eight-thirty in the morning.*"

"Really, Garrett." I was glad that Frannie felt compelled to intervene on my behalf. "It's a bit much. Why don't you save the song for the festival? I'm sure the children there will find it delightful."

"Oh, come on." Garrett continued to play. "Everyone loves this song. We're all young at heart, aren't we? Saul, I know you agree. Come on, everybody, let's sing together!" Then he leaned halfway over the back of his seat and began strumming while singing even more loudly into my face. "'You are my sunshine, my only sunshine—'"

It was right then that the bus lurched to an abrupt stop—abrupt enough that Garrett, who'd been sitting facing backward so he could sing to me, lurched heavily into the seat in front of him, losing the grip on his ukulele and causing the strings to clang tunelessly.

"Hey!" he called out in irritation to Will.

"Sorry," Will said. But I could see his face in the rearview mirror above the driver's seat, and he didn't look sorry at all. He was wearing a little smirk. "But we've reached our destination."

I turned my head. Out the window, I could see a large, graceful brick building surrounded by lovely thick-trunked banyan trees, with a full parking lot and a soaring porticoed entrance, below which hung a banner that read:

WELCOME TO THE 1ST ANNUAL LITTLE BRIDGE BOOK FESTIVAL

Above that, carved into the stone façade of the building, read the words, NORMAN J. TIFTON PUBLIC LIBRARY.

Festive helium balloons in multiple colors had been strung everywhere, and people were streaming into the many double doors leading into the library, all wearing happy expressions and carrying swag bags much like the ones we'd been given and that Garrett kept dragging around everywhere. I was relieved to see that the majority of the people were women and young girls, which meant that my panel with Bernadette was going to be well attended—although many of them, I was sure, were coming early to grab seats for Kellyjean and Garrett's panel, or for Saul's or Jerome's, the final speakers of the day.

Will had stood up in the driver's seat and now turned back to face us.

"Here we are," he said. "If you follow me, I'll show you to the auditorium. We've got a green room where you can sit and relax before your panel, or, if you'd like, you can explore the festival. We hope you'll find a lot to entertain you." Then his gaze flicked to Garrett. "You can leave that here on the bus." He gestured to Garrett's ukulele.

Garrett had wrapped his hands protectively around his instrument. "But I—"

"I promise it will be safe." While Will's tone was perfectly pleasant, there was something deadly serious in his dark eyes. "We've already hired local musicians—as well as face painters and jugglers—to entertain the children attending the festival, so I don't think you'll be needing it . . . unless it's part of your presentation?"

But before Garrett had a chance to reply, Kellyjean interrupted in her loud Texas drawl, "Oh, no, he won't be needing that thing. We're going to be talking about writing and magic. You don't need a ukulele for that, do you, Garrett?"

"I guess not." Garrett mournfully laid the instrument back in its case.

"Psst," I said, poking Bernadette in the back as we shuffled off the bus behind the Colemans.

She was talking on the phone to her wife. Apparently, there was some kind of crisis involving Sophie, their eldest.

But since there was always some kind of crisis involving Sophie, I didn't think twice about whispering, after Bernadette mouthed, *What?* "Do you think Garrett uses that ukulele to seduce unsuspecting fangirls?"

Bernadette rolled her eyes. "Would you have been seduced by 'You Are My Sunshine' back when you were younger?"

"No. But my personality was about as sunny then as it is now."

Bernadette snorted as we disembarked, then said into the phone, "No. No, I never said Sophie could have her friend Tasha sleep over. Well, why didn't you mention this when we talked last night? Yes, of course I trust you, but they're *six years old*—"

As I moved away from Bernadette to let her argue with her spouse in private, I saw that there was an air of excitement outside the library that was almost contagious. Will hadn't been kidding: Little kids were running around with their faces painted like tigers and butterflies, and there were jugglers tossing colored balls high into the air amid the enormous roots of one of the banyan trees. Live music was coming from somewhere I couldn't immediately see, but it sounded about as festive as the wafting scent of cookies and brownies, coming from the Snappettes' nearby bake sale, smelled delicious.

"Jo! Jo, over here!" I heard some female voices squeal nearby, and when I turned my head, I saw the girls I'd met on the plane—Lauren and her friends—waving excitedly to me from one of the small lines that had formed to get into the building.

I waved back, which caused them to giggle and wave even more excitedly.

"I told you, didn't I?" Will had come up behind me. He was carrying a wooden sign that said PUPPET SHOW THIS WAY with an arrow pointing to the right. He seemed unconscious of the fact that there were a lot of people (such as myself) who'd have paid good money to see Will Price carrying a sign that said *Puppet Show This Way*, only now we were getting to see it for free. "You've got a ton of fans here."

"Uh . . . yeah." Did he really not know that the person those girls were waiting for was him? Of course they liked me, too, but he was the one whose signature Cassidy wanted on her chest.

"Are you nervous?" he asked. "I still get sick to my stomach every time I have to speak in public."

"Do you?" Why was he telling me this? Why was he even talking to me? I'd agreed—sort of—to pretend to have forgiven him for the weekend for his sister's sake, but not to be friends. So what was this? "I used to get nervous, but I don't anymore."

He nodded like he knew what I was going to say. "Practice?"

"Sure, something like that."

I'd lost my fear of public speaking after years of visiting schools and talking about writing the Kitty Katz series. Many school systems understood the impact that bringing an author into the classroom could have on impressionable young readers. Not only did it teach them that books were written by actual living human beings, it inspired many of them to read more, and even try writing their own stories.

But Will Price had obviously never been asked to do a school visit because his books, instead of inspiring kids, would only end up putting them into therapy. Take *The Moment*, for example. Johnny and Melanie's relationship? Completely toxic.

"Are you carrying that sign somewhere," I asked him in order to change the subject, "or are you just holding it because you're the festival's official puppet show sign holder?"

He looked down at the sign in surprise. "Oh, right. There's so much to do with Molly out of the loop. Which reminds me, since she's at the hospital, I'm going to have to moderate your panel this morning."

What?

Will Price was going to moderate a literary panel on female empowerment in young-adult fiction? Will Price, who routinely wrote books where the female characters became empowered only after being rescued from their tragic past by a man with whom they fell in love (who then died or, alternatively, was the one who rendered the heroine's past so tragic in the first place)?

My shock must have shown on my face since he asked, "Are you all right?"

"Oh, yes," I said faintly. "I'm fine."

But I was lying. My fear of public speaking—or something like it—had returned, with a vengeance.

CHAPTER TWELVE

LITTLE BRIDGE BOOK FESTIVAL ITINERARY FOR:
JO WRIGHT

Saturday, January 4, 9:10 a.m.–10:00 a.m.

Speaking Panel

"From *Little Women* to *Teenage Assassins in Space*, How Young-Adult Literature Focused on the Female Point of View Has Developed and Changed Through the Years." Bestselling authors Jo Wright & Bernadette Zhang in Conversation

(Moderated by ~~Molly Hartwell~~ Will Price)

Things only got worse from there.

I was sitting in the front row of the library's newly renovated auditorium, a gorgeous room featuring a well-lit stage, on which Will Price stood with a microphone.

Molly and her team—which I knew now included Will—had done a wonderful job of making the stage look like a warm and welcoming place for the festival panelists. There was a Persian carpet set across the middle of a raised dais, on which three black leather chairs had been arranged to look more like a living-room conversation nook than a literary panel. Someone (probably Molly) had even been thoughtful enough to set out a couple of large potted ficus trees and little end tables, complete with bottled waters and boxes of tissues in case a panelist needed to blow their nose—or possibly dry their eyes from weeping if things got too emotional.

The only way you'd know, really, that it was a set and not someone's home was the handheld microphone resting on the seat of each of the chairs . . . and of course the gigantic scrim behind the chairs, onto which was being projected a very professional graphic proclaiming the words *Little Bridge Island 1st Annual Book Festival*.

But it didn't matter how homey the set looked. It was where, my roiling stomach was telling me, I was about to die.

Why, oh, why, had I let Rosie talk me into saying yes to this gig?

Will was standing in front of the chairs doing a not-terrible job of welcoming the almost five hundred people in the audience. I knew there were almost five hundred people because I'd seen a sign on the wall that said MAXIMUM ROOM CAPACITY: 500, and nearly every seat was full.

Obviously they were all there for Will. I could see Lauren and her friends smack-dab in the middle of the audience—

close to the stage but not *too* close—gazing up at him, enraptured, as he thanked everyone for coming.

And who could blame them? He did make a very fine literary ambassador. Whoever was running the stage lighting from the back of the house was doing an excellent job of it, the spotlight bringing out the glossy highlights in Will's dark hair and causing shadows to form just right on . . . other parts of him.

Whoa. What was I doing, looking at those parts? I was a celebrated children's author of books that empowered little girls (even if I wrote about them through the voice of a feisty teenaged cat). The fact that I'd even noticed Will's "parts" was so beneath me, especially when there were so many young women around. The Snappettes were milling about in their cute little matching shorts and shirts, helping with crowd control and passing out festival programs to anyone who hadn't received one yet, and still trying to sell their baked goods.

Of course there'd been quite a few gasps of excitement and some scattered applause when Will announced why Molly wasn't there—everyone in the audience seemed to be invested in the birth of her baby.

But there was no getting around it: Will Price was the real draw at this festival.

And that's why when I got up onto that stage, I was going to be super, duper nice to him.

Not that I'd ever intended to be mean to him. Why should I? He'd apologized. The past was all water under the bridge. I was completely letting go of the whole *New York Times* thing and welcoming this new journey we were on together . . . whatever it was.

And I had to admit that *The Moment* was not the worst book I had ever read. The actions of its hero were morally questionable, and the heroine had no backbone whatsoever.

But the book was at least more entertaining than the Bible, the only other book in my hotel room, which I'd (spoiler alert) already read.

So I was going to be as sweet as pie to Will Price, whatever he said up there onstage, and as soon as Bernadette showed up—I had no idea where she was—I was going to tell her to do the same, no matter what infuriating thing he might end up saying as moderator. This was his town, and we were guests here. It was like in *Kitty Katz #15*, when Kitty and her best friend, Felicity Feline, were hired to puppy sit in the beach town of Dogsville. Did the two of them back down from that challenge?

No, because they were competent as well as gracious. Bernadette and I would be the same, because we were just as good a team.

Which was why it was a bit odd to me that Bernadette was taking so long with her phone call. We were almost five minutes into Will's welcome speech (which was mostly a long list of thank-yous to various sponsors and donors) when she finally showed up, breathless and looking a little shaky.

"Jo." She knelt in the aisle beside my seat.

"Bern," I whispered. "Where have you been? We're going on as soon as Will is done up there."

Then I saw her expression. As nervous as I felt, she looked a thousand times worse.

"What's the matter?" I whispered. "Was it the mango? Do you need some ginger ale or something? I think they have some in the green room. We could—"

She shook her head. "No, Jo. It's worse."

For Bernadette, there was only one problem worse than digestive issues. I knew without her having to tell me what it was:

Sophie, her eldest. It was always Sophie.

She waved to me to follow her. I did, the two of us creeping out a side exit into a hallway, letting the door to the auditorium close softly behind us so we wouldn't interrupt Will's speech.

"What's happened?" I asked, my stomach in knots.

"Somehow Jen got it into her head that it would be a good idea to let Sophie have her friend Tasha sleep over last night." There were tears in Bernadette's eyes. "Don't ask me why when Jen's never supervised a playdate on her own before. So of course this morning when the girls woke up at the crack of dawn, they decided to play Horsies and were crawling all around on our not-yet-totally-refinished wood floors, neighing. And now Sophie's got a splinter in her knee."

I was confused. A splinter? *A splinter?* "Can't Jen take it out? She's a doctor, for pity's sake."

"That's just it. She tried. But this is no ordinary splinter. It's huge—maybe an inch long—and it entered vertically, way too deep to reach with tweezers. Jen's had to take Sophie to the ER."

I bit my lip. It wasn't at all funny.

But it was exactly the sort of thing that *would* happen to Sophie.

"Sophie's going to be all right, isn't she?"

"Yes, of course she's going to be all right. It's a *splinter*. Only they're surgically removing it in exactly fifteen minutes. And Sophie wants me to be there with her via FaceTime while they do it. Jen swears Sophie can't feel a thing—they've numbed the area thoroughly. But she's already screaming bloody murder for me. I can't not be there for her, Jo."

"Of course you have to be there for her." I took a deep breath. I knew what I had to do. "I can do our panel on my own. Don't even worry about it."

"Are you sure?" Bernadette looked as if she might break into tears. "I so hate to ask!"

I hadn't even had a chance to break the news to her yet about Will being our moderator.

But I certainly couldn't do it now. She was frazzled enough already.

Being a writer could be hard sometimes.

But being a parent, I knew, was the hardest job in the world. I was grateful sometimes for my easy—if sometimes slightly lonely—life with only the responsibilities of my sweet elderly Miss Kitty and accident-prone dad to worry about.

"Of course," I said. "Go be with your daughter."

Bernadette looked relieved. "I knew you'd understand," she said, giving me a quick hug even as her cell phone chimed. "I'll be back before you know it."

"Of course you will."

There was no way she would. An inch-long splinter, buried deep in her six-year-old daughter's knee? I'd be lucky to see Bernadette again before lunch.

But I plastered Fake Jo's smile across my face and turned back toward the auditorium doors, opening them just in time to hear Will Price say, "So please join me in giving a warm Little Bridge welcome to *New York Times* and *USA Today* bestselling authors Bernadette Zhang and Jo Wright!"

The audience applauded with—I liked to think—more than mere politeness as I trotted up the stairs along the side of the stage and over to the three chairs where we were to have our chat. Will was standing in front of the middle chair, still clutching his microphone. He smiled as he saw me approach, looking as ridiculously handsome as ever . . . but that smile wavered as he saw no one following me up the steps to the stage.

Yep, I tried to tell him with my eyes. *I'm on my own. But everything is going to be fine.*

I kept Fake Jo plastered across my face and, waving to the applauding audience, willed the jitters I felt to calm down. Then I reached for the microphone on the seat of the chair to the right of Will and sat down as gracefully as I could.

But not, of course, before I noticed that on the screen behind me, the graphic had changed. Now instead of welcoming everyone to the Little Bridge Book Festival, it showed two gigantic headshots: one of Bernadette, and one of me—our glossy back-of-the-book author photos.

But mine was as I'd looked years earlier, when I'd first started out in publishing, with a hopeful, radiant smile, sparkling blue eyes, and loose curling waves of blond hair, way before Will had ever publicly trashed my writing.

Great. This was not helping at all.

I had no choice but to address it, and the fact that I was alone.

"Wow, would you look at that," I said into the mic, gazing up at myself. "This is what one night of partying on your island does to people. It killed the author Bernadette Zhang and it turned me from that sweet young thing into *this*." I gestured at my black hair and the sunglasses I had forgotten up until that moment that I was still wearing. No wonder Will hadn't been reassured by my gaze.

For a second or two the audience sat in stunned silence, as if uncertain what it had heard. But I knew the mic was on, because I'd heard my own voice reverberate quite clearly from the back of the auditorium. The acoustics were dynamite.

Then a wave of appreciative laughter came pouring toward me: they got the joke.

And right then the butterflies fled, and I felt fine. Everything was going to be all right . . . so long as I could Kitty Katz my way through it and keep up the furr-endly banter.

"I'm so sorry that you ordered *this*," I said, gesturing toward the photo and then myself again, "but got *this* instead. But I assure you, I *am* Jo Wright. It's just been a while since I updated my author photo. And I'm loving my stay here on your lovely island. Thank you so much for having me." I gave Will a slice of my smile to show that my thanks extended to him, as well, but he was only staring at me with a sort of stunned expression on his face, so I turned back to address

158   MEG CABOT

the audience. "Bernadette Zhang's been called away for a family emergency—all of you parents out there know how hard it is to balance work and family life. But she'll try to join us as soon as she can. In the meantime, Will and I are going to have a great conversation about female empowerment in children's fiction today, aren't we, Will?"

Come on, buddy, I urged him with my eyes. *Get it together.*

But he had sunk down into the middle seat as if he couldn't quite believe the mess he'd stumbled into.

Why? Because he had to talk to me alone, on a stage? Was I that scary?

"Um," he managed. "Yes. Yes, we will."

"Great!" Oh my God, he was totally leaving me dangling. "Okay, well, we might as well get started. Will, what was your favorite children's book growing up—one that contained a strong female lead character?"

"Uh." For such a big man, he looked as if his chair was swallowing him whole, he'd sunk so far back into it. "I don't—I guess, er—*Peter Pan?*"

"Oh, *Peter Pan.*" Peter Pan? Dear God, how was this happening? I glanced at the audience, although honestly the stage lights were so bright I couldn't see them, even with my sunglasses on. "All right. So the strong female lead you're referring to is Wendy?"

"Yes." He appeared to be growing slightly more confident, if the way he was straightening up in his chair was any indication. "Wendy."

Oh, no. Not Wendy.

But he was serious.

"Wendy," I repeated. "Okay. You're sure? The girl Peter Pan abandons at the end of the book after dragging her all the way to Neverland so that she can essentially function as a domestic servant for him and all the rest of the Lost Boys? You see J. M. Barrie's character *Wendy* as a symbol of female empowerment?"

While a large portion of the audience sat in silence—probably bored witless—a few people laughed, including, I noted, Frannie. She had a very distinct laugh that I could pick out anywhere.

But Will wasn't yet down for the count. He sat up even straighter in his seat.

"Peter doesn't abandon Wendy," he surprised me by arguing. "She has some agency. He asks her to stay in Neverland—"

"As a mother figure. In the book he informs her that his feelings for her are those of a devoted son."

"—and she turns him down."

"Because she doesn't want to sit around darning his socks all day, competing for his affections with Tiger Lily and Tinker Bell."

"Right. Which makes her a feminist character."

Although I was impressed that Will had actually given so much thought to a children's book, a form of literature he'd publicly declared beneath him, I couldn't pretend to agree with him, even to be polite. "I'm not saying there's anything wrong with Wendy's choice—I wouldn't want to stay in Neverland, either. I'm just saying hers was the only choice a man writing in J. M. Barrie's day could conceive of for a female character. Fortunately today there are tons of great books for kids to read that show female characters having all the same opportunities and rights as their male counterparts—"

Will nodded. "Like in my books."

Whoa. I stared at him. "Excuse me?"

"Like in my books." He said it again! And went on to say more about it: "In my books, the female characters are treated as absolutely equal to the male—"

"Hold on. You do realize every single one of your books features an unrealistically perfect female character who is unfulfilled until she meets a man—usually a man whose heart has been badly damaged by some sort of 'evil' woman." I made quote marks in the air with my fingers when I said the word *evil*. "But then that man is healed by the perfect woman's love. And then, just as they're about to find blissful happiness together, the same thing happens: tragedy."

This got a nervous titter out of the audience . . . and one big horse laugh out of Frannie.

Will stirred awkwardly in his seat. "First of all, that isn't what happens in *all* of my books. You obviously haven't read them all. But secondly, even if that were true, what's so wrong with that? They're works of fiction, written to help readers escape reality."

"You're right, I haven't read all your books, but I know how they all end—you yourself call them tragedies. How is that escape fiction? Escape fiction is supposed to make you forget your problems and feel happy." Like reading about a funny teenage cat who earns her own money, I wanted to add, but didn't, because that would sound too self-promotional.

"But for some people, having a good cry over a sad story

does make them feel happy," Will insisted. If he was still nervous, it didn't show anymore. He was no longer slumped in his chair. Now he was leaning forward, clutching his mic with both hands, his elbows on his knees, looking intently into my face. "It was Aristotle who first coined the term *catharsis*, only he was talking about the emotional release or purge people experience when watching a tragedy take place live onstage. He felt that it could help to get them to move past their own stress or grief."

Whoa again. Also . . . was it my imagination, or was this guy even hotter when he was riled up about literature?

"So is that why you always write such sad endings?" I managed to keep it together enough to ask. "Are they an emotional release for you? Do they help you move past your own grief about . . . ?"

I let the end of the sentence dangle, hoping he'd fill in the blank. Come on, Will. What happened just before Novel Con that made you be so mean about my books? Let it out. It will be *cat-artic*.

But he only gave me an enigmatic smile and leaned back in his chair, crossing an ankle over his opposite knee. His body language could not have been more clear: *Back off.*

"I think we're getting a little off topic here," he said. "Aren't we supposed to be discussing female empowerment in YA novels?"

Whiskers.

"Right," I said, leaning back as well and reaching for the bottled water on the end table closest to me. "Yes, of course. Let's move on."

But my mind was a blank. I'd done this talk a thousand times with Bernadette as well as other authors, and even on my own, and suddenly I couldn't remember a single thing on the topic. It had nothing to do with the raw masculinity being exuded from the person in the chair opposite me. Nothing at all.

And I didn't need the water because I was feeling hot all of a sudden.

"What about you?" Will prompted. "What was your favorite children's book growing up—one that contained a strong female lead character?"

"Uh . . ." I hated this question, because the truth was, I didn't have one: I had a hundred. I'd read voraciously as a kid, using the library to escape my mother's illness and my dad's inability to cope with it. The names of dozens of books and authors raced through my head as I twisted the cap off the water bottle. Ouch. Why was this always so hard? I needed to remember to pick one and write it down on my hand before these things began.

"Wait," Will said, lowering his foot and leaning forward again. "Don't tell me. I think I know. Would you happen to have been named after its main character?"

I stared at him, startled. "What? No. Who?"

"Really?" He was smiling mysteriously again, like he'd got hold of some secret information about me. "You're not named after one of children's literature's greatest female characters of all time, Josephine March from *Little Women*?"

CHAPTER THIRTEEN

Wow.

I took a long pull from the water bottle, then said, "No, I'm not named after Jo March, as a matter of fact. My parents were huge fans of the musician Joe Cocker, so they named me after him, only they left off the *e* at the end because they thought that made it feminine. But since you brought her up, let's get this out of the way right now, since it's one of the most important questions in all of feminist literature. Who should Jo in *Little Women* have ended up with, Laurie or Professor Bhaer?"

Will's grin went from enigmatic to genuinely warm. "That's a trick question. The answer is obviously neither of them, since Louisa May Alcott herself remained single all her life, and was famously quoted saying that she never wanted Jo to end up married. She only did it because so many of her young female readers wrote to her asking her whom Jo was going to marry, assuming that marriage was the only conceivable happy ending for a woman. And economically, it was for most women at the time Alcott was writing."

I frowned, impressed. Bonus points for Mr. Price. He *had* done some reading. Or perhaps watched the latest film based on *Little Women*, possibly with his sister or because he'd been trapped with nothing else to do on a plane.

"But my personal feeling is Laurie," he went on. "Bhaer didn't respect the thing that mattered most to Jo, her writing, and Laurie did."

I was appalled.

"That is completely untrue," I said. "Professor Bhaer *did* respect Jo's work. He simply felt that her writing would be better if she wrote from the heart about the things that truly mattered to her, women's issues and family life, as opposed to the tales of mystery and horror she was writing under a pen name. And, strictly from a financial point of view, he turned out to be right, since her books on those subjects became her most successful."

"Which brings me to a question I've been wanting to ask you." Will's gaze was very dark and intent on mine—well, on the lenses of my sunglasses. "Have you ever felt that advice might apply to you?"

What was going on here? "What advice?"

"That instead of writing the stories you write—about talking cats—you might want to try writing from the heart about things that truly matter to you."

I was so stunned by this that for a moment I couldn't reply. I think the audience was stunned, too. I couldn't hear a sound from them—not so much as the rustle of plastic peeled back from a cookie purchased from a Snappette. At the very least, I'd have expected to hear a bark of outrage from Frannie, whose husband, Saul, had been writing quite successfully about gory vampire and ghost attacks for nearly forty years.

But . . . nothing.

Of course, it was possible they'd all left, bored to tears by our bickering. I still couldn't see a thing beyond the edge of the stage.

"I'm sorry," I said, when I could finally find my voice. "Are you implying that my *bestselling* children's books about a talking cat who helps the young kittens she babysits through major life difficulties like their parents getting divorced, and moving, and friendship troubles, and bullying, and sibling rivalry, and crushes, and going away to summer camp—just to name a few—aren't written from *my heart* and *don't really matter?*"

I could feel my body temperature rising, and the spotlights weren't helping the situation. The lenses of my sunglasses were beginning to fog up so that I couldn't even see Will anymore. I had to whip them off.

"That isn't what I—" Will began, but I was so annoyed, I forgot my promise to myself to be gracious to him in front of his adopted hometown audience, and interrupted.

"They may not matter much to *you*, but I can assure you that those subjects matter quite a lot to kids."

"I'm sure they do. I just wondered if—" Will appeared to be turning as pale beneath the spotlights as I was turning red.

"And when the tips on how to navigate them are delivered by a cute talking cat and her friends as opposed to printed out on some crappy pamphlet from the school counselor's office, they become a lot more palatable and accessible to those kids, especially for reluctant readers, which a lot of kids are."

My tirade had sent Will slowly sinking back into his chair, his eyes wide and his mouth slightly ajar.

"Sure," he said. "Of course. I know that. More than you can imagine. That—that isn't at all what I meant—"

Boy, he had not been kidding last night when he'd said that he wasn't good with words. "Well, then what *did* you mean?"

Instead of answering me, Will shaded his eyes with one hand so he could see out into the crowd. "I think now might be a good time to take some questions from the audience, don't you? Does anyone out there have anything they'd like to ask Ms. Wright or myself? I think we've got some members of the high school dance team moving along the aisles with microphones, so if there's something you'd like to ask, feel free to raise your hand, and one of them will be along to hand you a mic."

Ha! Way to save your fur from the fire, Mr. Price.

"Yes, please go ahead," I said into my microphone as, with my other hand, I slid my sunglasses back over my eyes, hoping they'd help me to see the Snappettes and their busy microphone maneuvers—and hide the anger I was still feeling toward Mr. Price. "I promise we'll be a lot nicer to you than we've been to each other so far."

This got another chuckle from the audience. I caught Will's eye, and was surprised to see him smile at me. This was his most genuine smile yet—no fake fan-friendliness, just unease. He seemed—well, he seemed almost *nice*.

"Uh, yeah, hi, my name is Lauren."

Whoops, yep, there she was. Lauren, right there in the middle of the audience, clutching the handheld mic that Chloe—it certainly looked like Chloe, her short blond bob gleaming in the houselights, which they'd turned up so that we could see who was talking—had handed to her. Today Lauren's hair was as flat-ironed as ever, and she was wearing an off-the-shoulder boho-chic top. Her friends Jasmine and Cassidy sat on either side of her, giggling and egging her on.

"So I just wanted to thank you both," Lauren said, in a high-pitched voice that trembled with nervousness. "It's been really great sitting here and listening to you. I'm an aspiring writer, and, uh, I feel totally inspired and, uh, empowered."

"Thank you, Lauren," I said warmly into my mic. I needed to make sure she knew all my antipathy was for Will, not her. "That is so sweet of you."

"Yes, uh, thank you, Lauren." Will didn't appear to have the slightest memory of having met Lauren yesterday. In fact, he kept looking at me and not her, which I found odd.

He glanced away as soon as my gaze met his, however.

"Thanks," Lauren said. "Well, what I wanted to ask both of you was how do you create such, um, realistic characters? Because both of you are so good at that. Your characters seem like real people. Or cats, in your case, Miss Wright."

I laughed along with the rest of the audience. Then I looked at Will, who was—again—looking at me. What was his deal?

"Would you like to answer first?" I asked him politely.

"Oh, no," he said. "Ladies first, please."

"Fine." I looked back at Lauren. "I think one reason readers find Kitty Katz realistic even though she's a cat is that she makes mistakes. She isn't perfect—or purr-fect, as she likes to say—but in the end, she always tries to do the right thing. I think if you write about characters who are perfect, they have no room to grow or improve during the course of the story, and then what do they learn about themselves? Characters learning new things about themselves is part of what makes the story entertaining. But if the character is already perfect, they have no room to grow. So then you have no story. Do you understand what I mean?"

Lauren nodded eagerly. "I do. That totally makes sense."

I looked questioningly at Will, and found him *still* staring at me. Now, this was just getting weird. "Will, do you have anything you'd like to add?"

"Uh, no," he said. "Just that what Miss Wright said is correct, Lauren. No one is perfect. We all make mistakes, sometimes terrible mistakes. My books are excellent examples of that. Jo mentioned earlier that my female characters find empowerment by being rescued by men, but I've never actually seen it that way. I've always considered that the male characters in my books, who are very far from perfect, find redemption through the love of smart, beautiful, complicated females . . . women like Ms. Wright, actually."

What? Had he just called me . . . ?

"So, in answer to your question, Lauren, yes, to create realistic characters, make them imperfect—but if you want your readers to like them, also make them sorry for their actions," he went on. "And perhaps also have your other characters find some way in their hearts to forgive them. Really, if you write stories that are anything like Ms. Wright's excellent books, you'll be fine."

Wait. Will Price had just called my books excellent? And me smart? Complicated? And beautiful?

Was this for the benefit of the audience and cameras, or for real? Maybe it was simply to make up for having stuck his foot in his mouth so badly before. I honestly couldn't tell.

Still, something in his dark eyes looked sincere.

Could he possibly really mean what he was saying? What—

"Sorry!"

One of the side doors to the auditorium burst open. I tore my gaze away from Will's face and saw Bernadette come running up the steps along the side of the stage.

"Sorry, sorry, I'm late, everyone!" She waved apologetically at the audience. "Family emergency, but it's all good now."

She threw herself, panting, into the seat beside Will. Then she picked up her mic, turned it on, and asked, grinning, "So. What'd I miss?"

CHAPTER FOURTEEN

I wasn't entirely sure what had just happened.

All I knew for certain was that Will Price had called me smart. Smart, complicated, and *beautiful*, as well.

People say all sorts of nice things they don't mean, of course, because they want something from you, or simply to be polite.

This didn't feel like that, though. It had felt genuine.

More than that, it had felt *good*. Will had apologized to me *again*, but this time it was on record, in front of witnesses. Witnesses who could actually hear him—all five hundred of them, even if they may not have understood what he was actually referring to.

He'd admitted he wasn't perfect. He'd made a mistake, and he was hoping to grow and learn from it, like a character in one of my books.

One of my *excellent* books.

Of course, he still hadn't told me *why* he'd said something so profoundly stupid (and mean) to that reporter. But that didn't make me feel any less like dashing from the auditorium the second our panel was over and running outside to yell, "Wheeeee!"

But of course I couldn't do that, because while I wrote children's books for a living, I was a grown adult, and there was one more panel and two speakers to go, plus our group signing, before the festival broke for lunch.

So instead I whispered, "Is Sophie all right?" as Bernadette and I walked from the stage together after our panel finished.

"She's fine." Bernadette beamed. "Didn't even need stitches, just a bandage and strict orders not to play Horsies in the dining room until the floors are sanded."

"Great." The audience was still applauding us as we returned to our seats—or perhaps applauding Garrett and Kellyjean, the next authors coming up to the stage.

"How did it go with *him* while I was gone?" she asked, nodding back at Will, who was still onstage. He had to moderate the next panel, after all.

"Oh, fine, fine," I said. I wasn't going to squeal, "He called me smart! And complicated! And beautiful! And said he likes my books!" because that would be absurd. Instead, I said, "Listen, I need to make a quick call of my own. I'll be back in a few minutes. All right?"

Bernadette looked surprised. "Of course! Is it your dad? Is everything okay?"

"Everything's great. I'll explain later."

I hurried up the aisle as the houselights, which had come up in order for us to find our way down the stage stairs, and Kellyjean and Garrett their way up, descended again. In the sudden dimness, however, instead of heading for the glow of the Exit sign, I found a vacant seat tucked in the last row, then sank into it. There, I switched on my cell phone, holding it low so that it wouldn't disturb anyone.

Then, as Will did his best to moderate Kellyjean and Garrett's continuing argument about the morality of young people using dark magic, I checked my messages.

Still nothing from Rosie.

But, as I sat there in the darkness wondering what could possibly have happened to Will to have made him change so much since I'd last seen him, something came over me, and I began to type. Words began pouring out of me.

And not just any words, either. The words to *Kitty Katz #27*, which I realized in that moment *had* to be about Kitty's breakup with her longtime boyfriend, Rex Canine.

This was going to be *explosive*. Rex was a fan favorite—readers adored that he was the star player on Cat Central High School's basketball team while also always being there for Kitty, no matter what jam she happened to find herself in with all those kittens she cared for on weekends to make money to buy the latest designer duds she loved so much (and to save to pay for tuition at Cat Community College, of course, where she intended to major in criminal justice).

But let's face it: Rex was boring. *So* boring.

This was partly my fault, because I'd been writing him that way for twenty-six books—well, twenty-one, since he hadn't shown up until book six, when Kitty's best friend, Felicity, tried out for Cat Central's cheerleading squad, and suddenly Kitty began going to all the school's games to support her.

Now seemed like the perfect time to move a secondary character up into the spotlight: Raul Wolf, Kitty's biggest rival. Editor of Cat Central High's school paper, Raul was always beating Kitty at the things she loved: debate, spelling, the science fair. And he could be pretty arrogant about it, too.

But what if all this time that arrogance had been hiding a sensitive side that Kitty never knew existed? Plus a dark secret she'd discover while puppy sitting for Raul's newly adopted baby sister, Mittens!

Suddenly Kitty is spending a lot of time with Raul Wolf, a boy she's never liked . . . until now. Because now that she's learned Raul's secret, Kitty is feeling emotions she'd never thought possible for a dog she's only ever considered her archenemy.

But what *is* Raul's secret? And what's drawing Kitty to him? Could it be that beneath that arrogant lupine surface beats the warm, passionate heart of a—

"Jo."

I screamed and nearly dropped my phone, on which I'd been typing frantically with my thumbs. "What?"

But it was only Bernadette standing at the end of the aisle by my seat. I was shocked to see that the houselights were back up and that everyone was filing out of the auditorium behind her, all wearing amused looks on their faces at the way I'd reacted to Bernadette calling my name.

"What's happening?" I looked around and saw that the stage was empty. Will was nowhere to be seen, and neither were Garrett or Kellyjean. "Is there a fire?"

"No, silly. The panels are over for the day." Bernadette was laughing at me. "It's time for the book signings."

I was stunned. I looked down at my phone and realized that not only had two hours gone by, but I'd written ten pages.

Single spaced. With my thumbs. Without any M&M's.

"Oh my God. Sorry. Let me just get my—"

Bernadette held out her hand. "Your bag? I have it here. Come on. Everyone wants to get the signings over with so they can go out on Will's boat. We're supposed to have lunch on it, remember?"

Still feeling dazed, I rose from my seat and hurried toward her. "Sorry," I mumbled. "I was just—"

"On a call, I know." Bernadette continued to look amused. "What on earth were you doing way back here?"

"Actually," I said as we filed out with the last of the audience, "I was writing."

"Writing to whom? Your agent? Did she get back to you with the details about you-know-who?"

"No, I mean really *writing*. I was working on Kitty number twenty-seven."

Bernadette spun on me, the smile on her face going from wry to delighted. "No way! But I thought you were hopelessly blocked on that one."

"I thought so, too. But something just . . . came to me. It's the weirdest thing."

"Can you tell me what? Or is it too soon?"

Bernadette and I were both superstitious about discussing story ideas too soon. Sometimes, simply by mentioning it out loud, a narrative could feel already "told," and then the drive to write it down could be lost forever.

"I think it's too soon," I told her. "But I feel like it's a keeper. I have no idea why, but suddenly, I'm unblocked."

"Oh, I think I know why."

"You do?"

"Yeah. Kellyjean told me *all* about it."

We'd exited the building and were walking down the library's front steps toward the parking lot, where the signing tents were set up. But now I stopped dead in my tracks.

"Oh, I'm sure she did." Kellyjean had the biggest mouth. "Listen, I can assure you that I still don't believe in magic. That thing last night with the wishing was only because I had a little too much to drink."

Bernadette looked perplexed. "What are you talking about? Kellyjean didn't mention anything about wishing. All she told me was what Will said to you at our panel, before I got there, about your books being good, and you being beautiful. She thinks you better watch out." Bernadette reached out to tap me teasingly on the shoulder. "She really is convinced he's in love with you."

I felt my cheeks growing hot, and not because we were in Florida and it was so warm outside.

"Kellyjean doesn't know what she's talking about," I said.

Bernadette looked confused. "Why? Did he not say those things?"

"Well, yeah, he said them, but not because he's in love with me." I had to dodge some little kids who were running around with balloons, their faces painted to look like sharks and angelfish. "I don't know what's going on with him. He seems to have the biggest case of Foot-in-Mouth Disease on the planet. One minute he's saying something super mean, and the next, he's saying something super nice. Honestly I think the only reason he says the nice things is because he has to, since he's hosting this thing."

"Oh, Jo, why do you always have to be so negative?" Bernadette asked. "I get that you're a tough New Yorker, but just for once could you let yourself entertain the idea that a man—a man with an actual job—might admire you?"

I rolled my eyes. "You mean why can't I be more like Kitty Katz, who takes every bad situation and turns it into a *pawsitive*? Because I'm not Kitty Katz, I'm only her creator. I want to be more like her, really, I do. But she's fictional. No real person can be that purr-fectly imperfect."

"Nobody's asking you to be purr-fect. But you could try being open-minded."

I sighed. The enormous banyan trees that sprawled across the yard mostly blocked our view of the signing tents, but I could see that quite a lot of people were gathering around them. I figured they were heading toward their cars to leave. Although Little Bridge seemed lovely, and it was nice so many people had packed into the auditorium to listen to us speak, it was unlikely many of them would buy books. That's the way book festivals worked. Authors were an oddity at which people loved to come out and gawk. Only a few cared enough to sample the product they were selling.

"Fine," I said. "I'll be open-minded. Will Price admires me. He admires me so much, he—"

Bernadette held up a warning hand. *"Don't.* Don't start that again. He said he was sorry. Maybe he really did have a bad day that morning at Novel Con. It could happen to anyone. Maybe—"

But I never did get to hear what Bernadette thought might have happened to make Will say such awful things about my books, because at that moment we cleared the trees and saw that the hordes of people in the parking lot weren't heading toward their cars at all. They were crowding instead outside the author tents. . . .

No, not crowding. Lining up.

"Holy cattails," I said, once again freezing in my tracks. "Are all these people here for—?"

"There you are!" Chloe came running toward us, breathless in her little red-and-white dance shirt and shorts. "I've been looking everywhere for both of you! Are you ready for the signing? Do you need bottled water or anything? Because there are a ton of people waiting, and it would be great if we could get you seated and started, because we've got a conch chowder lunch lined up for all the paid attendees over by the lighthouse, and we really want to get them over there before the chowder gets cold."

Bernadette and I exchanged shocked glances. *What?*

Maybe I really should start being a little more pawsitive after all.

CHAPTER FIFTEEN

LITTLE BRIDGE BOOK FESTIVAL ITINERARY FOR:
JO WRIGHT

Saturday, January 4, 1:00 p.m.–2:00 p.m.

Book Signing

With Clive Dean, Jerome Jarvis, Victoria Maynard, Garrett
Newcombe, Will Price, Jo Wright, and Bernadette Zhang

All of Little Bridge Island turned out for the book signing. Or at least it seemed that way. The line of people with books in their hands seemed to stretch endlessly.

Not that I was complaining! Hadn't this been my dream when I was secretly writing *Kitty Katz, Kitten Sitter #1: Kitty to the Rescue* in between shifts as a server in one of New York City's many, many beer 'n' burger joints, certain the book would never get published, yet also hoping against hope that it would? To be faced with a line of people who, in this day and age, actually read books—and not just any books, but *my* books?

It was like I'd died and gone to heaven.

Or at least it would have been, if I hadn't ended up being seated next to Will.

This time it wasn't his choice, though. The festival seated its authors alphabetically by last name.

So I found myself at my own little white-cloth-covered folding table with Will to my right and Bernadette to my left.

At first this was fine. I'd done so many signings with Bernadette, I knew exactly what to expect from her: she was warm with readers, but never phony; signed quickly but not like she was in any big rush (which, of course, we were, because of Chloe's dire warning about the conch chowder); she allowed fans to take selfies, letting them come behind her signing table to snap a quick photo, and even allowing them to come back for a retake if someone's eyes turned out to be closed or they didn't like their smile.

This was pretty much standard signing procedure. Bernadette and I always tried to be pleasant so no one ever felt slighted, but quick. We couldn't afford to stop to chat too long (like Jerome, Kellyjean, and Saul) or draw an elaborate illustration next to our signatures (like Garrett), because if we did, we'd never get through everyone in line, and then the worst would happen: some adorable child or teen would walk away disappointed, their book unsigned.

Will, on the other hand, didn't seem to care about any of these things. He hardly lifted his dark head from the books he was signing, barely stopping to smile or say hello to his die-hard fans—some of whom were so moved by the experience of meeting him at last that they'd begun to weep in line before even getting to his table, working themselves into sobs by the time they reached him. He was in such a rush to get through the line that he didn't, I noted, even respect his readers enough to sign his entire name, just his initials, *WP*, with a swoosh.

This was *appalling*, especially since his name was already so short—no longer than mine, and I always wrote out the entire thing. I felt it was the least I could do, even for readers who weren't purchasing any of my books new at the event, only bringing along copies from home.

I totally understood that an author like Saul, who'd been in the business long enough to have published hundreds— literally *hundreds*—of short story collections, novellas, and even entire series of novels under multiple pen names might put a limit to the number of books he'd sign for his fans at one event. His line would never end if he agreed to sign *every single thing* he'd ever written for *every single* Clive Dean fan who showed up, although he was always so tickled to see some of his very old books—from the seventies!—that he'd sometimes sit and chuckle over them, asking the fan where he or she had gotten it, how they'd managed to hold on to it so long, and whether or not they liked it as much as his new work, that his line would be held up even more.

It was Frannie who'd finally put her foot down. Three books per fan. Three books per fan—more if the fan bought the books new at the event—was all Saul was allowed to sign, or they'd be at every signing forever, and Frannie would never get back to the hotel for lunch or dinner.

But how could I apply the same rules to some sweet, adorable kid who'd brought along all of her tattered but much treasured editions of *Kitty Katz, Kitten Sitter*, the pages soft as velvet from being so well thumbed, smelling delightfully of vanilla, the scent of old paperbacks? Especially when they said, as they often did, that mine was the first chapter book they'd ever read, or it had come as a gift from Grandma, or gotten them through a difficult time?

I couldn't be so hard-hearted.

Instead, each got a personalization, a *You're Purr-fect!* or *Thanks Furr Reading!* and an XOXO *Jo Wright,* even if the book was clearly stamped as having been purchased second-hand at a used bookstore or library sale and there was no possible way I'd ever earn a cent of royalties from the sale. If someone—especially a child—was taking the time to come to a book event, that meant I needed to make the experience as special and memorable as possible, so that child would stay a reader forever. It wasn't just my responsibility: it was my *duty*.

Will Price apparently did not share this belief, however. He didn't even have qualms about denying his fans selfies, giving them a crisp British, "I wish I could, but I'm a bit pressed for time today," before turning to the next person in line.

I wouldn't have believed it if I hadn't witnessed it for myself—and if he hadn't confessed to me earlier his fear of public speaking.

I knew I shouldn't judge him too harshly. Maybe, I told

myself as I smiled for selfie after selfie—my readers, most
teenagers and older now, were as obsessed with getting the
perfect shot as Bernadette's—Will's rudeness to his fans had
something to do with whatever had happened to him and his
sister back when he'd been so rude about me at Novel Con.

Maybe when I finally found out what it was, I could make
Kitty discover that the same thing had happened to Raul
Wolf, and that's why he was such an arrogant jerk—albeit
one who was a teenaged wolf instead of a grown man who
really should have known better than to take his problems
out on his fans and innocent female authors.

That would only work, of course, if whatever had happened to Will wasn't too dark for Kitty Katz readers. My
audience expected a certain amount of humor from my
books, as shown by the fact that I couldn't get anyone in publishing interested in my books about the apocalyptic Mari-
anne Dashwood and Colonel Brandon or the girl with the
dying mother and broke musician dad.

It was toward the end of the signing—or at least the end
for Will, because he'd whipped through his line so fast—that
I began to notice something:

He kept glancing my way.

Not staring at me like he had during our panel, but darting
little looks, like he was watching what I was doing.

Then, as Will watched me, little by little, he started to . . .
there's no other way to describe it:

Copy me.

He began actually to put on the brakes, look up at his
readers, and smile at them. He even agreed to pose for the

selfies they kept begging him to allow them—though I noticed he kept his arms at his sides and his hands on the table,
obeying the Never Touch a Reader rule.

It was amazing. It was like watching an alien learn to adapt
to life on our planet. Will was *learning*. Learning how to be
human!

I couldn't help feel like *I* was doing this. *I* was teaching
Will how to act like a human being . . . or at least a professional writer in the twenty-first century.

But how had he never learned before? He was my age and
had been doing signings for at least as long as I had. Had no
one ever told him that he was being rude?

Actually, it was possible. This was occasionally the case
with famous authors: No one at their publishing house
wanted to insult their highest grossing author by suggesting
that their writing (or behavior) needed improvement. The
author could be so angry, they might flee to another publishing house.

But hadn't anyone in Will's *family* ever noticed his bad
manners before? Or had he been raised by *actual* wolves,
like Raul?

When I got a break in my line, I turned my head to see
if Bernadette had noticed any of what had been going on
beside me.

She had. She was watching Will with raised eyebrows—
and also hadn't missed how Garrett, one table over from Will,
was doing the complete opposite: he kept draping his arms all
over any reader who asked for a photo, no matter what age,
drawing them close to him and then "magically" drawing a

commemorative guild coin from their ear, grinning up into the camera lens, and shouting "Dark Magic" at whoever was taking the picture.

None of his young readers' parents objected, though. My free promotional bookmarks (Don't Fur-get: KK#27, Coming Soon!) weren't nearly as big a hit. No one wanted a bit of colored cardboard when they could have an actual *coin* (especially one magically drawn from their ear).

I got distracted from Will a second later, however, when a familiar voice said, quite close to me, "Oh my God, you guys, I just can't thank you enough for what you both said today!"

I looked up to see Lauren and her friends standing in front of both my table and Will's. They were in full resort wear— sunglasses, wedge sandals, and ruffly rompers over which they'd thrown floaty kimonos. Lauren was lugging a wheelie suitcase behind her and had clearly waited until both my line and Will's had died down enough so that she could be last and have a nice, long chat with us.

I knew what the wheelie suitcase contained, though I wasn't certain Will did. Will did not seem to understand anything about being a living human being and not a wolf, which was why I took the initiative and replied, "It was our pleasure, Lauren. We're so happy you could come."

"Oh, Lauren wouldn't have missed it for the world." Jasmine was sucking coconut water from a straw out of an actual coconut while hugging a pile of brand-new copies of Will's *When the Heart Dies*. Beside her, Cassidy was clutching a well-loved edition of *The Moment* as well as several new volumes she'd apparently purchased to give away to friends.

"Lauren's going to skip going to the beach with us this afternoon to stay in the hotel and write, she's so inspired."

"Well," Will said. I could tell by the way he was tugging at his shirt collar that he felt uncomfortable—as uncomfortable as he'd been at the airport yesterday morning, when he'd been swarmed by this same group of girls. "That's the way to do it. Discipline. Stories don't write themselves."

I had to disagree—respectfully, of course. "I think it's okay to skip writing for a day and go to the beach with your friends when you're on Little Bridge Island for the first time."

"No." Will shook his head. "When inspiration hits, you have to take advantage of it."

"Not when you're her age." I still hadn't the foggiest notion how old Lauren and her friends were, but I knew they were way younger than I was. I also knew how many parties and trips to the beach I'd missed because I'd had to work to pay for things that other kids hadn't, like my college tuition and our apartment's electric bill. One of the reasons I wrote about cats instead of humans was because I had no idea what it was like to go to a high school dance or basketball game: I'd never been to one. I'd been too busy working. But no one knew what a cat high school dance or basketball game was like, so I couldn't get them wrong. "She has plenty of time for writing. Right now she's on vacation on a beautiful island with her friends. She should enjoy it."

Will looked stern. "When inspiration strikes—"

"Oh, you two are so adorable together." Kellyjean, who had finished up with her line, came sauntering over, her eyes sparking playfully over what she considered her brilliant witticism. "Ha-ha! Am I right? Aren't these two always arguing just like an old married couple?"

I thought I might evaporate from embarrassment right there, and Will didn't look particularly pleased, either, judging by the way he white-knuckled the pen he was holding.

"Oh, come on," Kellyjean went on. She never knew when to quit. "You agree with me, right, Garrett?"

Garrett did not appear to appreciate Kellyjean's comment any more than Will or I had. He was finishing up one last autograph—which of course included an elaborate *Dark Magic School* illustration—for an eager young fan. "Um, not really," he said.

Lauren seemed to decide it was time to bring the subject back around to what mattered most: herself. She lifted her wheelie suitcase and placed it, with a thump, on my table, then opened it.

"I really hope you don't mind," she said, "but it's always been my dream to get these signed by you."

I watched as she began removing from the suitcase, one by one, all twenty-six books in the Kitty Katz, Kitten Sitter series, then stacking them in front of me.

"You don't have to personalize them," she said, apparently noticing my stunned expression. "But if you could sign them all, that would be great."

"Of course I'll personalize them." I couldn't quite believe what I was seeing. I'd suspected upon noticing the suitcase that she might have brought *some* of the Kitty Katz books with her, but not *all* of them. "You brought these all the way from *Canada*?"

"Not just these." Lauren twinkled at Will, who was also watching her with disbelief as she dug more deeply into the suitcase. "I've got some for you, too, Will!" Out came every book that Will had ever written, as well, each almost as battered and well loved as the copies of *Kitty Katz*. "Your books mean so much to me. Kitty Katz made me want to be a writer, but your books, Will, taught me what it means to be a woman."

Oh. *No.*

"Well, thank you." Will began scribbling away. "It means so much to me to hear you say that."

Which was exactly what *I'd* been saying to every reader who'd come up to my table in response to their telling me that a Kitty book had meant something to them. Was it possible that Will was doing the one thing so many of my girlfriends had assured me that Justin—or any man—would never, ever do: change?

No. It couldn't be.

Except it *did* happen sometimes . . . but usually only in books. In *The Moment*, for instance, Johnny Kane was turning from a lawless criminal into a tender lover for Melanie West.

"You're very welcome," I said to Lauren, practically hurling her books back to her as I signed each one, I was so eager to get out of there and tell Bernadette what had happened. Because of course Bernadette, finished with her signing line, had wandered away to order a drink from the cocktail wagon. (Yes! The Little Bridge Book Festival had a cocktail wagon that served alcoholic beverages to festival attendees, right there in the parking lot.) "Am I, uh, going to see you later?" I couldn't just take off and run when this girl had been such an awesome fan and bought so many of my books (in the past, not new at this event—not that I had any new books for her to buy). "Maybe tonight, at the banquet?"

"*I'll* be there." Jasmine was sucking noisily on the remnants of her coconut water. "I don't know about Lauren. She's going to be too busy writing."

Their other friend, Cassidy, who'd been watching Will sign the half dozen copies of *The Moment* she was buying for her friends, apparently having decided against the chest-signing request, looked up and said, "Oh my God, *yes*. On TripAdvisor it says that Cracked, where they're having the party, has like the *freshest* seafood on the whole island."

"You really ought to come tonight, Lauren." Garrett was still working on his drawing for a young fan, a small boy in an actual wizard cape whose father looked as thrilled to be receiving a Garrett Newcombe original as he did. "I agree with Jo that you should take all the advantage you can of being in such a beautiful place. It will definitely give you something to write about when you get home to Canada."

Lauren raised her perfectly plucked—or possibly waxed or threaded—eyebrows. "Do you really think so?"

"Oh, definitely." Garrett examined his drawing, then, apparently dissatisfied with his work, bent to add a finishing touch. "I know Will here thinks the way a book gets written is with discipline, and of course that's true. But you'll never be able to write anything if you haven't experienced anything to write about."

I was a little irritated to hear Garrett "You Are My Sunshine" Newcombe, of all people, so perfectly sum up my own thoughts on the matter.

But I was less irritated when I saw how much it made Will frown . . . especially when Lauren beamed at Garrett and asked, "You really think so?"

"Oh, I know so. Plus, I'm going to be performing an act of dematerialization at the dinner that you aren't going to want to miss. It'll be an experience I suspect you'll want to write about."

"Dematerialization?" Lauren glanced at her friends, who were giggling at each other, most likely because of the number of times the word "dematerialize" had been used. "Okay, cool. I'll be there."

Garrett smiled at Lauren like a kindly uncle, then handed the kid in the wizard cape the book he'd been drawing in. "Here you go, Dylan. And here's an official *Dark Magic School* number eleven commemorative guild piece to go with it."

"Gee, thanks!" Dylan—and his appreciative father—looked ecstatic.

It was at that moment that Chloe came bouncing over. She'd been working with the other Snappettes at managing the line, putting Post-it notes on the covers of all the readers' books so we'd be sure to spell their names rights (it was important, if someone had a name like Michelle or Alyssa, that we knew how many *l*'s or *s*'s it had).

But now that almost everyone had departed for the scheduled conch chowder luncheon, she was leading around a dark-haired boy who wore an expensive-looking Leica camera around his neck.

"Miss Wright, this is Elijah." Chloe pointed at the boy. "He's the festival's official photographer."

Elijah nodded at me coolly. "Hey," he said.

"Would it be all right if he got a few pics of you and Will in action, signing some books?" Chloe asked.

"Absolutely." I posed with my pen hovering over the last of Lauren's books, while Will did the same. Elijah began snapping away in a manner that really did seem quite professional.

"How's Molly doing, Elijah?" Will asked.

"Good, I think," Elijah replied, as his camera clicked. "Katie called a little while ago from the hospital, and said Miss Molly—I mean, Miz Hartwell—is four centimeters dilated, whatever that means."

I heard all the mothers left in the tent—Frannie, Kellyjean, and Bernadette, as well as a few others—make sympathetic sounds.

"Is it a boy or a girl?" Kellyjean asked. These kinds of things were important to her. In the Salem Prairie series, werewolves were always getting witches pregnant, and vice versa. Birth control did not exist in Victoria Maynard's supernatural universe.

"They want it to be a surprise. I mean, to everybody else. They know. *I* know, because Katie told me." Elijah was evidently someone important in the lives of Molly and the sheriff and his daughter. "But I'm not supposed to say. So, uh, Miss Wright, if you wouldn't mind scooting your chair a little closer to Mr. Price's—" To my dismay, he walked over and moved my signing table a few inches nearer to Will's.

"And, Mr. Price, if you could scoot closer to Miss Wright so I could get both of you in one shot . . . that's right—"

Will obligingly moved closer to me. So close that I could smell his cologne, which had a fresh, clean, citrus scent, and feel his body heat against mine. So close that I could see that he'd already begun to grow a five o'clock shadow even though it was nowhere near five o'clock. So close that I spied a few dark chest hairs curling out from the opening of his shirt.

And that wasn't all that was happening, either. Something about the combination of his scent and how tantalizingly masculine those dark hairs looked was making me feel warm. Much warmer than I knew it was in the tent, since electric fans had been set up to cool off the area as we signed, even though the temperature was really quite pleasant.

Still, sweat was beginning to break out along the back of my neck and along the insides of my thighs beneath the skirt of my dress.

This was not a good situation. This was not a good situation at all.

"How are you?" Will asked.

I blinked at him, startled. "Who? Me?"

He grinned, not glancing away from the camera. "Yes, you. How are you doing? All right, then?"

"Er." I was about to burst into flames, but other than that, fine. "Yes."

"Now if you could just lean across the tables." Elijah was talking to Lauren. "Like you're asking them a question, the way I saw you doing a few minutes ago?"

"Me?" Lauren looked delighted. "Of course!"

Lauren leaned across the table, her long, straight hair sweeping across the white tablecloth, brushing my hand a little bit and enveloping both Will and I in the scent of her apple-blossom shampoo.

This was preferable to the scent of Will in which I'd been enveloped before, but was doing nothing for the heat I was feeling. Was he not feeling it? He didn't appear to be, and neither did Lauren. They both looked cool as cucumbers, smiling away as Elijah clicked, clicked, clicked—

"Okay!" I sprang up from my chair and backed away from Will. Thankfully air rushed in and began to cool all the places that had begun to become slick with heat. "You have enough photos for now, right, Elijah?"

Elijah looked down at the screen on the back of his camera. "Uh . . . yes. Yeah, these are great. Thanks."

"Great." I grabbed my bag from beneath my signing table and darted away before anyone could think of some other reason to force me to sit back down next to the good-smelling nuclear reactor that was Will Price. "Well, I guess I'll see you all at dinner—"

"Oh no you don't, Miss Jo Wright." Kellyjean was suddenly at my side, snaking an arm through mine. "We're not letting you slink back to the hotel to work for the rest of this beautiful day."

"Uh." I had to lean my head to the side in order not to be struck by the rim of her enormous beach hat. "No, I really do need to get back to the hotel. I'm super behind on *Kitty*

Katz number twenty-seven. I finally got a good idea for it, so I'm just going to go work on—"

"You're not doing any such thing." Kellyjean's grip on my arm was surprisingly forceful. "You're going to go out on Will's boat with us this afternoon for lunch. Weren't you the one telling that little girl over there that if she wants to be a good writer, she has to have experiences worth writing about?"

"Um." I flung a desperate look in Bernadette's direction for help, but she only grinned at me, evidently enjoying my discomfort. *You did say that,* she mouthed, and pointed finger guns at me. "Yes. But Lauren is twelve and a new writer, and I'm in my thirties and—"

"Hey!" Lauren had zipped up her suitcase and was now flinging me a disbelieving look. "I'm nineteen!"

"Oh, sorry, nineteen. But I'd really just like to—"

"No excuses." Kellyjean's hold on my arm had turned to a death grip. "You're going to *love* it. We're going to drink wine, and maybe do some sunbathing—"

"Oh, that's too bad." In spite of the strength of Kellyjean's grip, I tugged to pull my arm free. "I didn't bring my swimsuit."

"I brought it." Kellyjean patted her gigantic beach bag while keeping hold of my arm. "I took it out of your room last night while I was setting up my diffuser, since I knew you'd forget it. Wasn't that smart of me? Now you have no excuse not to come with us."

Bernadette, to whom I flung one last desperate glance for

help, only smiled at me. "Sorry, Jo," she said with a shrug. "It's on the itinerary."

I gave up. Kitty Katz knew when it was ungracious to turn down an invitation—even an invitation she was dreading—and so did I.

"Gee, great," I said, faking an enormous smile. "I can't wait."

The Moment by Will Price

We made love on the floor in front of the fire. Our bodies met like long-lost friends, our limbs entwined, our lips clinging. Her hair hung around my face like a shimmering waterfall of liquid gold, the smell of her filling my senses like an opiate. For a while, I forgot what I had done.

Afterward, though, when she lay panting against my bare chest, and the flames in the fireplace had died to only a red glow, I remembered.

CHAPTER SIXTEEN

LITTLE BRIDGE BOOK FESTIVAL ITINERARY FOR:
JO WRIGHT

Saturday, January 4, 2:30 p.m.–4:30 p.m.

- Sailing Aboard *The Moment* -

Will Price invites fellow authors for a sail around Little Bridge
Island aboard his 60' catamaran. Lunch will be served.

O kay. The boat was pretty cool.

What was I saying? The boat was *amazing*.

I'd never been on a boat before, unless you counted the boat to the immigration museum on Ellis Island, which every kid who goes to school in New York City eventually ends up taking.

But that was just a ferryboat, and it had only gone back and forth across the Hudson River.

This was a multimillion-dollar catamaran sliding across the crystal-blue sea off the coast of Florida. The bright sun shone down on my bare arms as the warm wind whipped the hair that had come loose from my ponytail. As I leaned against the rail, watching the water glide beneath us—so clear that I could see the sandy bottom and seaweed beneath us—I felt as if all the worries and snarky thoughts in my head were being blown away by the beautiful tropical breeze.

I couldn't remember the last time I'd felt this happy. Maybe never?

The weirdest part was that I'd basically been forced onto this boat against my will, and yet I didn't care. Not only did I not care, I *loved* it.

"Can you believe this?" Bernadette, a plastic cup of rosé in one hand, a plate of what was being served for lunch down in the galley—delicately fried conch fritters, lemon herb chicken wings, roasted vegetable quinoa salad, watermelon and straw-berry kebabs—in the other, made her way toward me. She'd changed from her book panel clothes into a one-piece and shorts, even throwing on the bright yellow Little Bridge Book Festival visor that had been in our swag bag (to protect her face from the sun, she said).

That's right, Bernadette Zhang, author of the dystopian monster hit Crown and Stars series, was wearing a *visor*.

"It's *amazing*," I said.

We were headed for what Will had called "one of his favor-ite spots," which apparently took some navigating to get to. The island of Little Bridge was shrinking behind us. Ahead stretched only water—but water unlike any I'd ever seen before. Ribbons of turquoise and aquamarine and the palest green—other places almost white, the water was so shallow, the sand beneath it shimmering in the hot midday sun—surrounded us. Occasionally a small island of green popped up from the horizon like an oasis in a desert.

"Mangroves," Bernadette explained. Always in educator mode, Bernadette read from her phone about what we were seeing. "They thrive in areas of low tide and provide essential habitats for a myriad of wildlife, including wading birds. Hey! We might see a flamingo!"

But none of these mangroves appeared to be Will's special spot, since he was steering around them.

That was the other thing: Will didn't have a hired crew or anything. He was steering his own boat.

Was there something sexy about a guy behind the wheel of a large and powerful boat?

A guy who looked like Will? Yeah, okay, I'll admit it: Yes. Yes, there was.

"So, aren't you glad now that Kellyjean talked you into coming?" Bernadette set down her lunch plate and attempted to photograph a particularly lovely patch of shimmering blue water that stretched to meet the equally blue sky at the horizon—two blues so deep that you could hardly tell where one stopped and the other began.

"Oh, I'm glad, all right." I took a sip from my own cup of rosé that I'd been handed upon boarding *The Moment*—yes, Will had named his boat after his latest book, which had apparently helped pay for it—and let my gaze roam away from the water, toward the boat's bridge deck, where Will was steering. Shirtless, I might add.

And let me tell you, that view was every bit as enticing as the ocean.

Fortunately he couldn't see me looking at him, because I had my sunglasses on. I'd invested in a good pair of polarized sunglasses with mirrored lenses when I'd first started shopping in Florida for places for my dad. At the time it had only been to help combat the glare of the sun when I was being driven around by Realtors, but now they were paying off in ways I'd never expected. For all Will knew, I could have been checking out some birds flying in the sky above him.

Instead I was checking out him. He was deep in conversation with Jerome, who was fascinated by the boat's navigation system and wanted the console explained to him. Will appeared only too happy to oblige, which suited me fine, as well. Now he not only couldn't tell I was observing him, he was too busy.

I was doing all of this observing for research purposes only, of course. It would help me turn Raul Wolf into a fully realized and complex character. I needed Raul to be someone that readers would come to love and fully support Kitty Katz dumping Rex Canine for.

No other reason. No other reason at all.

At least I'd have been able to do this if other people hadn't kept interrupting me.

"Can you believe this boat?" Garrett appeared from belowdecks, holding a can of hard seltzer in one hand and, unfortunately, his ukulele in the other. Like Will, he was shirtless.

Unlike Will, however, Garrett had not had the sense either to wear a hat or stay beneath the shade of the bridge, so his pale skin was already burning under the sun's intense rays, even though Kellyjean had offered him use of her SPF 100 wholly reef-safe and biodegradable sunscreen. The rest of us had let her spray us down, but Garrett had declined.

"I never burn," he'd informed us. "I'm one-eighth Cherokee."

He also, I noted, shaved his chest. Either that or waxed it. He was miraculously smooth everywhere except his legs, underarms, head, and face.

"This boat has got a bedroom bigger than the one I have back home!" Garrett had apparently been exploring *The Moment*, which Will had urged all of us to treat as our second home for the afternoon. Garrett, however, was the only one who'd taken that literally and not as mere politeness. "How much do you think this thing set him back? Just ballpark."

"You already told us last night it was two million." I took another sip of my wine.

"Yeah, but now that I'm seeing it, with all the bells and whistles, I'm guessing three million, easy. And then he goes and names it after his book about a murderer!"

"Excuse me." I glared at him. "Some of us haven't finished the book yet. I don't know if Johnny did it or not."

"Oh, please. Don't you read the end of the book first?"

"No, I do not. What is wrong with you?"

"I'm all about craft, baby. I don't care about the story."

I pointed at him. "Don't call me baby, you—"

"Shhh." Bernadette pointed toward a number of lounge chairs a few yards away where Chloe, her friend Sharmaine, and Kellyjean were all draped in their swimsuits, eating their lunch, their backs toward us. "There are impressionable young people in the vicinity."

"Fine." I lowered my voice. "But don't call me baby."

"Jeez." Garrett rolled his eyes. "So tense. But fine, I won't. Still, you have to admit, that's weird, too, right? What's Will's deal with teenaged girls?"

"Gee, I don't know." Bernadette sipped her wine. "He's related to one?"

"But don't you ladies think this thing with the cheerleaders is suspicious?" Garrett should maybe have laid off the hard seltzers, since his face was getting redder by the minute. "Because I do."

"They're not cheerleaders," I heard myself saying. "They're on the school dance team. And Will is donating money to them to help out during the festival. I don't think that's weird. I think it's nice."

Whoa. What was wrong with me? Why was I coming to Will's defense?

Garrett was too wrapped up in his own concerns to notice.

"I imagine you two have heard the rumors," he went on, as if I hadn't spoken.

Bernadette's eyebrows were raised almost to the sweatband of her visor. "Rumors? What rumors?"

"About a certain author." Garrett was smiling now. "A certain famous *male* author."

Bernadette side-eyed me as she lifted her lunch plate. "I can't imagine what you mean."

"Price, of course. You know the real reason why he wants all these young girls around, don't you?"

"Why, no, Garrett." Bernadette took a bite of watermelon kebab. "But I'm sure you're going to tell us."

"*Research!* Will Price wants to make the move into writing children's fiction!"

Bernadette and I exchanged glances. Garrett must have noticed that we were smirking, since he cried, "Oh, *come on!* How can you not see it? It couldn't be more obvious. It's why he's paying you, Jo, such a huge stipend to be here. I'm surprised you two didn't catch on this morning during our panels. He couldn't have been more thrilled that Molly went into labor! It gave him the opportunity to sit there and grill us about what it's like to write for kids."

I choked a little on the sip of wine I'd taken. Apparently Garrett took this for disbelief, since he insisted, "You must have noticed how competitive Will is! He's already conquered writing for adults, so why wouldn't he try to take over the world of children's lit, too? God." Garrett shook his head at what he perceived as our extreme stupidity. "The truth has been staring you two in the face this whole time, and you refuse to see it."

Bernadette blinked at Garrett one or two times, then burst out laughing. She tried flinging a hand over her mouth both to keep from being overheard by Kellyjean and the Snappettes and to keep Garrett from noticing how hilarious she found his statement, but it didn't work.

"I don't see what's so funny." Garrett looked wounded. "You know I'm right."

"I'll tell you what's funny," I said. Unlike Bernadette, I wasn't laughing. I wasn't smiling, not even a little bit. "Last night you were insisting that the reason I'd been given such a big stipend was to lure me here because Will is in love with me. Now you're saying the only reason Will's hanging around with any of us is because he wants our help to break into children's lit—as if he'd need any help with that. Will could write the alphabet on a piece of paper and someone would publish it. Get your story straight, Garrett. If this is an example of how you plot your books, I don't understand why anyone reads them at all."

"Wha—?" Garrett looked even more hurt. "Jo. Where's all this animosity coming from? Are your feelings hurt or something, because Will might not actually be that into you after all? I'm only trying to *warn* you girls that the guy is up to no good, and you—"

"Oh, God, Garrett. Shut *up* already."

I must have spoken a little too loudly, since Chloe leaned her head around the back of her sun lounger and asked, "Hey ya. Is everything all right back there?"

"Oh, yes," I called to her. "Sorry. Everything's fine. Just talking about books."

Garrett was glaring at me. I had clearly lost a friend—if he and I had ever been friends. But I felt like that ship had sailed—to coin a phrase—yesterday morning on the author bus when he'd so aggressively sang at me with his ukulele.

"Oh, books!" Chloe sounded excited. "My favorite subject!

Are you sure you have everything you need? Can I get anyone more fruit kebabs?"

"No, we're all good, sunshine." Garrett tipped his hard seltzer toward Chloe in a toast. "You and your brother are the perfect hosts."

"Oh, thanks for that," Chloe said with a wide grin. "Cheers." Then her head disappeared back behind the lounger.

"Well, since you two seem to object so much to my company, I guess I'll go spend time with people who actually appreciate it," Garrett huffed at us. Then he began stalking over to the women on the sun loungers.

"Garrett," Bernadette called after him. "Garrett, no, wait—"

But it was too late. Garrett sat down, set his drink in a cup holder, and began strumming his ukulele.

"Hey, ladies," he said to Kellyjean, Sharmaine, and Chloe. "You know what you remind me of, lying there, looking so pretty in the sun? A little sea shanty I happen to know. 'Farewell and adieu unto you Spanish ladies. Farewell and adieu to you ladies of Spain—'"

"Oh, God." Bernadette looked at me, all signs of humor gone. "Now look what you've done."

"*Me?* You're the one who laughed in his face."

"I know." Bernadette seemed regretful. "I think I've had too much rosé."

"Well, I'm starting to think Garrett might be one of *those*."

"One of what?"

"You know, one of those guys who insists every other guy

in the room is no good, so he can make himself look great in comparison."

Bernadette gazed at Garrett thoughtfully. "If that's his goal, it's definitely not working."

"Why don't you keep an eye on him, while I go warn our host?"

"Wait." She caught my hand as I started for the bridge. "*What* are you going to do?"

"Warn Will that he needs to look out for Garrett." At Bernadette's bug-eyed expression, I elaborated. "Don't you think at least one member of the festival board should know the truth about him?"

"The truth about what?"

"What you heard about him at Novel Con. The guy's sitting there serenading Will's sister—his *teenaged* sister."

"He's playing the *ukulele*, Jo. You yourself said that a guy playing the ukulele wouldn't have impressed you when you were their age."

"Yeah, if he'd been an *ordinary* guy. But Garrett's a bestselling author. That definitely would have impressed me enough that I'd have overlooked the ukulele thing. Did you or did you not tell me that there were rumors flying around about a bestselling author hitting on all the girls at last year's Novel Con?"

"I did. But I also said I didn't have any proof of who it was."

I nodded at Garrett, who'd finished up his song about Spanish ladies and launched into something even worse, a ukulele version of a reggae tune. "I think it's pretty obvious who it was. And if Chloe were my little sister, I'd want to know."

"Oh, God." Bernadette rolled her eyes. "Fine, okay, go. But don't blame me if your plan backfires."

"Backfires how? What do you think Will might do? Throw Garrett overboard?" This would actually make the cutest illustration for a Kitty Katz book *ever*. I could just see Raul Wolf tossing Rex Canine over the railing of the town ferry, into the Bay of Dogsville.

"Oh my God." Bernadette's voice, sounding incredulous, broke into my fantasy. "I know what you're doing. You're going to put all of this into a book, aren't you?"

"What?" I looked away in case she somehow glimpsed the truth through the mirrored lenses of my sunglasses. "No! Of course not."

"Yes, you are." Bernadette shook her head in disbelief. "I know you. This is all going into *Kitty Katz number twenty-seven*."

"Oh, please!" Too late. She'd seen right through me. "You really *have* had too much rosé."

"If you break up Kitty and Rex," Bernadette called after me, "your fans will hate you. You're going to be the scourge of Goodreads!"

Worth it, I thought, but didn't say out loud.

The Moment by Will Price

She was half asleep. I kissed both of her eyelids. "I have to tell you something."

The eyelids rose. She smiled. "Tell me what?"

I leaned up on one elbow and swept some of her hair from her face. "The truth. I have to tell you the truth"

Melanie sat up. Her hair fell forward, over her full, round breasts. Her eyes were like twin blue ponds, fathoms deep. "There's nothing you can say to me, Johnny, that will change the way I feel about you."

What could I do after that but make love to her all over again?

CHAPTER SEVENTEEN

The wind began to die a little as I wound my way up the steps to the bridge. It was too bad Frannie feared the ocean so much that she had forced Saul to go to the conch chowder lunch instead of joining us on *The Moment*. She was really missing out on a delightful day on the water. And also on what was about to happen.

"So when you see a pair of channel markers," Will was saying to Jerome as I joined them in the cockpit, "you steer the boat between them. Except when you're returning to dock, then you steer the boat right of the red ones—red, right, return."

Jerome gazed in the direction Will was pointing, looking more relaxed than I'd seen him in ages. Possibly this was because he was on a luxury yacht with a beer in his hand, but you never knew. "Sure, sure. I will definitely need this information at a future point in my life."

Will grinned. "Well, you probably don't get many channel markers in Iowa."

"I wouldn't know. I saw *Jaws* as a kid and vowed never to go near the ocean again. This is my first exception since."

Will laughed—the most genuine laugh I'd ever heard from him. It was easy to see he felt more comfortable out on the water than he did on land—more comfortable and maybe more himself.

"No great whites here. The water's only a few feet deep in most places. We could practically walk back to Little Bridge, if we wanted. How are you, Jo?"

"Oh. I'm fine." I kept my gaze glued to the ocean through the windshield, because otherwise, it might have strayed in dangerous directions. Jerome was rocking a perfectly acceptable dad bod, but Will? Oh my God. No wonder he'd been nominated for *People*'s sexiest man alive: beneath all that linen resort wear, he had the lean, muscular build of an Olympic swimmer.

Not only that, but his manscaping game was on point. He had to be manscaping, because I didn't know many guys whose body hair grew naturally from a silky-looking mat across their chest into a nice thin line down their stomach before disappearing into the waistband of their board shorts, like an arrow or the trunk of a tree . . . a tree whose root I was getting more and more interested in investigating.

Whoa. Cool it, Jo.

"So I was heading down to the galley for more wine and thought I'd come up to see if you guys needed anything," I lied. But since I'd waitressed for so many years, I felt like it came out sounding very natural and convincing.

"Oh, aren't you sweet?" Jerome's mischievous grin told me that he, at least, saw right through my lie. "As a matter of fact, I am getting a little low." He rattled his empty beer can. No glass was allowed on board *The Moment*, so we were all drinking out of cans or plastic. "I was just thinking about heading downstairs to get myself a refill. Why don't I bring back some for all of us?"

I recognized right away that someone must have tipped off Jerome about Kellyjean's plans for Will and me. *If y'all can, try and leave them alone together*, I could almost hear her telling everyone in her Texas twang. *It's time those two crazy kids fell in love!*

But instead of getting mad about her interference in my personal life, I decided to take advantage of it. "Sure. Thanks, Jerome."

Jerome, wearing an expression of mild amusement, slid from the swiveling co-captain's chair on which he'd been sitting and walked away. I was fairly certain he wouldn't be back. I couldn't blame him, really.

But it didn't matter. Will and I were finally alone. This was my chance to do the research I needed for *Kitty Katz #27*. And Will made it all too easy.

"Is Garrett playing that damned ukulele again?" he asked, peering out the windscreen and down at the sundeck. His sunglasses were perched on top of his head. Maybe he'd forgotten where he'd left them.

"Oh. Um." My gaze was on his legs. This was the first time I was getting to see them bare, since he was wearing shorts.

They were as fine as the rest of him, tanned and muscular and ready to be wrapped around me. "Yes."

"I thought I told him to leave it on the bus."

"You did." His feet looked amazing as ever. "But he brought it anyway."

Will shook his head, bringing my attention back to his face. "Is it just me, or is there something a bit peculiar about him?"

I slid into the chair that Jerome had recently vacated, keeping myself from saying, *Funny. He says the same thing about you.* I had to handle this just right. "Well, he certainly does seem to like serenading members of the opposite sex. Maybe in his past life he was a lovelorn troubadour."

Will frowned, still squinting through the windscreen down at the little group on the sundeck. "He doesn't seem very good at it. And aren't Kellyjean and Bernadette both married?"

"Um." I nibbled on a hangnail. This was going to be harder than I'd thought. "Yes. But I think it might be your sister and Sharmaine he's singing to."

His dark-haired head twisted toward me fast. "My *sister*? She's in high school."

"I think Garrett's aware of that. It doesn't appear to bother him."

Instead of storming off the deck and down the stairs to throw Garrett overboard, however, Will only leaned back in his swivel chair with a chuckle. "Well, good luck to him. If he actually tries anything, Chloe'll kill him."

This was an unusual take. "*Chloe* will?"

"Oh, yes. She and her friends on the dance team have started learning capoeira."

"I'm sorry. Capo-what-a?"

"Capoeira. It's an Afro-Brazilian style of dance, combined with martial arts. The girls have gone mad for it. Could cause significant cranial damage with a single kick, from what I'm told."

"Wow," I said. "So I guess your sister can take care of herself."

"Certainly well enough to handle the Garretts of the world."

I recalled what the sheriff's daughter had mentioned the night before about Will's fears that his sister might be kidnapped . . . probably something I should have remembered before I'd come rushing up to tell him about Garrett.

But he still didn't seem to be experiencing any anxiety on Chloe's behalf. Probably because the only possible threat in the area was Garrett, and he wasn't actually all that threatening. We were in the middle of the Florida Keys backcountry. There wasn't another soul around for miles, or at least it seemed so to me.

Which reminded me . . .

"Where are your parents?" I asked, definitely not eyeing his naked chest over the rim of my plastic wineglass. "Why does Chloe live with you and not them? Or are they here and I haven't met them yet?"

What I did not say was, *None of the interviews I've ever read about you have mentioned your parents. Not that I've read many, of course. Okay, I've read them all.*

"Our mother passed away," Will said shortly, then busied himself with doing something to the console that made the boat engines quieter. He must have noticed my suddenly stricken expression, however, since he added quickly, "A long time ago. Chloe was just a toddler."

Whoa. There was nothing in any of Will Price's bios about his mother dying tragically young.

Then again, most publications limited bios to one hundred words or less. It's why mine read merely, *Jo Wright was born in New York City. She is the author of over twenty books, including the #1* New York Times *bestselling Kitty Katz, Kitten Sitter series. She lives in Manhattan with her cat.*

"I'm so sorry," I said to Will, meaning it. "That must have been terrible. How did she die?"

Of course you're not supposed to ask "How did she die?" when someone mentions that a loved one has passed away. That's rude and none of your business and also probably painful for them to talk about. At least that's how it had been for me, until time and therapy had softened the blow of my mother's passing.

But if you're a nosy writer trying to put a story together that's more than a year late and you're talking to the person responsible for making it late (more or less), then it's okay to be rude.

Or at least, that's what I decided in that moment.

Will threw me an expressionless glance. For a few seconds I thought he wasn't going to answer, but finally he said, "Embolism."

"Oh." I winced. "That's awful. And your dad?"

"My dad." Will said the word like it tasted bad. "My dad. He was—how can I put this?—ill-prepared to assume the responsibility of single parenthood."

"Oh." I nodded. "Like Johnny's dad?"

Now the look he threw me was startled. "Johnny?"

"Yes. Johnny Kane. From *The Moment*. Or are you telling me that's *not* an autobiographical work?"

Slowly, he began to grin. "So. You're reading it."

"Of course I'm reading it. It's a free book that someone left in my hotel room. How could I not read it?"

The grin widened. "And what do you think of it?"

"Well." It was always so delicate when another author asked what you thought of their book, especially when that author was your sworn enemy, and yet you couldn't put their book down. "Johnny and Melanie certainly seem to have had a lot of trauma in their lives. But that isn't stopping them from having a lot of sex with each other."

The grin froze. His gaze became very still—almost wary— on mine. "And what do you think about that?"

"Well, on the whole, I'm a fan of sex, as long as it's be- tween consenting adults." What was happening here? Why was he looking at me that way? "But since I haven't finished the book yet, I'm reserving judgment. I presume you're going to kill Johnny off at the end, since you're such a big fan of *catharsis*."

The wary look left Will's face, and the grin returned. "Oh, you never know. I might surprise you this time."

"I doubt it. Anyway, I thought we were talking about your

dad. I hope he didn't die in a mine collapse like poor Johnny's father."

"Not exactly. But like poor Johnny's father, my dad only loved three things: his wife—my mother—gambling, and alcohol. After she died, he threw himself into the latter two with impressive abandon."

I was genuinely shocked. Not only because the normally tight-lipped Will Price was suddenly opening up to me, but because none of this matched what I'd assumed I knew about him. "Will. That's . . . that's really horrible."

He gave a nonchalant shrug of those enormous shoulders, as if nothing he was saying mattered. "I suppose. But however bad it was for me, it was much worse for Chloe. At least I got to spend a dozen years or so with a loving parent, who introduced me to so many wonderful things—books and reading. My mother loved them. Chloe didn't have that. I tried as best I could in my mother's place, but—"

He shrugged again, this time with a helplessness that almost broke my heart. I couldn't believe I was feeling sorry for Will Price, of all people.

"That's a lot of pressure," I said gently.

He didn't look very convinced. "I suppose. When I got into university, I didn't even want to go. Who was going to take care of Chloe?"

This sounded so much like something Johnny Kane would wonder about his sister, Zoey, I began to ask myself if *The Moment* wasn't slightly autobiographical after all.

"My dad agreed," Will went on, staring sightlessly off into

the sea. "He thought university was useless. He wanted me to take over his construction business, which was failing thanks to his betting habit. What a mess I would have made of that, eh?"

I blinked. I couldn't believe how wrong I'd been.

Not about everything, of course: Will Price really had been raised by wolves. But only one of them, and not exactly in the privileged luxury I'd always imagined.

Feeling like it might be appropriate to lighten the mood a bit, I said, "I can sort of relate. My dad is great, but he's a musician. He's still devastated I didn't go into the family business."

"Really?" Will glanced back at me and smiled. "Did he try to force you to learn the piano?"

"Worse: violin. Even with all my literary success, my dad is still holding on to the hope that someday I'll come to my senses."

"You do understand, then. Parental expectations can be . . . difficult."

"Yes," I said. "But look how well you've done for yourself." I gestured widely at the boat. "Your dad can't still think that you made the wrong choice."

The smile disappeared as his gaze shifted moodily back toward the windscreen. "Well, I'll never know. He died before I graduated university. Heart attack."

For once I was the one rendered speechless.

I understood now why there wasn't any mention of this in any of his bios. It was something every single journalist he'd encounter would want to ask him about: What was it like to have suffered so tragic a loss at such a young age, then gone on to become so meteorically successful writing books about survivors of equally terrible loss? (Although Will Price would never allow a character to die of something so mundane as a heart attack. Being hanged for running over your lover's husband would be more likely.)

Deeply regretting all the times I'd gouged out his eyes in photos in airplane magazines, I finally managed to stammer, "I . . . I'm so sorry, Will."

So original. But then, what else were you supposed to say upon learning something like that?

Then, because I didn't know what else to do, I added lamely: "My mother died when I was young, too."

Oh, God, *why? Why* had I told him this?

Will looked startled. "I thought she was a homemaker who loves baking cookies for you and your dad."

Now I was the one who was startled. "No. Where did you— Oh!" Comprehension dawned. "No, that's Kitty Katz. *Her* mom is a homemaker who loves baking cookies and cupcakes for—"

"Kitty and her three little baby brother kittens. Right." He was grinning again. "And Mr. Katz supports them all by working nine to five at Katz Savings and Loan."

I gaped at him. What was going on? Will Price had read my books? Obviously I knew he was familiar with them. He must have seen the bits that Nicole Woods had stolen, since they'd been quoted in every article about her plagiarizing the two of us.

And since he was on the selection committee for the

book festival, he'd have to at least heard Molly talking about them. Or possibly his sister had left *Kitty Katz #15: Kitty Quinceañera*, lying around the house, and he'd picked it up and learned about Kitty's best friend Felicity's rockin' fiesta de quince años.

But read one? Actually *read* a whole book of mine, the way I was (finally) reading one of his?

"But in your interviews," he went on, looking confused, "you always say Kitty's family is based on your own."

"Yes. Well." I twisted uncomfortably in the co-captain's seat. Wait—he'd been reading my interviews, too? No. Chloe had probably read them to him over the breakfast table or something. That made more sense. "Sometimes it's easier to say things like that when reporters ask you questions about your personal life, don't you think? Because the truth is such a bummer."

He raised his eyebrows at me. "The truth about my upbringing, yes. But yours? It's sad about your mother, but you seem extremely well adjusted . . . except for what you've done to your hair."

I flung a hand defensively to my head. *"What?"*

"Don't worry. I like the change. It suits you." He was grinning again. "All I'm saying is that unless you have post-traumatic stress from being forced to learn the violin all those years ago, your upbringing seems quite normal. Why wouldn't you want to talk about it during interviews?"

"Because I don't want to share the worst pain I've ever felt in my life with some stranger I've only just met. Why would I want to keep reliving the pain of my mom dying of cancer when I was fourteen, and how awful that was, and how my dad spent every penny he had—that he wasn't giving away to his bandmates—trying to save her, all to promote a book? I know *you'd* call that cathartic, but to me, that's private. That's not for public consumption."

Why was I telling him all this? But he had just told me his darkest secrets, so I might as well admit mine.

He didn't look the least bit fazed, however.

"Of course. Makes perfect sense. The part about your dad, though, you did mention in one interview. I believe it was last year. Your father had just broken his arm slipping on some ice." At my shocked expression, he added, "I only remember because I was on a flight and I happened to pick up a magazine and—"

"Sure." I was mortified. "Yes. I remember. It was right after it happened. The journalist called while I was in the hospital waiting room."

Wait. What was going on?

None of this made any sense. Will Price had been reading my interviews *himself*? Willingly? Not because Chloe had been forcing him to over bowls of Cheerios?

Why?

CHAPTER EIGHTEEN

I'd have to think about that later . . . and the fact that nothing I'd believed to be true—well, hardly anything, anyway—was actually true.

Right now, all I could think to say was, "I . . . I'm so sorry about your parents, Will. That's truly awful. But . . ." My gaze alighted once more on Chloe, looking golden and lovely on the deck below. "But your sister turned out all right in the end, didn't she?" Yes, that was it! Concentrate on the pawsitive, like Kitty.

"Mercifully, yes." He avoided my gaze, performing another maneuver on the console, and the engines became even quieter. The boat was slowing to a stop. "Thanks to some kind neighbors. They were angels through the whole thing. Took care of her after our father died until I could finish school and the book I was working on—*When the Heart Dies*, as it turns out. I knew I was going to have to earn money somehow, and I remembered all the books my mother had loved when I was a kid. I was sure I could write something similar and get it published."

Of course. Why not? He was Will Price.

Then again, to be a published author, you had to have more than a little confidence in yourself. Otherwise you'd never have the courage to share your writing with the world, much less continue trying to do so after the inevitable rejections and bad reviews.

"I never expected it to do so well," he went on. "But fortunately for me, it did, so I was able to support us. I was—well, I was a little more prideful than I should have been. I thought I could raise Chloe by myself and balance a burgeoning writing career at the same time."

"Gosh," I said drily. "You, prideful? I can't imagine that."

He grinned. "I know. What I didn't expect was . . . well, how little time I was going to be able to spend at home, because of all the publicity." He grimaced at me with sarcastic humor. "The books sell the best here. You Americans really do love your tragic love stories, don't you?"

I was glad he wasn't a mind reader and didn't know how many emails Bernadette and I had exchanged over the years with *When the Fart Cries* in the subject line.

"Well, every American except you," he added, and I realized I hadn't done a very good job of hiding my thoughts, so I returned his cynical smile. "It wasn't fair on Chloe," he continued. "I was barely ever around. I hired nannies to take care of her instead of doing it myself."

I gazed down at the teenaged girl relaxing on the sun lounger below with her friend. Bernadette had performed her duty perfectly, somehow luring Garrett away from the girls, and now she, Garrett, Jerome, and Kellyjean were gathered on one side of the deck, gazing out at the water.

"She really does seem okay to me," I said.

"Thank you. But that's only because you're meeting her now. A few years ago, she'd tell you herself, she was a mess."

"She did tell me herself. She said it was my books that saved her life."

He looked uncomfortably shamefaced. But he didn't shut down. "She was telling you the truth. I thought that, because I could afford it, that I should put her in the best school that money could buy, because that's what people with money did. So I enrolled her in the most expensive girls' school in town, thinking she'd get the best education—the kind I'd always wished I'd had, where they teach all the classics."

I smiled, thinking of Chloe, in her little Snappette uniform, tackling *Ulysses*. "And how did that go?"

"Exactly as I can tell you're thinking it did." He shook his head glumly. "She never said a word to me about it, of course, because she's not the sort who would. But the other girls there all came from families with money, and they were brutally unkind to Chloe because she didn't. Meanwhile, I was paying tens of thousands of pounds a year for Chloe to go to a school that was only making her miserable, and then I found out she couldn't even read."

That stopped me cold. "Wait . . . couldn't *read?* What do you mean, she couldn't read?"

"She was in her teens, but could barely read or write. The teachers were passing her because I was paying her tuition in full and on time, and she was obviously gifted in other ways—dance, for instance—but she wasn't learning a thing."

"How is that even *possible?*"

He shrugged. "I came home unexpectedly from some book event to find her weeping over her tea about the teasing and how hard the coursework was, and that's when I discovered it: she couldn't even read the back of a bottle of brown sauce. So I got her tested and—"

Something clicked in my brain. Suddenly so much made sense. "Dyslexia."

"Exactly. None of her teachers or nannies had noticed. *I* hadn't noticed."

Good grief. No wonder he'd been so worried about what Chloe had told me. No wonder he was personally hosting so many events at this festival! Like his character Johnny, he must have been drowning in guilt.

"But Chloe not being able to read wasn't your fault," I said. "You were busy trying to support her. How could you—"

"I should have known." There was a heated look in his eyes. He was angry, but this time at himself. "She's my sister. Anyway, I told her she never had to go back to that wretched school again—that we could go anywhere in the world that she wanted. And that's why we're here."

"Here?" I gestured toward the island of Little Bridge, which I could see only very dimly in the distance. "*Here*, as in Little Bridge Island here?"

"Yes. She'd heard about the dance team. Apparently it's quite good. They dance on television in a holiday parade in New York City every year. It's quite an honor, I'm told."

He must have meant the Macy's Thanksgiving Day Parade. I reflected on how exciting that would be for a certain kind of teenaged girl—not the kind I'd been, of course—and felt a little envious of Chloe and her friends. The only thing I'd wanted to do in high school was get out as quickly as possible.

"And of course the weather is significantly better than it is back in England," Will went on. "Did you know the temperature here has never once fallen below freezing? And there are statistically more hours of sunshine in Little Bridge than there are anywhere else in America."

I couldn't tell whether or not he was pulling my leg. Will had never struck me as much of a practical joker, but I was finding it hard to believe he was being serious, even though he wasn't smiling. "You moved here because of the weather? And because your teenaged sister wanted to be on the school's dance team?"

"Yes. Why not?" He glanced at me quizzically. "What other qualifications do you need to live somewhere? You live in New York City, a place I've been to quite a few times, and I must say, the weather's never been exactly optimal. We certainly couldn't do this." He waved his arm to indicate the boat, and before I could open my mouth to point out that Manhattan is an island with easy access not only to boats but also the ocean, he went on, "Little Bridge has got a slower pace of life, and the people have all been very kind. Plus it's got quite a good school system. Besides the dance team, they put Chloe into a special program and had her reading in no time. That's when—"

I knew exactly what he was going to say next. "She discovered my books."

He looked surprised. "Yes! How did you know?"

"I, uh, have been told my books are very accessible."

This was an understatement. Kitty Katz had helped many children—and some adults, too—not only learn to read, but learn English as a second language. And it wasn't only because the animated series based on the books followed the original stories so closely and was shown in twenty-nine countries. There was something about that little kitty and her furry friends that made reading fun.

"Well, they certainly did the trick for Chloe," Will said. He was smiling again. "The difference was like night and day. Your books were the first ones she ever read all the way through. She was immensely proud of herself for finishing them. She has a special shelf of honor for your books in her bedroom."

"That's wonderful to hear," I said.

And it was. Suddenly, everything made sense. Readers always held a special place in their heart for the first book they ever read (or at least, the first book they ever read and enjoyed, the one that got them hooked on reading). That's why Lauren, at nineteen, had hauled a suitcase of my books all the way from Canada for me to sign.

But there was still something gnawing at me.

"But if you knew Chloe loved my books so much during Novel Con," I said, "why were you so nasty about them?"

The smile was replaced by a look of surprise. "I wasn't nasty about them."

"Excuse me, but yes, you were."

Now he was not only not smiling, he was frowning. "It's true that I said something about your genre that wasn't as educated as I ought to—"

"Category."

"I beg your pardon?"

"Children's books aren't a genre, they're a *category* of books. Mystery or romance is a genre." Garrett must be wrong about Will hoping to break into children's books. He knew absolutely nothing about them. "Fiction and nonfiction are categories of books. Young adult and middle grade are age categories of children's books—"

"*All right*, Jo, I get it. I said something stupid about your books. I shouldn't have, and I've been sorry for it ever since. Don't you ever say things that you don't mean? Or wished you'd said, but couldn't find the right words—or any words at all?"

I blinked at him. "I'm very, very rarely at a loss for words." Except when it came to my current manuscript.

He raked a hand through his overgrown curls. "Well, consider yourself lucky. I find myself saying the wrong thing—or worse, nothing at all—quite a lot. And it wasn't until *after* Novel Con that Chloe discovered your books. It was just before the conference that I found out how badly she was struggling in school."

Wait. "*What?* You found out your sister couldn't read and you went to—?"

"You think I wanted to leave her just then and come all the way to the U.S. to give the breakfast speech at some book conference I'd barely heard of?" Will looked frustrated enough to steer his own boat into an iceberg on purpose just to end the conversation, if there'd been one nearby. "My publisher said if I canceled it would be some sort of publicity disaster."

He was right about that. Speaking at the Novel Con breakfast was a privilege that writers with decades more experience than Will and I hardly dared to dream of. The only forgivable excuse for canceling was death—of a loved one, or of oneself.

"I guess," I said slowly, "it would have been unprofessional to renege, especially with the plagiarism scandal going on. Everyone kept telling me I had to go, too, or it would look like I was letting what Nicole had done affect me."

He glanced away from the windscreen and toward me. "So you understand."

I wanted to say that I did. I knew I should let it go. My therapist back in New York had been telling me for months to let it go: *Leave the past in the rearview mirror. You can't move forward if you're always looking behind you.*

But I couldn't. Even after knowing what he'd been through, I couldn't. My mother's Sicilian blood wouldn't let me.

"I'm sorry," I said. "But that still doesn't explain why you were so mean about my books, especially after—well, after I thought we got along so well in the green room."

I was appalled to find that tears had sprung to my eyes.

Which was ridiculous, because I obviously didn't care what he thought.

Fortunately I was wearing my sunglasses, so I was sure he couldn't see the sudden waterworks.

Except maybe he could. Because suddenly he tore those large, tanned hands away from the console, slid from his captain's chair, and reached out to seize me by both arms. His dark gaze swept my face, searching for . . . what?

"Jo, I—" His voice was broken, ragged even. He seemed to want to tell me something else, but couldn't—really and truly couldn't—find the right words.

Was there such a thing as verbal dyslexia? Because if so, Will had it, or at least some kind of oral impairment that seemed to make it impossible sometimes for him to grasp the words he was searching for.

"What?" I asked. I had to work to make my voice sound coolly incurious, because the truth was, my emotional state and his proximity—the raw heat coming off his body, the feel of those hard hands on my arms—had my heart jackhammering in my chest. This close, I could see that he needed a shave more than ever.

And I wanted to feel the scrape of that dark, prickly facial hair all over my neck, those hard hands on every inch of my body.

What was *wrong* with me? I couldn't stand this man.

Or at least that's what I was thinking right up until the moment I pulled him close and started kissing him.

CHAPTER NINETEEN

Yeah, okay, so what? None of us are perfect.

It wasn't my fault that I grabbed Will and started kissing him. I couldn't help it. Sometimes actions speak louder than words, and he was just so . . . kissable.

At least that's what I was thinking—to the degree I *could* think—as I pressed my mouth to Will's, and felt those cool, strong hands slide from my arms to my waist, pulling me closer to him as the sharpness of his facial hair pricked my skin. *This*, I thought in some detached part of my brain, as my body strained to press even closer to his. *Yes, this.*

Being kissed by Will was like crawling into a cool, soft bed with newly washed cotton sheets.

It was like sunshine on your face, after weeks and weeks of gray, drab rain.

It was like diving into the clearest, bluest pool of sweet warm water.

It was like coming home.

It was definitely something I could get used to.

Except that I couldn't. I *couldn't*. I couldn't go around kissing Will. What was I, *insane*? It was wrong, all wrong! I knew it was wrong. . . .

And yet I stood there, kissing him—and letting him kiss me back. . . .

Until I finally came to my senses, and pushed him away. Possibly with a little too much force, since he backed into the console and may have jiggled a few of the controls, because the boat engines made a loud whirring noise. He turned quickly to adjust them while I held on to the back of the co-captain's seat, trying to catch my breath.

"Okay, *that*," I said, when I finally found my voice, "was messed up."

Will glanced at me in surprise. "I rather liked it."

"No," I said, horrified more at the way I was feeling—which was as if I'd just run a marathon, not that I would ever do something so stupid—than by what had actually happened. "We can't—I mean, that can't happen again. That was . . . that just can't happen again."

"Granted, I've heard you're on the rebound," Will said. "But frankly, I'm willing to take the risk."

"Oh my God." I wanted to dive overboard. "I'm sorry."

"What are you apologizing for? I said I liked it."

"Thank you. I'm flattered. But we can't—" I had never been in a situation like this. I had no idea what to do, much less what to say. "I mean, you're . . . and I'm—"

"After all that bragging," he said, folding his arms across his chest and leaning against his seat, a small smile playing across his lips, "you're the one at a loss for words."

He was right. I was sputtering. I made a concerted effort to control myself.

But it was hard, because I still felt all melty inside, and my knees were like Jell-O.

I slid back onto the co-captain's seat and tried to pull myself together.

"Look," I said. "I'm sorry. I honestly don't make a habit of going around doing that."

"Well, that's a shame." He still had that little smile on his face, as if he thought I were the funniest thing in the world. "Because I found it very enjoyable."

"Well, it's not going to happen again," I blundered on. "Because this is a book festival and I'm pretty sure I just violated about a million of your sexual harassment policies."

He actually laughed at that. Laughed!

And then he said the thing that astonished me most of all, even more than my having kissed him, which had been very astonishing indeed:

"Jo, you can kiss me anytime." He reached out to take my hand in his. "I—"

But before Will could get out whatever it was he wanted to say—or pull me toward him to plant another one of those spine-melting kisses on me, which I had to admit was what I was hoping for, even though I still hated him, I one hundred percent definitely did—a man's voice called out from below, "Look!"

Unfortunately, I turned my head to look.

Garrett was pointing over the side of the boat at something he really wanted us to see. Something sleek and shining that was arcing through the surface of the water just beside *The Moment*. Not just a single something, either, but dozens of them, each glistening and leaping in the bright sun, splashing through the water, having a grand old time.

It took me a second or two to register what I was seeing because I'd never seen them in the wild before. Or anywhere, really, except on screens.

"Are those . . . *dolphins?*" My voice came out a little throatier than I'd intended, mainly because Will was still holding on to my hand, and I could still feel the heat radiating from his body, and my heart was still banging against my ribs like a mallet thanks to his proximity.

"Yes," Will said. He didn't sound amused anymore. "Yes, that's what I wanted to bring you out here to see. There's a wild pod of dolphins that swims around here. I can't always find them, but we got lucky today, I guess. I thought you might like to see them—"

"Jo!" Garrett's voice cut through the moment—or whatever it was Will and I were having—like a rusty saw blade. "Get down here! You don't want to miss this!"

That's when Will seemed to realize what he was doing, and unfortunately—very unfortunately—dropped my hand.

"He's right," he said. "Why don't you head down and take a look? You ought to be able to get a lot of nice photos for your social media."

CHAPTER TWENTY

What is wrong with you?" Bernadette demanded.

"Nothing." I was standing in my hotel bathroom, attempting to apply a new layer of black eyeliner. "Why do you ask?"

"Well, for starters, because you were making out with Will Price on his boat this afternoon."

"No, I wasn't."

"I saw you with my own two eyes. Is sucking his face all part of the making-him-regret-his-life-choices plan, or have you decided to forgive him?"

"Hmph! Not likely, since I've yet to hear any sort of explanation from him for what he did that makes any sense. For a bestselling writer, the guy has a really hard time formulating words with his mouth."

Although, to be honest, it turned out his mouth was capable of doing a whole range of other, much more interesting things.

"Who *are* you?" Bernadette asked. "And what have you done with my friend, Jo Wright?"

For a second I was worried she was reading my mind about

the things Will had done to me with his mouth, but no. She was sitting on the fluffy armchair in my hotel room, her feet up, thumbing through my copy of *The Moment* while waiting for me to get ready for dinner.

"You're actually *reading* this?" she cried in horror, holding up the bookmark I'd been using to keep my place.

"Yeah." I turned back to the mirror, feeling only slightly cringey. "So what?"

"You're reading a Will Price book *and* you've been making out with him? Now I honestly do think the real Jo has been kidnapped and replaced with a reptilian humanoid by the aliens."

"Why?"

"Because from what you told me, the guy has had a pretty crummy life. Losing his parents at a young age, struggling to raise his younger sister all on his own, and doing, from what I can tell, a pretty good job of it. And yet still all you can think about is the *one* time he let slip a negative opinion about your books. Do you know how many negative things you've said about *his* books—before, of course, you became one of the reptilians?"

"Uh, I said them to *you*, remember? Not to reporters from one of the world's most-read newspapers."

Bernadette went on as if I hadn't even spoken. "Not to mention, he's more than made it up to you, falling all over himself to apologize, sending you first-class tickets here, making sure you got the best suite in this hotel, plus the biggest stipend of all of us at this festival. He even arranged for a pod of wild dolphins to cavort playfully in the sea for you.

What more do you want from the guy? I'm actually starting to think this whole thing isn't because you want to put him into *Kitty Katz number twenty-seven*, but because Kellyjean is right: you actually do want to jump his bones."

I threw her a scornful glance, though secretly I was horrified, because his bones were extremely appealing. "Oh, *please*."

"I don't see why it's so out of the question. He obviously has the hots for you, and you don't seem to find him physically repulsive. Why not punish him, you know, *carnally*, and enjoy yourself while you do it."

"Because it still doesn't make any sense." I slammed my eyeliner down onto the sink. "I don't have any siblings, so I don't know what it's like to have to single-handedly raise one. But if I *had*, I wouldn't have left her alone to go to Novel Con after finding out she's being bullied and flunking out of school due to a learning disorder."

Bernadette rolled her eyes. "Jo. He's a man. Who knows how they think? I mean, listen to this." She began to read from *The Moment*: "'She wore a black shantung dress, matronly enough to befit her status as a widow, but close-fitting enough to reveal her tiny waist and full breasts—breasts that, I happened to know, stood up on their own without needing any support.' Ha! She doesn't even need a bra to keep her full breasts standing at attention? What the hell? Could it be any more obvious this was written by a man? And *USA Today* had the nerve to call this an instant classic."

"Yes," I said, my mind flashing back to Will's hands, which had strayed fairly close to my own breasts earlier that afternoon. "It's ridiculous. But we both know that we live in a patriarchy. Now, turning to something along the same lines, how do I look?" I stepped from the bathroom and spun around so that Bernadette could inspect my ensemble.

"Hmmm." She ran a critical eye over the sleeveless jump-suit (black, of course) that I was wearing beneath a tuxedo-style jacket. The rumor among us authors was that the dinner at Cracked was supposed to be dressy. "Are you sure about the shoes? What if we walk?"

I glanced down at my strappy black stilettos. "Why would we walk? The author bus is taking us."

"Do you really want to get back on the author bus after what happened with Garrett? The map they gave us says the restaurant is only a few blocks away. If you'd wear lower heels we could walk and avoid the author-bus-drama experi-ence completely."

"Good point."

I was slipping back into my mules—which I was getting heartily sick of—when my phone purred to let me know I had a text message.

> **GabbyKittyK2010:** Hi, Jo, just letting you know everything is good with Miss K! I've been feeding her twice a day just like always when you go away, and also making sure she gets her special treats and belly rubs. Also you and Will Price make a great couple!!! ♥♥☺♥♥☺

"*What?*"

Bernadette was so startled by my outburst, she dropped *The Moment*. "What happened? Is it your dad?"

"No." I showed her Gabriella's text. "What could she be talking about?"

Bernadette squinted at the screen. "I don't know. Did you post any photos of you and Will together from the panel?"

"Of course not." I snatched back my phone and began frantically to reply to Gabriella. "Why would I do that?"

"Uh, because you're a professional writer, and as the guy you definitely don't want to have sex with pointed out, you're active on social media?"

"Yeah, but post a picture of me and Will Price together? Give me a break. Hold on, I'll find out what she's talking about."

> **Jo Wright:** Thanks so much for taking such good care of Miss Kitty as always, Gabriella. What photos of me with Will Price? Where did you see them?

"Come on." Bernadette rose from her fluffy chair and straightened the houndstooth jacket she was wearing with a pair of pleather pants. These, with her purple faux-hawk, made for a particularly striking evening look. "That kid today took tons of photos of you and Will at the signing. Would it be the worst thing in the world if some of them got posted online? Because from what I saw on the boat this afternoon—"

"Stop it." I watched as three blinking dots appeared on my phone screen, indicating that Gabriella was writing back. "There's nothing going on between Will and me, because Will can't even find the words to—hold on, Gabriella just wrote back."

GabbyKittyK2010: It's on BuzzFeed!

1 Attachment

---

33 Ways You Know You're Gen Z

#19 The Author of Your Favorite Books from Childhood Is Hooking Up with the Author of Your Favorite Books as a Teen and You're Like, "Yeah. Makes Sense."

I screamed in horror and threw my phone against the bed.

"What? What's it say?" Bernadette dove to fish my phone out from beneath the pile of throw pillows where it had landed, then read the link Gabriella had sent. "Oh, is that all?"

"Is that all? *Is that all?* Bernadette!" I paced the room, clutching fistfuls of my hair, which for once I was wearing down, since it was dry. "This can't be happening."

"Why? You look cute in the photo. And check out the way Will is smiling at you. If I didn't know better, I'd think the two of you were hooking up, too."

I screamed some more, this time into my clenched fists.

"Oh, come on." Bernadette couldn't seem to stop smiling. "This isn't the worst thing. At least they've got you paired up with Will and not Garrett. Could you imagine if everyone was saying you were hooking up with *that* guy? One-eighth Cherokee, my butt."

I looked up from my fists. "Bernadette, I can't go tonight."

"Because of *this*?" She waved my phone. "What are you, twelve? Jo, you have to go. First of all, you told that little suitcase girl that she had to go—"

"Lauren. Her name is Lauren."

"Fine, Lauren. She was going to stay in her hotel room and write tonight, but you told her she had to go. Imagine how disappointed she'll be if you're not there. And secondly, no one's going to have seen this."

"My eleven-year-old cat sitter saw it."

"Well, okay, but no one at the book festival is going to have seen it. They were too busy enjoying themselves out on the water or eating clam chowder or whatever they were doing today. It'll be— Oops, your phone is purring, you're getting another text. I think it's your agent."

"Oh." I rushed over to grab the phone from Bernadette. "Finally! I've been waiting all weekend to hear from her."

> **Rosie Tate:** Sorry for the tardy reply, I was traveling. Can't apologize enough for Will Price being there when I know I swore to you that he wouldn't be. But it looks like you're getting along well enough now. Saw the piece in BuzzFeed. 😊 You two are trending at number ten in the U.S. on Twitter right now!

I thought I might start hyperventilating when another text from her arrived.

> **Rosie Tate:** I have never heard a word about Will's personal life. I honestly don't think he has one. All the guy seems to do is write and then work to promote what he's written.

Rosie Tate: P.S. I ran into the head of Netflix children's programming in Aruba and pitched her a Kitty K reboot. She said she didn't hate the idea! Let's talk on Monday.

Rosie Tate: P.P.S. How's the writing going? I'm only wondering because your editor emailed me Friday to ask when she can expect a first draft.

I drew back my arm to throw my phone off the balcony, but Bernadette pried it out of my hands. "What? What did she say?"

"Nothing." I sank down onto the bed in defeat. "Just . . . Will and I are trending."

"Trending?"

"On Twitter. We're number ten in the U.S."

Bernadette's lips twitched. I could tell she was trying not to laugh, but she couldn't control herself. "I'm sorry," she said, and dropped my phone in order to whip out her own. "But I have to tell Jen. This is just too funny."

"I'm glad that my agony is so amusing to you."

"You're not in agony," Bernadette said as she typed. "If you were really that unhappy about what was going on, you'd pack up and leave."

"I can't. Like you said, I owe it to Lauren to stay."

"Oh, just admit that part of you is getting something out of this—whether it's inspiration to write *Kitty Katz number twenty-seven* at last, or . . . something else." She waggled her eyebrows as she said *something else.* "I haven't seen you this heated up over a guy in . . . well, ever. Even when you and

Justin were breaking up, you hardly talked about it, because you just didn't care. Face it, Jo. Love or hate, whatever is going on with you and Will Price, there's *something* there. And something is better than what you felt for Justin by the end, which was nothing."

I dropped my head into my hands in shame. I didn't want to admit that Bernadette was right. There was "something" between Will and me. I saw it every time I looked into his eyes. It struck me like a heat-seeking missile.

"Fine," I said grudgingly. "I'll go tonight. But we're not staying long. And if anyone starts joking about this BuzzFeed thing—"

Bernadette held up her hand in the traditional claw-fingered Kitty Katz salute. "We leave. I swear. And I'm not kitten around."

I winced. This was going to be a long night.

The Moment by Will Price

With her golden hair piled on top of her head, small diamond pendants dangling from her earlobes like icicles, Melanie reminded me of a princess from a storybook. Her white dress, covered all over with diamonds smaller than the ones at her ears, shimmered like the snow outside. She was without a doubt the most beautiful woman I'd ever seen. Whenever I looked at her, I felt my chest tighten with emotion . . . an emotion that only had one name: love.

Don't ask me how, but I'd done it. In a few short moments, we'd walk down the aisle together, and she would be mine.

CHAPTER TWENTY-ONE

LITTLE BRIDGE BOOK FESTIVAL ITINERARY FOR:
JO WRIGHT

Saturday, January 4, 8:00 p.m.–11:00 p.m.

- Building Bridges Dinner -

Please join all festival attendees for a night of fine
drinking and dining by the sea at Cracked on the Pier.

Jooooooooo!"

Of course the first person we ran into when we got to
the restaurant was Kellyjean. She was resplendent in a red-
and-gold kimono, her long blond hair flowing loose around
her shoulders, her skin glowing from her day out on the water, despite her organic sunscreen.

"Wow, Kellyjean," I said. "You look like a tequila sunrise
threw up on you."

"Oh, stop!" She gave me a playful but clearly delighted slap. I wasn't certain Kellyjean knew what a tequila sunrise was. "Where've y'all been? You almost missed it!"

I was worried she meant that we'd missed a group reading aloud of the BuzzFeed article until Kellyjean, seeing our confused expressions, laughed and said, "Sillies! I'll show you!"

Then she grabbed Bernadette and I each by the shoulder, and wordlessly pushed us not inside Cracked, but around the side of the restaurant, onto the pier. It was weirdly crowded there—not just the fenced-off deck with white-clothed tables reserved for diners at Cracked, but the rest of the pier, as well.

A huge crowd had gathered onto the weathered dock, everyone staring off into the west where the sun was slowly sinking into the sea with a blaze of color almost as vibrant as Kellyjean's ensemble.

I glanced around suspiciously. "What's happening?"

"Yeah," Bernadette said. "What's everyone looking at? Someone get mugged?"

"The sunset."

The voice at my side was deep. I'd have recognized it anywhere even without the British accent, so I didn't need to turn around to see that Will had come to stand beside me, but I did anyway.

Yep, there he was, looking tall and ridiculously handsome in a dark linen suit and another crisp white button-down shirt that showed off his deep tan. How many of these did the guy own? Hundreds, probably.

"What do you mean, the sunset?" I glanced back at the horizon. There were sailboats and yachts gliding around on glassy water in front of us, each as crowded with people as the dock we were standing on. "Are you trying to tell me that *all* of these people are out here just to watch the sun set?"

"Yes." He had on the little half smile he seemed to wear habitually, except when he was frowning with anxiety—or displeasure—over something. So it was impossible to know if he'd seen the gossip about us online, unless of course he'd seen it and found it amusing. I didn't think that Will was the kind of person who'd find that kind of thing amusing, however. "It's a nightly tradition here in Little Bridge."

"Watching the sunset?" I was baffled. "But the sun sets every night. Why on earth would anyone stand around and watch it?"

Will's smile deepened as he glanced at me with what I could only call a pitying expression. "Because it's beautiful. I know that might be a difficult concept for a New Yorker to understand, but some people do find nature soothing."

After making a face at him, I turned back toward the sea. I supposed there was something slightly relaxing about watching the boats bob on the smooth surface of the water, and the sun sink lower and lower behind them into the sea. There was only a small crescent of it left now, since Bernadette and I had arrived so late to the party.

"But that's not the best part," Kellyjean declared, so loudly that I jumped. I'd forgotten she was standing so close to me. "Tell them the best part, Will."

"They say that when the last rays of the sun hit the sea," Will explained, "if you see a green flash, you'll have good luck for a year."

"What?" I couldn't believe it. More magic?

"I've heard of that." Bernadette already had her phone out and was snapping photos of the brilliant sky to send to Jen and her kids. "It's like a mirage or optical illusion or something."

Will nodded. "Right. It only happens at sunrise and sunset, when meteorological conditions are exactly right."

"Of course," Kellyjean said, with a chuckle, "my kids will tell you that according to the *Pirates of the Caribbean* movies, it's something else entirely. Brad and I probably shouldn't let them watch so much—"

It was at that moment that the last ruby-red sliver of the sun slipped beneath the water. Then three things happened all at once:

First, a roar went up from all the people gathered on the boats, rippling over us like a wave, and applause broke from everyone on the dock around me.

Second, a flash of green shot out from the exact spot the sun hit the sea, dazzling my eyes despite the polarized lenses of my sunglasses.

And third, I snatched instinctively at the person standing closest to me. It was just a coincidence that that person happened to be Will.

"Did you see that?" I gasped.

"I saw it," Will said quietly. His gaze fell from the waterline to my fingers, digging deep into his arm. Then those dark eyes moved from my fingertips to my face. His lips curled into a smile. "Beautiful."

I hastily dropped my own gaze. Of course he was talking about the rare meteorological phenomenon we'd just witnessed, and not me, because this was real life and not some cheesy Will Price novel—but I lowered my hand from his arm, suddenly flustered.

"Saw what?" Bernadette glanced up from her phone, where she'd been scrolling through her photos. "What are we talking about?"

"I saw it!" Kellyjean was practically hyperventilating. "Oh my Lord, I saw it! Two falling stars and the green flash, all in one weekend? No one back home is going to believe this when I tell 'em about it."

"Oh, man." Bernadette looked like she wanted to pitch her phone into the ocean, she was so disappointed. "I can't believe I keep missing everything."

Will, as soon as I'd dropped my hand, had begun to turn away, heading into the restaurant along with most of the rest of the crowd from the festival.

I felt weirdly disappointed. But why? It's not as if I believed in this stupid magic stuff, and certainly not as if I cared about Will. Unless . . . unless Bernadette was right, and I'd caught feelings for him.

But that was impossible! He was Will Price, and I hated Will Price, even if he was a really good kisser and it turned out there was a fairly reasonable explanation for why he was the way he was.

But if I hated Will Price so much, why, when he hesitated

and looked back at me—and only me—did my heart give a stupid little Kitty Katz schoolgirl flutter?

"Aren't you coming in?" he asked, those thick dark eyebrows of his raised questioningly. "We should probably toast our upcoming year of good fortune, don't you think? I've ordered some very good champagne for the party—the real stuff, actually from Champagne, France."

Ordinarily, that kind of statement coming from Will Price would have annoyed me so much, it would have made me want to punch him—or at least one of the cardboard cutouts of him in a bookstore. Did he think I didn't know that real champagne came from France?

But for some reason, this time, I only felt amused—maybe because I finally knew why he was the way he was. He couldn't help it. He was Raul Wolf, who'd lost his mom at a young age and then been raised by a beast.

I lifted my sunglasses—I didn't need them anymore now that the sun had set—so he could see that I'd narrowed my eyes at him in a sarcastic smirk. "Oh my gosh, *really*, Champagne, France? Catch me before I faint."

His eyes widened. It's possible I was the first person in a long time, if ever, to make fun of him to his face. Then he smirked back at me. "I'd be happy to."

Zing! went my heart. Okay, this was not good. But it was fun.

Inside Cracked, the party was in full swing. Loud, upbeat bossa nova music boomed from the stereo system, while servers bustled back and forth with trays of drinks. On one side of the restaurant, a wall of French doors had been thrown open to reveal the deck overlooking the shimmering sea and still fiery red sky. On the other stood a set of buffet tables so loaded with platters of shellfish I feared they might collapse.

Of course all the donors and readers were gathered on the deck, admiring the view and chatting with one another away from the thump of the music, while all of the authors were crowded in front of the food. I've never seen an author—no matter how bestselling—pass up an opportunity for free food. None of us could forget those prepublication days when we were barely scraping by. Many writers never left those days.

So I wasn't particularly surprised to see Frannie—despite her previous reservations about the locally caught fish—practically inhaling a plate of steamed clams, while beside her, Saul was slurping up raw oysters. Not far from them, Jerome was picking away at a stone crab claw, while Kellyjean had evidently abandoned her vegetarian lifestyle for the evening and joined Bernadette in attacking the shrimp cocktail. All wore rapturous expressions, like they'd died and gone to author heaven.

Only Garrett remained out on the deck, talking with a great deal of animation to Lauren and her friends. Fortunately, their mothers were with them, so I wasn't worried about anything untoward going on . . . especially given the fact that Garrett was wearing a floor-length purple velvet cape over a pirate shirt and what appeared to be matching pirate pants and boots.

I was going to have to process that later. The sight was entirely too disturbing to deal with now.

"Shall we have a toast?" Will fortunately distracted me by

asking, snagging two glasses of champagne from the tray of a passing server and handing one to me. "To our good fortune in the new year?"

"Sure." I clinked my glass to his, figuring it would be ungracious to tell him that I didn't believe in luck any more than I believed in magic. Will seemed to have really fallen hard for the whole Florida Keys lifestyle, though, what with the boat and the linen shirts and the belief in the local superstitions.

"What kind of luck are you hoping the green flash will bring you?" He had to raise his voice to be heard over the music.

"Oh, uh." No way was I telling him about my wish from the night before . . . or that it had sort of come true already. "I guess what I'm really looking for is a little, uh . . . real estate luck." Yes! This sounded good. "I've been checking out places in Florida for a few months now for my dad, and he's hated every single house I've chosen for him."

"Really?" Will looked surprised. "What seems to be the problem?"

"I don't know. My dad's just hard to please. A real New Yorker through and through, I guess."

"Hmmm." Will glanced at the ceiling as he sipped his champagne. "So not at all like his daughter, then."

It took me a second to realize he was joking. Will Price, author of some of the most maudlin love stories ever published, was trying to be comedic.

"Oh, ha-ha," I said, swatting at his shoulder. "Very funny."

Laughing, he dodged my hand . . . and spilled some of his

drink onto his sister, who'd come bouncing over to speak to us.

"Chloe, I'm sorry." Will snatched up some napkins from a nearby table and attempted to dry off his sister's bare arm, but she waved him away impatiently.

"Will, you said the team could do our dance number during the cocktail hour to entertain everybody." She pointed at a small stage that had been set up along the railing on the restaurant's deck, probably for live music during a normal night. It was really more of a platform than a proper stage, though it had a gazebo-style roof over it, from which hung an assortment of stage lights, and large speakers on either side. Sharmaine and some of the other Snappettes were leaning against these speakers, looking surprisingly sullen for girls wearing red-and-white dance uniforms.

Will nodded. "Yes. What about it?"

"Well, Garrett Newcombe is saying that Molly told him he could do some kind of magic trick first."

Will glanced around until he spied Garrett, still yukking it up in his pirate costume with Lauren and her friends and their moms. Then his eyes narrowed menacingly. "She never said anything to me about it."

"I know." Chloe's dark eyes were flashing as balefully as her older brother's. "And I don't want you to call and bother her about it since she's just had her baby. But can you tell Mr. Newcombe that he has to wait to do his trick until we're done with our number? Sharmaine is having us all over for a slumber party barbecue after this and her mom wants us there before her dad burns the ribs. You know how he is."

Will put down the champagne glass he'd been holding. "Happy to," he said, his jaw set in a way that would have made me uneasy if I'd been Garrett. "If you'll excuse me a moment, ladies."

Then he began striding toward Garrett, who was still absorbed in conversation with my readers and their moms, and had no idea what—or who—was about to hit him.

"Um," I said to Chloe, feeling slightly alarmed by the purposeful look I'd seen in her brother's eyes. "Do you think we should do something?"

Chloe had pulled her cell phone from the waistband of her dance shorts and was gazing down at the screen. "About what?"

"That." I nodded at Will as he tapped Garrett on the shoulder, then began interrogating him, a conversation I sadly couldn't hear due to the volume of the music inside the restaurant.

Chloe glanced over her shoulder. "Oh, no," she said with a shrug. "They're fine. How are you tonight, Miss Wright? Did you enjoy your time on *The Moment*? Those dolphins were brilliant, weren't they?"

"Um," I said. I couldn't take my gaze off Will. He had Garrett's full attention, the smaller man waving his hands around as he spoke, the hem of his cape flying as Lauren and the other girls, along with their mothers, backed slowly away. "Yes, they were."

"Did you hear about Mrs. Hartwell?" Chloe was scrolling through text messages on her phone. "She's had a little boy.

Well, not so little, actually. He weighs ten pounds! Just shoot me, am I right? Only joking. Here, see?"

She showed me a photo of a newborn baby. Molly's son looked exactly like every other newborn I'd ever seen, except perhaps slightly more red-faced and indignant at having been thrust out of the womb into the real world.

"Oh," I said politely. "Sweet."

"Yeah, I think so. They're calling him Matthew after a character out of a book—*Anne of Green Gables*. Do you know it?"

Startled at the burst of emotion I felt at this news, I looked down, hoping my hair would hide my suddenly tear-filled eyes. "Yes. Yes, I know it. That's very nice."

"Is it?" I needn't have worried about Chloe seeing my eyes, since she hadn't glanced up from her phone. "I haven't read it yet. There are lots of books I haven't read yet that everyone else has, but I'll get to them soon enough. I'm not surprised Mrs. Hartwell named her baby after someone in a book. They met in the library, you know, she and her husband. Katie says they hated each other at first, but then they fell in love. Isn't that the most romantic thing you ever heard?"

I took an extra-big gulp of my champagne and looked frantically around for help. "Yes. Definitely."

What was happening to me? Why did I feel so weepy over a photo of a baby and the story of how his parents had met? I wasn't particularly keen on babies—except for Bernadette's, of course. They were lovely. But other babies? They were fine to look at, but I'd never wanted one—not once the whole time I'd been with Justin. All babies ever do is cry and take your attention away from your writing, and of course your adorable cat.

But now, suddenly, the idea of having one didn't seem like the absolute worst thing in the world . . . maybe only the second or third.

Fortunately, Frannie was weaving her way toward me through the crowd, which was getting thicker and thicker as more people headed inside for the buffet. "Oh my God, Jo," she said, waving a plate beneath my nose. "These shrimp. You've got to try one."

Chloe looked down at the plate Frannie was holding. "Oh, the buffalo shrimp? Yeah, those are good!"

"Good?" Frannie's beautiful red manicure was no longer visible beneath the orange sauce of the shrimp she was rapidly devouring. "They're insane!"

Kellyjean sidled up to us. "Are y'all talkin' about the shrimp?"

Frannie beamed at her. "Divine, aren't they?"

"I'm about to ask the chef for the recipe!"

I didn't get to hear how Frannie replied to that, however, because Will reappeared, touched Chloe on the shoulder, and leaned down to tell her something. I couldn't hear what it was because the music and level of chatter in the restaurant was too loud.

It didn't take a genius to figure out that whatever it was he'd said had pleased her, though, since Chloe gave him a dazzling smile in reply and rose up on her sneakered toes to give him a kiss on the cheek. Then she darted away through the crowd to join her teammates by the outdoor stage. A second later, they'd all lost their scowls and begun scurrying around, preparing for their big number.

"Well," I said to Will. "You've made some people very happy, anyway."

He shrugged with exaggerated modesty. "Only doing my duty as temporary board chair. Speaking of which, I see that you haven't yet been fed. Should we get you a plate?"

Unfortunately, he said this right in front of Kellyjean, who sucked in her breath excitedly.

"Yes, you should!" She waved a hand excitedly. "Don't forget the shrimp! Do you want me to snag a table? They're going fast. I'd be happy to save y'all seats."

"That's quite all right, Kellyjean." Will smiled. "I think we'll manage."

And we were. Will was able to use his credentials as temporary board chair to slip to the head of the enormous line that had formed at the buffet and secure us two heavily laden plates of food. Then I used my cred as the author of a beloved and heartwarming children's series about talking cats to get us seats at a table.

"Ms. Wright! Ms. Wright!" Lauren bellowed from across the deck when she saw me. "Over here! Come sit with us!"

Lauren was sitting at a table not far from the stage with her two pals, Cassidy and Jasmine. Dressed to kill, the girls were in head-to-toe sequins and had hung purses and wraps over the backs of the empty chairs beside them, but when they saw me approaching, with Will not far behind, they reached to remove them.

"Are you sure these seats are free, girls?" I asked before I sat down.

"For *you* they are." Lauren's worshipful gaze went from me to Will and then back again.

"Especially *you*," Cassidy said, batting her long faux lashes at Will.

I wasn't convinced. "Aren't you saving them for your mothers?"

"Oh, they're in line for the bar," Jasmine said in a scornful tone. "They'll be gone for *ages*."

Will looked alarmed. "But there are servers going around with wine and champagne—"

"Our mothers only drink vodka sodas. Saves on calories." Cassidy patted the seat of the empty chair beside her. "Why don't you sit *here*, Will?"

"I'll just sit here next to Ms. Wright, if that's all right," Will said, and dropped hastily into the seat beside mine.

"Your loss." Cassidy fluttered those lashes in a way I didn't blame Will for finding alarming.

"Oh, wait until you taste those shrimp!" Lauren was closely examining everything on my plate. "They're amazing."

"Are they?" I sampled one. The ensuing taste explosion was a welcome surprise. "Oh my God, you're right!"

"See?" Lauren beamed with pleasure. "I told you."

"Lauren's glad she took your advice and came, aren't you, Lauren?" Jasmine grinned wickedly at her friend. "Especially since now we get to sit with the third highest trending couple on Twitter."

CHAPTER TWENTY-TWO

I choked on the mouthful of shrimp I'd just swallowed.

Looking concerned, Will asked, "Are you all right?" and patted me lightly on the back while signaling a passing server for water.

"Well, you'd probably be number one," Jasmine said, mistaking my suddenly streaming eyes for dismay, "if Timothée Chalamet hadn't been spotted on a beach in Ibiza with Harry Styles earlier today."

"Oh, please." Cassidy looked disdainful. "Everyone knows Harry and Timothée are just friends."

The server arrived with the water Will had requested. I thanked her and, taking the glass, quickly gulped down enough liquid to keep from dying at the table from asphyxiation.

Dying of embarrassment was another matter.

"Are you sure you're all right?" Will asked me.

I nodded vigorously, still unable to speak. Scanning the crowd, I finally found Bernadette seated a few tables away with young fans of her own. She was too engrossed in conversation with them, however, to notice the distress signals I was sending her with my eyes.

"Well, that's good," Will said to me. "I know we've got some of the best seafood in the world here, but you might not want to inhale it. Now, who did you say is trending?" he asked the girls curiously.

As Jasmine sucked in her breath to reply, I felt my life flash before my eyes.

But fortunately an enormous burst of static came from one of the nearly four-foot-tall speakers sitting not far from us, and everyone's attention shifted to the stage, where Chloe stood in front of five of her fellow dance team members—the stage was too small to accommodate more—each in a power pose, their pom-poms on their hips.

"Um, hello, may I have everyone's attention?" Chloe asked into the microphone she was clutching. "Hi, welcome. I'm Chloe Price, co-captain of the Little Bridge Island High School Snappettes. We're so honored to be here helping out during this first-ever Little Bridge Island Book Festival. Are you enjoying yourselves so far?"

This was met with cheers and applause from not only everyone on the deck as well as inside the restaurant but even farther down the pier, where people who weren't attending the book festival had stuck around after sunset to continue enjoying the warm night air and ocean breeze. Now they were also gleefully watching the stage at Cracked, which was suddenly covered in cheerleaders.

Chloe looked encouraged by this positive response, and

said into the microphone, "Great! Well, we couldn't be happier to have all of you here, and to show you our appreciation, we wanted to perform a piece we've been working on. It's called 'Dances to Songs About Writing and Books.'"

What. The. Kitten.

I threw Will a quick, questioning look. He smiled and leaned over to whisper in my ear, "Chloe begged me to allow them to perform this. And after what I did to you at Novel Con, I'm not exactly in a position to judge someone else's artistic choices, am I?"

I tried to grin back at him but failed, not because I didn't agree with him—I did—but because his warm, sweet-smelling breath had tickled my neck, causing gooseflesh to rise on the backs of my arms, and other parts of me—parts I didn't want him anywhere near, but also very definitely did—to snap to tight attention.

Fortunately, he didn't seem aware of any of this, since his gaze was on the stage, where Chloe had laid down her microphone, lifted a pair of pom-poms, and moved into formation with her fellow dance team members just as the loud bossa nova music from inside the restaurant suddenly went silent.

I'm certain the only expression I was able to make after that was one of utter astonishment, especially as the first chords of "Kitty Katz to the Rescue"—the theme song from the short-lived animated television series *Kitty Katz, Kitten Sitter*—boomed from the speakers near us.

Then the Snappettes dropped their pom-poms, placed their hands upon one another's shoulders, and broke into a perfectly synchronized kick line to the riotous, high-pitched all-girl band chords of:

> *Which li'l kitty is the head of her class?*
> *Which li'l kitty's got lots of sass?*
> *Which li'l kitty is tons of fun?*
> *Which li'l kitty is number one?*
> *Here Kitty, Kitty, Kitty, Kitty,*
> *Here Kitty, Kitty, Kitty, Kitty,*
> *Here Kitty, Kitty, Kitty, Kitty,*
> *Kitty Katz!*

I could hardly believe what I was hearing, much less seeing. But there it was, right onstage in front of me.

I glanced around the deck to see how other people were registering what was happening, but none seemed to be quite as astonished as I was. Most looked delighted . . . especially when "Kitty Katz to the Rescue" ended and Elvis Costello's "Every Day I Write the Book" came on. The less manic pace of this song gave the girls a chance to show off more balletic stuff . . . at least until Don Henley's "All She Wants to Do Is Dance" began to boom from the sound system.

Then the team launched into what I could only assume were the capoeira moves Will had been describing earlier, since the many spins and jumps in the choreography sent the girls flying off the stage and onto the deck. Those seated nearby had to duck for fear of having their heads kicked off.

The crowd loved it, however. Jasmine wasn't the only person who raised her phone and began filming. I clapped along with everyone else, but when the performance ended—with the girls performing flips off the stage and landing in perfectly timed splits to the theme song of *Salem Prairie*, Kellyjean's series on Netflix—I still had questions.

"'All She Wants to Do Is Dance' is based on a book?" I shouted at Will. I had to shout because the crowd had burst into a standing ovation. I was standing along with them, clapping loudly enough to hurt my hands. The girls deserved it for their grand finale alone.

"*The Great Gatsby*," Will shouted back, looking as proud of his little sister's ingenuity as he was her athletic prowess. "And *The Ugly American*. Oblivious rich Americans dancing as the world around them burns—sound familiar?"

"Oh." I couldn't believe I'd listened to this song so many times and not realized the Molotov cocktails referenced in it were actual bombs and not drinks. "Of course."

"Totally putting this on the 'gram," Jasmine was yelling to no one in particular. "Otherwise no one's going to believe me back home when I tell them about it."

I knew how she felt. Not that I hadn't loved every minute of it. I wasn't the only one, either.

"Oh my God, Jo!" Frannie and Saul appeared at my side. "Can you believe this?" Tears of laughter glistened in the corners of Frannie's eyes. "I swear they were better than the Knicks City Dancers!"

"They were," I agreed. I'd never been to a Knicks game, because sports—aside from cooking competitions on the Food Network—were not my thing. But I knew Frannie had never missed one, so if she thought this, it had to be true.

"This is some book festival." Saul had a bright orange streak of buffalo shrimp sauce on his black shirt, in sharp contrast with his image as the king of horror fiction. "Way better than Novel Con. The meals and entertainment are much higher class, and you don't have to fight for taxis afterward to get back to your hotel. The lines for booze are shorter, too."

I had to stifle a laugh at this. A quick glance up at Will showed me that he was holding back a chuckle as well. His gaze, bright with suppressed mirth, met mine.

And suddenly that same odd sensation I'd felt before—first when I'd stepped off the plane into the hot, humid air and onto the rickety steps leading to the Little Bridge Island tarmac, and then when I'd kissed Will—swept over me again. A certainty that this was where I belonged . . . a conviction that I was home.

Which was completely absurd.

What was happening to me? I wondered as I tore my gaze from Will's and searched once again for Bernadette in the crowd. Was I drunk again? No, that wasn't possible. I'd only had one glass of champagne.

Food poisoning, then. My God, Frannie had been right all along. Why had we eaten the locally sourced seafood?

"Are you all right?" Will asked curiously.

I realized the horror I'd been feeling at my shocking self-revelation—that I liked this island, and even more startling, was beginning to like Will—must have been showing on my face.

"Oh, fine," I said, waving away his concern. "I'm fine. Just—" I looked around quickly for an excuse and found it on the table. "I'm so *thirsty*." I snatched up my empty champagne glass.

"I think I can rectify that for you." Smiling, he signaled once again to one of the servers.

Phew. That had been a narrow escape. Now so long as the girls at our table kept their mouths shut about how Will and I were trending as a couple on social media, I might actually make it through the rest of the evening and back to the hotel without—

"What'd you think?" Chloe came bounding over, her pompoms clutched tightly under her chin, her expression anxious.

"You were great!" Will threw an arm around her shoulders and kissed the top of her ponytailed head.

"You really were," I said, meaning it, as Frannie and Saul and Lauren and her friends all added their kudos as well.

"I don't know how you remembered all that choreography," Lauren said.

"Oh." Chloe beamed. "We practiced tons. I'm glad you liked it."

"I'm going to incorporate some of your moves into Felicity Feline's next cheer routine," I said, only half joking.

But Chloe took me seriously, her mouth falling open. "Oh, Ms. Wright, do you mean that? That—that would be amazing! That would be the biggest compliment ever!"

I glanced uncertainly at Will, only to see that he'd covered his mouth with a hand to hide his grin.

"Well, yes, I mean it," I said to Chloe. "If I have your permission to steal your moves. I know people can be a little sensitive about—"

"Oh, you *totally* have our permission! We'd be honored! Which moves do you mean? I can make a list for you, if you want. I think it would be great if in your next book, Felicity is working on a back handspring—"

"Wow, folks, wasn't that great?"

We were all startled by a man's voice coming from the speakers on either side of the stage. I looked over to see Garrett standing in the stage lights, his hair looking wind-tossed and a bit sweaty from the island humidity—probably because he was wearing a cape, and the temperature was in the seventies.

"Let's give those girls another round of applause, shall we?" Garrett beamed as everyone in the audience, looking confused, stared at him, then finally let out a polite patter of applause. "That was really great. For those of you who don't recognize me in this amazing ensemble." He did a full turn to show off the pirate outfit and cape. "I'm Garrett Newcombe, bestselling—and award-winning—author of the Dark Magic School series for kids."

A number of children who were in the audience let out appreciative little shrieks and darted forward, eager to push through the crowd so that they could see the author of their favorite new series doing—well, whatever it was Garrett was about to do.

"Thank you," Garrett gushed with what I felt was completely fake modesty as these same children sank to their knees in front of the stage. "Thank you so much. And thank you, too, to the board and staff of the Little Bridge Island Book Festival for hosting such an amazing event tonight. Are you all having as much fun as I am?"

The kids kneeling in front of Garrett exploded into appreciative cheers, and that same sentiment was echoed around us—except by Bernadette, who'd come weaving through the crowd toward us, Kellyjean and Jerome trailing not far behind her.

"What the hell is he doing up there?" Bernadette hissed into my ear as soon as she reached my side.

"I have no idea," I whispered back. "I thought you would know. Is this part of his shtick?"

"How should I know?" she asked, slipping into a chair beside me. "I thought magic was his shtick."

"So if his shtick is magic, why is he dressed in a pirate costume?"

"Oh, hon, that's not a pirate costume." Kellyjean sank into one of the chairs near us and peeled off her shoes. She was wearing her jeweled sandals, and once again they were rubbing her feet the wrong way. "He's dressed as Professor Eurynomos, the hero of his books. Haven't y'all read them? My kids can't get enough of 'em, even though I don't approve of any books that glorify—"

"Shhh!" One of the children sitting closest to us put his fingers to his lips and shushed Kellyjean.

Frannie, her eyebrows raised, looked mockly offended.

"Well! I guess we've been told off. I certainly hope this doesn't take long, though. There's a Knicks game tonight, and I don't want to miss the tip-off."

Grinning, I caught Will's eye. He grinned back. I felt a jolt of white-hot desire shoot through me, and quickly looked away.

Oh, this was not good. This was not good at all.

"Tonight," Garrett was going on, up on the stage, "I'm going to introduce all of you to the mystical art of dematerialization— or, as some of you may be more familiar with, teleportation. But in order for me to do so, I'm going to need a volunteer to assist me."

The hand of each child in the audience shot up. "Me!" every single one of them cried. "Me, me! Oh, please, pick me!"

"Hmmm." Garrett looked out at the dozen or so children practically convulsing in front of him in their eagerness to be chosen. "I think not. I need someone very special to assist me. Someone highly skilled in the psychic sciences. Someone who *believes*. And while all of you children seem delightful, that someone is . . ." Garrett began scanning the audience on the deck, his index finger extended so he could point out the person he sought.

"Oh, no," Kellyjean muttered as that finger swung in our direction. "I'm not havin' anything to do with this. Dark magic is wrong, and he knows good and well I would never—"

"*You*," Garrett cried, his roving finger pointing directly at me.

The Moment by Will Price

"And now, by the power invested in me," said the preacher, "I declare you man and wife. Johnny, you may kiss your bride."

Never in my life had I heard sweeter words. And never in my life had I seen a sweeter sight than the face of my new wife, Melanie, as she turned to me, eyes radiant and shining, ruby lips parted in a smile and ready for our first kiss as a married couple.

At least until a voice rang out from the back of the church:

"She'll be no bride of yours, Johnny!"

I turned just in time to see her husband, alive and well, burst through the chapel doors, a gold-plated pistol in his hand.

When the shot rang out, I knew there was only one thing I could do—only one way I could make things right. I threw myself in front of the bullet he meant for Melanie.

CHAPTER TWENTY-THREE

M e?" I looked around, certain Garrett was pointing at someone else.

But no. The finger he'd jabbed in my direction was now crooked as he motioned for me to approach the stage.

"Yes, *you*." Garrett grinned—a grin that made my blood run cold, despite the warm ocean breeze—because there was no denying it: I was the person he was talking to. "Come on, Jo, don't be shy. Ladies and gentlemen, please give a big round of applause to Ms. Jo Wright, author of the internationally bestselling Kitty Katz, Kitten Sitter series. She's graciously agreed to be my assistant this evening."

"What?" I glanced around, panic swelling inside me. "No, I didn't." I found myself looking desperately up at Will. "I didn't!" Don't ask me why it was so important to me that Will knew I had never agreed to be Garrett's magician's assistant. At that moment, it seemed vital. "I don't even believe in magic," I blathered. "Why would I agree to help with his trick?"

"Don't believe in magic?" Of course Garrett had overheard

me. Now he feigned outrage as he repeated my words to the crowd, who'd begun to murmur among themselves. "Well, we can't have that, now, can we? Kids, what do you say we make a believer out of Ms. Wright?"

"Hocum-pocum," the kids cried. This was apparently something from the books Garrett wrote. "Harry-scary!"

"Oh, for Pete's sake," Kellyjean said, rolling her eyes. "That isn't even an authentic incantation."

Oh, God. This was a nightmare.

It wasn't because I was shy, of course, or even that I didn't believe in magic that I didn't want to get up onstage.

It was because I didn't want to have anything to do with Garrett, or the stupid trick he was performing to promote his brand.

But I could think of no gracious way to get out of the situation, especially when all of the little kids in front of the stage—and some not-so-little kids, too, like Jasmine and Cassidy—were yelling, "Come on, Ms. Wright! Do it!"

"Yes, do it, Ms. Wright," Garrett said, egging them on. "Don't be a party pooper!"

Ugh, those words. Those two little words. How could he possibly have known how much those two little words would get to me? Especially since they'd been flung at me so often, first in high school and then later, through college and even after, when friends (but not my *real* friends, because they had known me better) had nagged me to come out with them to have fun.

But I couldn't, because I'd been too busy working my many side hustles in order to make ends meet, and then later, when I'd needed to meet my deadlines. If that made me a party pooper, so be it.

"Fine," I grumbled, and started for the stage . . . until Will stopped me by laying a hand on my shoulder.

"It's all right," he said. He looked worried, like a host whose dinner party roast chicken was going up in flames. "You really don't have to do this. You don't have to do anything you don't want to do."

"Thank you," I said, smiling at his attempt at chivalry. "But I can handle it."

Then I began making my way toward the stage to the sound of cheers and applause from the audience.

"Ah, there she is, ladies and gentlemen," Garrett said as he offered me a hand to help me up the single step to the stage. "Isn't she lovely? I think she'll make a perfect assistant."

I leaned close to Garrett's face as if I was going to kiss his cheek, but instead, I grabbed a handful of his cape and, pulling hard on it, whispered into his ear, "If you do anything weird, I'm going to take this cape of yours and wrap it around your neck and pull until you're dead. Understand?"

"Ah-ha!" Garrett let out a high-pitched giggle and jerked away from me, startled. "Let's not waste any more time, shall we? The spirit world is crying out for release! And I have just the tools they need."

From deep within a pocket of his pirate pants—or professor pants, I guess—Garrett withdrew a pair of handcuffs. The stage lights winked dramatically on the bright silver metal, causing the kids in the audience to gasp.

I, however, was not as impressed.

"If you think you're putting those on me," I whispered to him, "you have another—"

"I've brought you up here, Ms. Wright," Garrett went on dramatically, speaking to his audience and not to me, "to examine these manacles and assure our audience that they are indeed genuine. I shall then have you secure *my* wrists with them and perform before your very eyes the same daring act that my well-known character Professor Eurynomos will famously perform in *Dark Magic School number eleven*—available everywhere books are sold on January the twenty-second: the feat of dematerialization."

The kids in the audience went wild, screaming and kicking their feet while shouting, "Dematerialization! Dematerialization!"

I had to admit, Garrett's shtick was pretty good. Even the adults in the audience were getting into it. Everyone was smiling and buzzing to one another, especially Saul, probably the toughest critic in the place, since he'd written numerous books featuring the occult (although they were all for adult readers). Over on the dock, people who weren't attending the book festival, and so couldn't get into Cracked, were jostling with one another for a better view.

Even Will, when I stole a glance at him, was grinning, enjoying the spectacle. Garrett may have been a writer, but he had a strong streak of showmanship in him. My dad would have been impressed.

I decided the wisest course of action was to play along so

I didn't look like a "party pooper," even though I still didn't trust—or like—Garrett.

"Okay," I said. "Let me see them."

"The manacles, madam." Garrett slapped the cuffs into my hands. "And the only existing key." He withdrew from the same pocket a tiny key on a long silver chain. "You will hold on to this until I return from the spiritual plane to which I shall travel while attempting to free myself. You and only you, Ms. Wright, shall have the means to free me. If I fail—though I pray to the gods of darkness I shall not—you must use this key to save me."

He dropped the chain holding the key around my neck.

"Fine," I said, playing along. "I accept the honor."

Then I made a great show of inspecting the handcuffs, holding them up to the stage lights and squinting at them while locking the clasps and then unlocking them with the key, much to the squealing delight of the children.

"Well?" Garrett asked me. "Does everything seem to be in order?"

"It does."

They really did appear to be an ordinary pair of handcuffs, not the trick kind my mother gave me when I was little—a pair that broke after approximately five uses—back when I still believed in magic.

I returned the cuffs to him, conscious of the cold metal of the key resting against the skin of my chest. "Regulation handcuffs."

"Thank you, madam. And now, if you will do me the great honor—" He held his arms out to his sides. "Please search my pockets to ensure I have no other key in my possession and am not cheating this fine audience gathered here tonight."

I took a quick step backward. "Uh, no. I'm not searching your pockets." The jerk.

"Ms. Wright." Garrett wore a look of mock dismay. I knew his feelings weren't really hurt. But he was good at pretending they were. "You were doing so well until now. Why won't you reach into my pockets and make sure I don't have a spare key? Surely you aren't frightened of the power of my *magic*, are you?"

Ugh, he was disgusting. I knew he thought he was being funny—a number of people in the audience were laughing, even if the "joke" went straight over the heads of the kids, though they laughed as well, since they could hear some of the adults laughing.

But Garrett's joke wasn't funny to me. It was gross and inappropriate, especially in light of the rumors I'd heard about him.

Of course, they were only rumors, and it was wrong to judge people based on gossip . . . something I probably should have kept in mind where Will Price was concerned.

But there was no way I was playing along with his little game. I was inhaling to tell him so when a deep voice rang out from the crowd.

"I'll do it."

I hardly had time to register who the deep voice belonged to before its owner stepped up onto the stage.

It was Will, of course.

"Uh." The smile disappearing from Garrett's face, he lowered his arms. "No, that's okay. I'll just—"

"Turn your pockets inside out?" Will asked coldly, reaching over to do exactly that. He thrust both hands inside the pockets of Garrett's trousers and wrenched them outward. "There. Look, folks. Nothing to see here. Nothing at all."

Garrett's cheeks were turning pink under the bright glare of the stage lights, but he managed to keep it together, even as I'd begun grinning like a maniac because Will Price had come to my rescue.

Not that I'd *needed* Will to come to my rescue, of course. I had been one hundred percent purr-fectly capable of handling the situation of Garrett Newcombe and his inappropriate suggestion that I put my hands down his pants.

But the idea that Will had *thought* he'd needed to come rushing up onto the stage and protect me from Garrett's disgusting pants proposal?

So sweet!

Until I realized that I wasn't the only person who'd noticed. Both Jasmine and Cassidy had lifted their phones to start filming, and so had a few total strangers in the audience. I had the sense that we were mere seconds away from the incident being submitted to BuzzFeed as more evidence that Will and I were an item.

Worse, I was beginning to think this wouldn't be the worst thing . . . especially as I took Will by the arm and attempted to push him off the stage, and I felt the hardness of his bicep beneath the soft material of his linen jacket.

"Thanks so much, Will," I said. "But if you could just go back to your seat, I can take it from here—"

"Are you sure?" He looked—well, furious was the only word to describe it.

Furious on my account. This was a first. I couldn't remember a man ever being furious on my account, except possibly my dad when he read what Will had said about me in the *Times*.

I was going to have to remember what this felt like so I could slip it into *Kitty Katz #27*.

"I'm sure," I said, steering Will back to his seat. Fortunately he let me. "It's all good."

It wasn't all good, especially with Bernadette winking knowingly at me over the rim of her martini glass. But I just had to get through the next five minutes—or however long it took for Garrett to finish his trick—and then I could return to my seat and continue flirting with Will—I mean, enjoying my evening.

I hurried back up to the stage and found Garrett standing there, his hands stretched out in front of him. "Ms. Wright. If you will."

"Of course." I snapped the cuffs into place—extra tightly, since Garrett wasn't my favorite person at the moment.

He didn't flinch, however.

"And now," he said, raising his chin. "If you will do me the honor of untying my cape and using it as a curtain to cover me while I dematerialize."

I stared at him. "What?"

He rolled his eyes at my ineptness. "Untie my cape and use it as a curtain to cover me while I—what, children?"

"Dematerialize!" roared the kids in the audience.

"Honestly, Ms. Wright," Garrett said, in mock indignation. "It's almost as if you had no knowledge whatsoever of the spirit world."

Realizing this was evidently a well-known part of Garrett's act, I untied the strings that held Garrett's cape secure beneath his chin and then, when the garment fell from his shoulders and into my hands, held the heavy purple velvet to my side, high enough so that the audience couldn't see what he was doing behind it.

"Professor Eurynomos will see all of you soon," Garrett called to his audience as he pressed an emergency release button on the side of the handcuffs and slipped them back into his pocket, "when he returns from the other side of the spirit world!"

"Really?" I whispered to him from behind the cape. "This is your big magic trick? I was expecting something a little more dramatic."

"No, Jo," Garrett said to me with a pitying smile. "That isn't the magic trick. *This* is."

And then, still hidden behind the cape I was holding before him, Garrett walked to the deck railing behind him, swung his legs over it, and dropped into the sea.

CHAPTER TWENTY-FOUR

I'm not going to lie: I screamed.

Then I dropped the cape, pressed my hands to my cheeks, and cried, "Oh my God!"

It's not my fault that this only added to the drama of what most people in the audience thought they had seen: a man disappear before their very eyes. Only those farther down the pier saw what I had—Garrett drop over the deck railing.

And only those closest to the stage heard what I had—the splash as his body hit the water below.

One of those people happened to be Will. As everyone around him applauded Garrett's amusing trick—and my apparently even more amusing reaction to it—Will came sprinting from his chair and headed straight to the deck railing where I was standing, still paralyzed with horror.

"Did he still have the handcuffs on?" Will asked me as he gazed into the water, looking for some sign of Garrett.

"N-n-no." For once I was the one who could barely get my words out. "They were trick cuffs. He put them in his pocket."

Will looked relieved—but only slightly. "Thank God."

Will and I weren't the only ones leaning across the railing to peer down at the water where Garrett had gone in. Farther down the pier, others were doing the same thing, pointing down at the cold waves and calling, *There he is!*

And then, *No, that's just a fish. No, wait, there! No, that's not him, either.*

The drop from the dock to the water wasn't far—less than seven or eight feet—and the water directly beneath the Cracked deck was lit by harbor lamps so that diners could gaze into it while they ate. The water was so clear that I could see all sorts of different fish swimming beneath the waves, and a variety of sea grass, too.

The only problem was that there was no sign of Garrett. And beyond those circles of light cast by the lamps? Only a vast, literal sea of darkness.

"Do you think he got sucked beneath the dock?" I asked Will worriedly.

"The current here is strong, but it flows the other way." Unfortunately, Will pointed toward the darkness. "I'm more concerned about him being carried out toward the Gulf of Mexico."

I swallowed. I wasn't Garrett's biggest fan, but I didn't like the idea of anyone being helplessly carried off by the current into all that black nothingness—especially when dressed only in a pirate costume.

"Oh my God," I said to Will. "I had no idea. I swear to you, I had no idea he was going to do this!"

"I know." Will laid a comforting arm around my shoulders. "How could you? None of us did."

It wasn't until I felt the warmth from his body seeping into me that I realized I was shivering, despite the warm night air. Maybe what Garrett had done was sending me into shock.

"Hey, you two." Bernadette came up onto the stage. "Hate to crash the party, but any word on when Garrett is going to return from the spirit world? Some of us would like to head back to the hotel and hit the hot tub. And Frannie's complaining about missing her Knicks game."

Will instantly dropped his arm from my shoulders.

"No, no idea." I pointed at the water. "Garrett jumped in, and now we can't see him anywhere."

"He *jumped?*" Bernadette looked down into the water. "Yikes. That's a little more hard core than usual."

Will raised his eyebrows at her. "He's done this before?"

"Oh, yeah. Well, not the jumping part, but the dematerializing thing. He usually rematerializes sooner than later, though."

We all looked around. The restaurant staff had apparently decided Garrett's trick was over, because the boss nova music was playing again and the servers had returned, passing out drinks and key lime pie tartlets for dessert. Members of the audience who weren't aware that Garrett had jumped into the water had resumed their party chatter. Jasmine and Cassidy were recording dramatic reaction videos of Garrett's trick while giggling maniacally. There was no sign of Lauren, which was odd. But I saw her mother with the other girls' mothers over by the bar, so I assumed she was around somewhere, too.

Only Garrett's most die-hard fans—the children sitting in front of the stage—remained in their places, patiently waiting the return of Professor Eurynomos. . . .

"I'd say it sounds like he's purposefully pulled another one of his disappearing acts, then," Will said. "Except that the only ladder leading up from that water is about a quarter mile down the dock. Would Garrett have been aware of that?"

"Hmmm." Now Bernadette was beginning to share my worried look. "You'd think he'd have researched that beforehand."

"You would think so." Will's dark eyebrows were lowered as he continued to scan the surface of the sea.

"As far as tricks go," Bernadette said, "I'm not finding anything particularly magical about this one."

"Neither am I," I said. "Do you think we should—I don't know—call someone?"

"Yes." Will slipped a cell phone from his suit pocket. "The coast guard."

CHAPTER TWENTY-FIVE

A half hour later, I was watching as a helicopter flew low along the water's surface a few hundred yards from the pier, sweeping the waves with spotlights. Closer by, coast guard cutters patrolled the harbor as well, the officers on board hoping to spot the missing magician.

Meanwhile, on land, deputies from the sheriff's department had arrived to question everyone who'd witnessed Garrett's "trick" . . . but most especially me, since I'd been closest to him when he'd disappeared.

"Did he fall?" the officer sitting in the chair opposite mine asked. "Or was it more like a dive?"

"Neither," I said. "He swung his legs over the railing and *dropped* into the water."

"So," the deputy said, looking down at the little notebook he was scribbling into. "Deliberate."

"Definitely. He didn't fall. He was trying to disappear."

The deputy looked confused. "Yeah, that's the part I'm not getting."

The name tag on the front pocket of his shirt said *Martinez*.

From the top of the same pocket peeked a cigar with a blue *It's A Boy!* ribbon around it. I'd seen Sheriff Hartwell glee-fully handing them out, as well as showing off photos of his newborn son, when he wasn't busy coordinating the search on the ground for Garrett, "in case his body washed up on shore."

Overhearing this phrase had sent a chill down my spine. The sheriff and his fellow officers seemed pretty certain that Garrett had either fallen by mistake or purposefully jumped to harm himself. Why else would anyone go into the ocean fully clothed at night in January?

"Disappear?" the deputy repeated. "Why would he want to do that? Was he running away from something?"

"No. It was a magic trick. Garrett is a writer." *Was* a writer? No, *is*. Definitely *is*. "He writes about magic, and he does disappearing acts to entertain the kids. The thing is," I said to the deputy, "Garrett is the last person I know who'd ever want to hurt himself."

I couldn't think of a more delicate way of saying that Gar-rett Newcombe was a complete narcissist who thought he was God's gift to women. Case in point, he wouldn't even stop singing to them on the author bus when they asked him to, repeatedly.

"Oh, yeah?" Deputy Martinez looked up from his note-pad. "How long have you known him?"

"Um. Well, not that long." Had it really only been yester-day that I'd met Garrett on the plane? "But I'm still pretty sure he isn't the type who would ever do anything to hurt himself." Others, yes—particularly attractive females. Himself, never. "He just really wanted to put on a good show to promote his books."

"Yeah, his books." Deputy Martinez nodded. "I understand they're about kids who go to wizard school? Wasn't that what those Harry Potter books were about?"

"Yes," I said. "But Garrett's are different. The kids in his books go to evil wizard school."

"Okay. Got it."

I saw Deputy Martinez write *Evil Wizard School* in his notepad.

Oh, God. When he put it that way, the entire thing seemed sillier than ever. This man's job was to save people. Mine was to write stories about talking cats. What was I even doing with my life? I needed to make some changes, and fast.

"See, that's why Garrett was pretending to disappear," I said, trying desperately to make the officer understand. "Because he was acting like one of the wizard professors from his books."

"Right." Deputy Martinez snapped his notepad shut as if the case were closed. "Except that he wasn't pretending, was he? He really did disappear. And I have to be honest with you, Ms. Wright. When people around here go missing in the water at night, we generally don't find them until daybreak. It's simply too dark out there to see them . . . especially when, if what you're saying is true, they disappeared on purpose, and don't want to be found. Here." He handed me a business card. "If you can think of anything else, please let us know."

"But . . ." I stared in disbelief as he rose from his chair. "That's it? You're calling off the search?"

"Have to, ma'am." The deputy tipped his hat. "We only have the one helicopter, and we've got to share it with the hospital. There's a resident who just had a heart attack and needs to be medivacked up to Miami for an emergency bypass. We don't have a cardiac surgeon on staff at the local hospital. We need to concentrate on saving the people who want to be saved. Have a good night."

Then he was gone, leaving me feeling dismayed—unlike the rest of the festivalgoers. Most of them were delighted by the turn the evening had taken, especially the children, who could not have been more excited by the magical disappearance of one of the authors and the subsequent appearance of both a helicopter and multiple boats in the water with flashing lights on them. If anything, these had only made Garrett's trick more spectacular. Dylan, the young boy whose book he had spent so much time signing earlier in the day, seemed to be in ecstasy.

"It's no good looking for Mister Newcombe, you know," he kept telling anyone who'd listen, even as his exhausted-looking parents attempted to convince him to return with them to their hotel. "He's in the spirit plane. He'll rematerialize when he feels like it . . . probably when we all least expect it!"

"I hope that kid's right," I said to Bernadette.

She raised an eyebrow. "You mean about Garrett being in the spirit plane?"

"No. About him showing up when we least expect it."

"Oh, right. Except that when he does, I think he's going to regret it."

She wasn't kidding. The sheriff's deputy wasn't the only one who didn't appear to appreciate Garrett's prank. Will was stomping around with a furious expression on his face, and Frannie kept glancing at her watch, muttering, "If I miss the game because of this, I'm going to kill that little weasel when he finally rematerializes."

"True, but you gotta hand it to the guy," Saul said. "He certainly knows how to work a crowd. I'm thinking maybe my next book should be about a guy like him. You know, a novelist who strikes a bargain with the devil in order to become a bestseller."

Kellyjean shivered. "That'd fall into the horror genre, all right."

"If you do write it," Jerome said, a beer in one hand and one of the sheriff's It's A Boy! cigars in the other, "be sure to make him survive his publicity stunt so that the fellow hosting the event he's crashed can murder him." He nodded toward Will, who was on his cell phone a few yards away, glaring into the darkness beyond the deck railing. He truly did look murderously angry.

"Oh, sure." Saul was sipping on a Baileys he'd snagged from the restaurant's bar. "Everybody'd want to kill him. That'd be part of it. Only they can't, see, because he's got the devil on his side. And—"

I tuned their voices out and focused instead on Will. I couldn't tell who he was talking to on his cell, but he looked about as angry as a human being could possibly look and not actually be pounding his fists against something. I didn't want to interfere—it wasn't my place, and he definitely had enough to worry about—but I felt I should let him know what the sheriff's deputy had said.

So I drifted toward him, idly listening to the chatter of the teenaged girls still sitting at the table we'd shared. Chloe and her friends had long since left for Sharmaine's sleepover, but Jasmine and Cassidy were sticking around, apparently to see how the drama about Garrett played out.

"Look," Jasmine said, her pretty face glowing in the light from her phone screen. "It's number nine now."

"Really?" Cassidy peered down at her phone, then looked disappointed. "Oh, but only in the U.S."

"Right, but that's because there was that earthquake. We can get it to trend higher if we post that shot of you with the helicopter."

"Oooh, good idea."

"What," I asked them curiously, "are you girls talking about?"

Both faces popped up, startled.

"Oh, nothing, Ms. Wright," Jasmine said, grinning. "We're just trying to get our videos of Mr. Newcombe disappearing to trend number one."

"I've never gone viral before," Cassidy confessed. "It's exciting! Although I don't really have anything to promote."

"You do," Jasmine scoffed. "Your OnlyFans."

"Shhhh!" Cassidy, scandalized, glanced around. "My mom might hear you!"

I glanced around as well. "Where's Lauren?"

"Oh, she went back to the hotel. She said she felt inspired to work on her novel. Too bad, because she's missing out on everything." Then Cassidy looked guilty. "I hope you don't mind, Ms. Wright, but because of what happened here tonight, you and Will Price aren't trending in the top ten anymore. You're, like, not even top twenty."

I threw a quick look in Will's direction and saw with relief that he was still on his call and didn't appear to have overheard. He was, however, massaging his brow like a man who felt a massive headache coming on.

"Uh, thanks," I said to the girls. "That's okay. We'll talk some more later, okay?"

"Okay," they said. "Bye—"

But I was already hurrying over to Will, and reached him just as he was slipping his phone into his suit pocket.

"Hey," I said gently, laying a hand on his arm. "Are you all right?"

He lowered his fingers from his face and blinked down at me in surprise, as if he couldn't imagine why I'd be standing beside him, let alone expressing concern for him. "Of course," he said, reaching up to pat my hand. "I'm fine. How are *you*?"

On the word *you*, his fingers gripped mine, sending a wave of warmth through me.

"I'm fine," I said. To my regret, he'd released my hand as quickly as he'd grasped it. "It's you I'm worried about. I'm really sorry about . . . well, all of this. I know it's not how you were hoping the night would go."

He gave me a kind but all too brief smile. "Thanks, but I'd hardly call any of this your fault. In any case, I just got off the phone with Henry. He's bringing the bus around. You should be able to leave for the hotel and forget this nightmare in a few minutes."

"Great."

Except that I didn't want to go back to the hotel. I wanted to stay there with him. I wanted to slip my fingers back into his, kiss those worry lines away from his forehead, and tell him everything was going to be okay.

Except what was I thinking? I didn't know if everything was going to be okay. I couldn't do any of those things. Had I lost my mind?

"Um," I said instead. "That sheriff's deputy I was just talking to said they have to call off the search. It's too dark out, and they need the helicopter to take someone who's had a heart attack up to the hospital in Miami."

"I know." He was staring moodily off into the darkness again. "They told me the same thing. They only have the one helicopter. One of the disadvantages of living in paradise, I suppose. For day-to-day life it's idyllic, but for emergencies it's not very convenient."

I looked down at my pedicured toes. "Right. I got the feeling from their line of questioning that they don't seem to think there really is an emergency here. They seem to think that Garrett—"

"I know." Will's tone was flat. "If Garrett does rematerialize, unharmed, the festival is in a heap of trouble. Apparently, there's a fifty-thousand-dollar fine for filing a false missing persons report."

"*Fifty thousand dollars?*" I looked up sharply, appalled. "That's a large—and very specific—amount."

"That's the amount it costs to launch a search and rescue like the one we saw here tonight." He gestured toward the coast guard vessels that were beginning to pull out of the harbor.

"Well, Garrett can afford to pay it back," I said. "Have you ever looked up his net worth?"

"No." Some of the tension had left Will's face. He even smiled a little. "Is that a thing people do?"

I wanted to say that his sister did it—or at least her friends did—but instead I said only, "Oh, well, I guess some people do. And believe me, Garrett can afford it."

Will's smile vanished. "Yes, but even if he did disappear on purpose, I don't think I—"

"Bus is here." Frannie swept by us, waving her phone. "Just got a text. Let's get a move on, Jo. Already missed the first half of the game, don't want to miss the second."

"The way I'd write it, see," Saul was saying, loudly, as he strolled past, following his wife, "is I'd have the guy—that'd be Garrett—stash some scuba gear beneath the dock so that after he goes in, all he has to do is swim over and grab it."

"Saul, that's been used so many times before," Kellyjean declared. "I've seen that in about a thousand episodes of *Magnum P.I.* alone."

"Wait, now," Jerome said. "Let the man finish."

"Right. You didn't let me finish. This scuba gear has been cursed by *Satan*—"

Scuba.

Scuba.

Of course.

CHAPTER TWENTY-SIX

That's it," I whipped around to say to Will. "Garrett scuba dives. He told me."

Will stared. "I beg your pardon?"

"Friday night on the author bus, when we were talking about going out on your boat, Garrett was bragging about how he's certified to scuba in open water. He offered to teach me, but I said I wasn't interested." My mind was racing. "Can you rent scuba equipment around here?"

"Absolutely," Will said. "It's Florida. You could rent a tiger if you wanted to. But you don't think—"

"I do." I turned and stabbed my index finger into Will's chest to emphasize my words. "I know where Garrett is."

"Jo, are you coming or not?" Frannie's voice shouted shrilly from the darkness of the parking lot where the author bus was waiting. "I'm going to miss the third quarter if you don't hurry up!"

I flattened my hand against Will's chest. I liked the warmth I could feel radiating from beneath the light material of his shirt, and the steady *ba-dum, ba-dum* of his heart. I didn't care what kind of videos Jasmine, behind us, might be recording. "Do you have a car here?" I asked him.

"Of course," he said. "But why?"

"Because it will be faster." I took his hand—the hand I'd been longing all night to hold. It felt solid and right in mine, like it had been made to fit in my fingers. "Come on, let's go."

"But where are we going?" Will looked more amused than upset—especially when I began tugging him toward the parking lot, ducking past the author bus where Frannie was frantically yelling at Kellyjean to hurry up, since she'd had to run back into the restaurant to get her wrap. Kellyjean had never, in all the time I'd known her, remembered to bring all her belongings when we'd left a place.

"Frannie, I'm going with Will," I called to her. "Let Bernadette know, will you?"

Frannie waved at me impatiently. She was too concerned about missing any more of her game to be curious about what I might be doing sneaking off in Will Price's car.

And what a car it was.

"*This* is what you drive?" I was so shocked I dropped Will's hand.

"Yes." In the glow of the parking lamps, I could see Will reaching into his pocket for his keys, a bewildered expression on his face. "Why, what's wrong with it?"

"Nothing's *wrong* with it," I said. "It's just not what I'd expected a guy like you to drive."

"What do you mean, a guy like me?" Will opened the passenger door of the bright red Tesla. "What did you expect?"

"Something more—well, gas-guzzling, to tell you the

truth. A Range Rover, maybe. Or a Porsche. Possibly a Ferrari."

"Ouch." He winced. "You really do have a low opinion of me, don't you? Do you think I'm actually that insecure that I'd need an expensive, gas-guzzling sports car to prove my masculinity?"

"Yes," I said cheerfully as I climbed inside the Tesla, noticing that, unlike his house, it was filthy. The floor pads were covered in sand. Something rolled under one of my feet. I reached down to lift it and found a grimy tennis ball. "Do you have a *dog?*"

"Chloe does." He'd swung into the driver's seat. "I promised her one after we moved. I felt like it was the least I could do."

"Of course you did." I dropped the slimy ball over my shoulder, into the back seat. "Let me guess: a Rottweiler."

He shook his head. "You really do hate me, don't you? Susie is a springer spaniel, and she's lovely."

"Susie?" I burst into incredulous laughter. "Your sister named her dog *Susie?*"

"Yes, my sister named her dog after your character, Susie Spaniel." His dark eyes twinkled at me. "You see? I really have read your books. I know all the characters. Kitty, her parents, her best friend Felicity, Susie Spaniel, Rex, Raul—"

I stopped laughing abruptly. Raul? He knew about Raul? This was getting uncomfortable. "I'm sorry. I just . . . that really is very sweet." Our gazes met, and I suddenly became aware of how very quiet it was in the parking lot—and how very alone we were. He was sitting so close that I could feel the heat coming off his body . . . that hard, lean body I'd already seen half naked earlier in the day. All I had to do was lean forward a little and put my hands on that—

These were completely unsuitable thoughts to be having while a man was missing.

"I should probably tell you where we're going, shouldn't I?" I said, in a voice that sounded much too high-pitched.

"That would be helpful," he said. "Yes."

"The Lazy Parrot Inn, please."

He'd started to turn on the ignition, but now he switched it off and twisted in his seat to stare at me in disbelief. "Your hotel? You think Garrett is back at *your hotel*?"

"Yes, I do."

"Why on earth would he go back there?"

"Because where else is he going to go? It's high season here. Every other hotel room is booked. Unless he planned this thing months in advance—which I highly doubt—he doesn't have anywhere else to hide."

"But the man would have to be an idiot to think that no one would look there."

"Well, no one has," I pointed out. "Until now."

Will frowned. "It's not possible. Only a fool—"

"May I point out that Garrett was serenading your teenage sister on the ukulele this afternoon, right in front of you? He *is* a fool."

"I don't believe it," he said. "But to prove you wrong, I'm willing to look."

"Oh, sorry," I said in my most sarcastic tone. "Is spending time alone with me such a burden?"

He grinned. "No. I enjoy your company—however repugnant you seem to find mine."

"You've been growing on me slightly," I admitted grudgingly. If only he knew the truth—like the fact that I was sitting there thinking about him naked.

He looked delighted. "Have I? What did it? It was my immense knowledge of feminist characters in children's fiction, wasn't it?"

I choked. "God, no."

"What, then? It was the boat, wasn't it? Most women find a man with a really big . . . boat irresistible."

"Don't be disgusting." Please, be disgusting. Be disgusting all over my body.

What was going on, anyway? Will Price wasn't the flirting type.

Although, to be honest, neither was I. Or at least I hadn't been for a really long time. Was this happening simply because I was alone in a car with an attractive man (whom I'd admittedly hated until a little while ago), or because the evening had been so stressful, it was nice to release a little tension? Or was there something else going on? If it turned out to be the stupid green flash—or worse, Kellyjean's essential oil—I was not going to be happy.

"What kind of car do *you* drive, anyway?" Will asked.

"What? Me? None. I'm a New Yorker. I don't own a car. I don't even have a license."

"What about your father?"

"My *father*? What about my father?"

"What does he drive?"

"Nothing."

Will raised his eyebrows. "So how is your father going to get around when he moves here?"

"My dad's not moving here. I'm looking at places for him farther north, in the Orlando area." I risked a glance at him, though it meant picturing him naked again. "Where's all this concern for my dad coming from?"

"Because you don't seem to have really thought through how to take care of yours, who seems like a good one. At least if he moved here, he could walk nearly everywhere he wanted to go. This is a small island. Your dad wouldn't have to drive anywhere."

While a lot of unexpected things had happened since my arrival in Little Bridge—having a heart-to-heart with (and then kissing) Will Price on his yacht; watching Garrett Newcombe disappear himself into the Gulf of Mexico—discussing my dad's future living plans with Will had to be one of the weirdest.

"Um," I said, as we pulled up in front of the hotel, "I appreciate your concern. But I suspect the real estate prices here in Little Bridge might be a little out of my dad's"—meaning *my*—"price range anyway."

"You don't have to buy," Will said. "Renting first is always a good way to tell if you like an area. Then you can buy later, once you know your way around the local real estate."

If someone had told me a week ago I'd be spending any amount of time with Will Price discussing Florida real estate, I think my head would have exploded. Now it simply seemed . . . normal.

Will had slid the car into the space in front of the hotel marked *Lazy Parrot Inn Guest Drop-Off/Pickup Only.* Now he got out, walked over to open my door, and said, "After you."

"Uh, thanks. And thanks for the real estate tip. I'll keep that in mind."

Maybe people with no parents really liked discussing other people's parental problems, I thought, as I watched Will go up to the young guy who was managing the hotel desk, lean an elbow against it, and say, "Hello. We were wondering if we could have the room number of one of your—"

Whoa. I darted forward and snatched Will by the arm.

"Nope," I said to the guy behind the desk. "Nope, no, we weren't. We're fine. Have a good night."

Both Will and the front desk guy looked startled.

"Very well, miss," the front desk guy said. "Have a nice night, yourself."

As I hustled Will out of the lobby and through the living and dining rooms, out into the courtyard, he whispered, "What are you doing?"

"What are *you* doing? You can't just go up and ask the guy at the front desk for Garrett's room number. He might tip him off that we're on our way! We've got to be *subtle* about this."

Will looked taken aback. "But then how else are we going to get his room number?"

"I already know his room number," I said. I had my arm wrapped around his as I hustled him around the edge of the pool. "I checked into this place at the same time he did.

Don't you remember? I was standing there in the airport yesterday morning holding a sign with both of your names on it. I know you saw me. You looked right at me and dropped your bag in fright."

Will froze, nearly catapulting me into the pool, because while he'd stopped walking, I'd kept on going, and my arm was still hooked through his.

Not anymore, however. Now we stood in the middle of the courtyard, which was empty of guests as well as hotel employees, and totally silent except for the gurgle of the hot tub and the musical chirps of crickets and frogs.

"I wasn't *frightened* to see you," Will insisted. "I was simply a little surprised."

"Well, I don't know why. You're on the festival board. You knew I was coming."

"Yes, but I didn't know what time your flight got in. And I didn't know you'd done that to your hair."

My hand went reflexively to my head. "I thought you said you liked my hair this way."

"I did. I do." The only light in the courtyard was from the lamps outside the doors to everyone's rooms, and of course the pool lights, which gave everything a blue, out-of-this-world glow. Still, I could see that Will looked upset—upset enough that he'd stuffed his hands deep into the pockets of his trousers, as if he were trying to stuff down something else . . . his emotions, maybe. "It was just a shock. You looked so different from when I'd last seen you . . . not in a bad way, just different. I'd heard from a few people that you'd been upset about what I said in the *Times*"—people? What people?

It could only have been Rosie, who'd probably run into his agent in Aruba or wherever it was all agents hung out when they weren't in New York, making deals. I was going to kill her—"and I was worried—"

"About what? That I'd dyed my hair black because of *you?*"

Actually, I had, although not directly. Midnight Black matched the way I'd been feeling for months about my career, my love life, and most of all, Will Price.

"No! No, not at all." At my derisive eye roll, he said, "Well, all right, maybe. I knew I had to apologize, and I wanted to do it right. I'd been rehearsing what I was going to say when I saw you. I didn't expect our first meeting to be in the Little Bridge Island Airport, though, so I'll admit, I ran. It was cowardly, but you looked"—he swallowed—"angry."

I tried to suppress a grin, remembering how I'd been about to spit on the whiteboard and erase his name from it. Then something he'd said hit me. "Wait a minute. You *rehearsed* what to say when you saw me? On the beach the night of the meet-and-greet—you *practiced* that?"

He winced. "I had a speech written out, exactly what I was going to say when I saw you. Only then you brought up Chloe—"

Now I could no longer suppress a grin. "And the fact that she said I'm her favorite writer?"

"That wasn't what I thought you were going to say she told you. I thought you were going to say she'd told you—"

"—how you hadn't noticed she had dyslexia her whole life. I know."

He winced. "Oh."

"I didn't put it together until today, when you told me on the boat. But I get it now."

"I told you. I've just never been very good with words. Not spoken words. I've always been better at writing. The things I want to say—somehow, they just never seem to come out right unless I'm typing them. Then it feels like I get everything right."

"Well, that's a matter of opinion." When he only stared at me in confusion, I added, "You can't possibly consider having two people fall in love only to have one of them get shot *at their own wedding* 'getting everything right.'"

One corner of his mouth turned up. "You really are reading my book, aren't you?"

"Of course I'm reading it. But I can't say I'm finding it very cathartic, or whatever I'm supposed to be feeling. What kind of twist is that supposed to be? How can Melanie's husband not be dead? Johnny saw his body. He was very, very dead. But now somehow he's risen from the dead and shot Johnny *at his own wedding?*"

Out from those pockets came his hands, big and stretched wide open, as entreating as his dark eyes. "I can't believe you're actually reading it."

"I still have about thirty pages to go. But I don't understand what's going to happen in the next thirty pages of a book where the first-person narrator has been shot dead."

"You do know what, Jo." One of those large hands reached out to clasp me by the wrist. "The emotional journey all protagonists take in every book: from being someone flawed, who's made mistakes—maybe serious mistakes—to being someone slightly less flawed." His other hand reached out to clasp me by my other wrist. "Someone who's learned from their mistakes and only wants forgiveness, and has maybe done one or two things to earn it . . . not only from the reader, but from their potential love interest, as well. Does that make sense to you?"

I blinked at him. I had to blink, because my eyes had suddenly filled with tears. I couldn't believe it, but Will Price—whose soppy books I'd been making fun of for years—had finally managed to make me cry.

"You're not talking about Johnny, are you?"

"Actually, I am," he said, as he pulled me toward him. "But also . . . maybe not. Because maybe I'm Johnny."

And then—don't ask me how—Will was kissing me again. Not just kissing me, but saying my name over and over—"*Jo, Jo, Jo*"—like one of Kellyjean's incantations.

But I didn't mind, because the sound of my name on his lips was an elixir, as intoxicating as the smell of the night-blooming jasmine hanging heavily in the air. I was kissing him back, my whole body feeling as if it were on fire. I was standing on tiptoe, my hands around his neck now that he'd released them to wrap his arms around my waist, pulling me so close that I could feel enough of him through the thin material of the suit he was wearing to be pretty sure—but not one hundred percent yet—that he was wearing boxers and not briefs. This was something I knew I was going to have to get to the bottom of, and quickly, when something occurred to me, and I tore my mouth from his.

"Wait a minute," I said, looking up into his dark eyes, the

lids half lowered with desire. "If you're Johnny, does that mean I'm Melanie?"

"Yes," he murmured, his lips traveling down my throat.

"But Melanie is a total idiot."

"She isn't." Now his mouth was burning hotly against the bare skin of my chest. "To quote *Kirkus*, she's the 'epitome of femininity, at once beautiful and strong' . . . like you."

It was hard to think properly with so much hard muscle pressing against me, but I managed to say, "I'm pretty sure the epitome of femininity isn't—"

But I never got to finish, because his lips returned to mine, effectively wiping all rational thought from my brain.

At least until the sound of a door being opened somewhere nearby caused me to pull my mouth from his and look past his shoulder. Then I saw someone I never expected in a million years come strolling into the courtyard.

"Lauren!"

CHAPTER TWENTY-SEVEN

Lauren, still dressed in her sequined top and miniskirt from the party, froze, her eyes looking ridiculously large behind her horn-rimmed glasses. She had a pizza box in one hand and an empty champagne bottle in the other.

Will and I had leaped away from each other at the sight of her, but she was the one who seemed the most surprised.

"Oh, hi, Ms. Wright," she cried. "And Mr. Price! How are you?"

"Um." I stepped quickly in front of Will so Lauren wouldn't see the bulge our kissing had created in the front of his trousers, which was truly impressive and which I had every intention of exploring at a later time. "We're fine. How are you?"

"Oh, I'm fine. Great, actually! Would you happen to know where the recycling is?" She waved the bottle and pizza box in the air.

With my brain not quite functioning properly yet due to the fact that my body was still tingling all over from Will's kiss, I pointed limply toward the tiki bar. "Over there."

"Oh, thanks!" Lauren trotted to the recycling bin. She was wearing platform heels on which she appeared to be having trouble balancing. She looked a bit like a toddler wearing her mother's high heels. It wasn't until I saw her go a few more steps that I realized it was because she was drunk.

I glanced at the open doorway through which Lauren had appeared. It was on the first floor.

A male figure filled it, peering out into the courtyard. Because his back was to the light inside the room, it was difficult to see who he was.

Difficult, but not impossible.

Before I could even figure out what was happening, Will was racing across the courtyard.

"Garrett," he said. "Get out here."

I saw the figure in the doorway jump—Will's voice, coming from the darkness, must have sounded to him like a gunshot—and try to close the door.

But Will was too quick for him. He reached room 102 in a flash, and thrust his foot inside the door just as Garrett was closing it. I have no idea what the soles of Will's shoes were made of, but it must have been sturdy stuff, because it kept Garrett from shutting the door on us.

"Don't even try it, Newcombe," Will growled as he pressed his shoulder against the door. "Did you know the entire Little Bridge Coast Guard was out there searching for you? There are probably still little kids sitting on that dock, waiting for you to rematerialize. And you're tucked up safe back here in your hotel room with a girl? Get out here and face me like a man!"

"I—I—I'm not feeling too well," I heard Garrett cry. "I think I caught a chill. I'll see you tomorrow at the event—"

"No chance." Will was shoving against the door as hard as Garrett, inside his room, was pressing against it to keep him out. "I'm going to take that sodding cape of yours and wring your neck with it."

"Mr. Price?" Lauren came tripping over from the recycling bin just as I, too, reached room 102. She looked curious, but also a little scared. "Is everything okay? What's going on?"

I had other things on my mind besides the fact that Garrett had been found alive and—for now, anyway—well.

"Have you been in there with Garrett all night?" I asked Lauren.

"Well, not *all* night." Lauren wobbled a little on her platform heels. "He and I caught a rideshare over from the marina. He's been helping me with my manuscript."

Of all the things I'd expected her to say, this was not one of them. *"Your manuscript?"*

"Yes." Lauren's eyes lit up behind the lenses of her glasses. "It's a modern retelling of *The Great Gatsby*, only with a female bisexual Gatsby, and set during the heady cocaine era of the 1980s. Mr. Newcombe thinks he can get his agent to represent me!"

I blinked, only this time, it wasn't because I felt like crying. Well, actually I did, but for different reasons than before. "I'll bet he does," I said, sending a baleful look in Garrett's direction. He'd given up trying to close his door on Will and finally come out of his room—but only when

Will, having also heard Lauren mention her manuscript, lowered his fists.

"It's not what you think." Garrett was wearing his hotel bathrobe over a pair of swim trunks and the bright yellow complimentary Little Bridge Island Book Festival T-shirt we'd all been given in our swag bags. He had both his hands up in a defensive gesture, as if he were afraid that Will might still jump him—a valid concern. "I'm just helping her with her book."

"Her *book?*" I don't think Will was capable of speech, he was still so angry, so I had to do all the talking.

"Of course he was just helping me with my book." Lauren seemed more bewildered than ever. "What else would we have been doing?"

"And the champagne? Lauren's underage, you know."

Garrett flung a startled look in Lauren's direction, but she parried quickly with, "No, I'm not. I keep telling you, I'm nineteen! And the legal drinking age in Manitoba, where I come from, is eighteen."

"Yes, well, here it's twenty-one." I narrowed my eyes at Garrett. "Something Mr. Newcombe, who is twice your age, knows perfectly well."

"I'm not *twice* her age," Garrett began to protest, but he shut up pretty quickly when he noticed Will's expression, which was as dark as a thundercloud. "Well, okay. *Almost* twice her age. But I wasn't going to try anything, I swear! You see, I consider myself something of a mentor—"

"I think what we need here is a little less explaining and

a little more apologizing," Will said. He was leaning against the doorframe to room 102, looking as threatening as a panther about to pounce. "Come on, get to it, Newcombe. You owe me fifty grand for that search, and you're going to bloody well pay up. Get your checkbook out."

Garrett let out a bark of nervous laughter. "What? You can't be serious."

"Would you prefer I call the sheriff's department?" Will reached into his trouser pocket for his cell phone. "I'm sure they'd be very interested to know where you are . . . and who you're here with."

"Wait." Garrett held up both his hands. "Wait just a minute here. I researched this. It's not illegal to fake your own death. It's not illegal anywhere in the United States."

"That may very well be true, but it *is* illegal to misuse emergency services."

"*I'm* not the one who called them," Garrett pointed out. "You did that. *You* people were the ones who thought I died. I was very clear with all of you before I jumped that I was going to be back. I said I would see all of you soon, when I returned from the spirit world, didn't I, Lauren?"

Lauren was looking less and less enthusiastic about the situation with each passing minute. "I mean . . . I guess you did say that, Mr. Newcombe. But I could also see how people might have been afraid that something bad had happened to—"

"Jo." Seeing that Lauren was going to be of little help to him in this situation, Garrett appealed to me. "You were standing right next to me. I said I'd be back, didn't I?"

"You did," I said. "What you didn't say was when, and also that you had scuba gear stashed under the dock and that you were going to swim to it, then use it to get over to the next dock and take an Uber back to your hotel with one of our teenage guests."

Garrett chewed on his lower lip. "I couldn't tell you all that, Jo. A good magician never reveals his tricks."

"I hate to be the one to break it to you, Newcombe," Will said. "But you're not a good magician."

"Oooh." I couldn't help but glance admiringly at Will. "Good line."

He didn't smile. He was still angry with Garrett, and in no mood to joke. "Feel free to use it sometime."

"I will. Maybe in *Kitty Katz number twenty-seven*, after Rex Canine and Kitty Katz break up, Rex will take up magic."

"Rex and Kitty are going to break up in your next book?" Lauren looked shocked. "But why? They're made for each other!"

"Well, the truth is, Lauren, characters grow and change, just like people." The warmth in the look Will shot me after I said this made my knees weak.

Garrett was appearing more at ease now that the conversation had shifted away from him. "That's true," he said. "So very true. Characters—and people—learn their lessons, and vow to do better next time. So I take it we're all in agreement: everything's good here? No need for anyone to call the police or write any checks?"

He made the mistake of laughing and raising a hand as if

to give Will a high five—then froze as the latter scissored a look in his direction that was as cold as the look he'd sent me had been warm.

"I think we're all in agreement," Will said acidly, "that you can be trusted to phone the sheriff's department yourself and let them know that you're safe, then show up tomorrow morning for the farewell brunch at the library to make sure everyone who saw your disappearing act from tonight knows the same thing."

Garrett lowered his hand. "Uh, sure. Yeah, I can do that. I'll go inside and make that call right now. And I'll see all of you in the morning."

I wanted to believe him. It seemed incredibly unlikely that he would lie about something so serious.

But then again, it was Garrett.

Which was why I slipped my hand through the crook of Lauren's elbow and said, "Great. Then Will and I will give Lauren a lift back to her hotel. Right, Will?"

Will didn't skip a beat. He slipped his phone back into his pocket and nodded. "Certainly."

Lauren was a little mystified by the turn of events, however. "Wait. What are we doing?"

"What hotel are you staying in, Lauren?" I asked as I steered her back toward the hallway leading to the lobby. "Will's car is parked right outside."

"Oh. We're staying at the Marriott Beachside." Lauren kept glancing back toward Garrett. "Mr. Newcombe isn't in any trouble, is he?"

"Not at all." Garrett was in a heap of trouble, as far as I was concerned. But I wasn't going to worry about that now. "Tell me more about your book. What's the title?"

"Oh! Well, I was going to call it *Gatsby's Girl*, but I looked that up on Goodreads and it's already taken. So I decided to go with *Gatsby!* with an exclamation mark—you know, like the musical *Oklahoma!*"

Lauren chattered on, seemingly completely unaware of the danger from which Will and I had just saved her. Or possibly not. Who knew? Maybe the rumors about Garrett were untrue, and he wouldn't have tried anything.

Except that, judging by what I'd seen with my own eyes, that seemed highly unlikely. He was a bestselling author in a position of power. She was unpublished, half his age, and more than a little tipsy. Really, Garrett was getting off easy. Judging from the expression I'd seen on Will's face as he'd been pushing on that door, the evening might easily have gone another way entirely.

In any case, Lauren was prattling away about the characters in *Gatsby!* when, as we stepped outside the Lazy Parrot, the author bus finally arrived.

"Jo! Will!" Kellyjean was the first person off the bus, most likely because she'd been the last person to climb on board, thanks to her missing wrap. She'd apparently found it, because a shimmery gold shawl was loosely tossed around her shoulders. "There you are! I was wondering where you two had disappeared to."

"Excuse me." Frannie pushed past her, anxious to get inside and catch the last few minutes of her ball game. "Hi, Jo, hi, Will. Excuse me, but I have to go. Bye."

"Bye." I watched as Frannie disappeared inside the hotel. "Um, so, yeah." I turned toward Saul, who was the next to disembark from the bus. "We found Garrett. He's fine. He was in his room here at the hotel the whole time."

"Oh, hey! That's great." Saul looked over his shoulder at Jerome, who was climbing down from the bus behind him. "Hey, Jarvis. Newcombe was in his room the whole time. Pay up."

Jerome let out a colorful expletive and reached into his pocket. "I fell right into that one," he said as he ruefully peeled a twenty from the wad of bills in his wallet and handed it to Saul.

"So how'd he do it?" Bernadette was the last author off the bus. She was carrying a to-go cup of what looked like champagne. "Did he have someone waiting under the dock with a boat?"

I shook my head. "Scuba. Saul was right."

"Darn it!" Saul looked angry. "I'm hardly ever right about anything, and the one time I am, Frannie isn't around to hear about it. Well, anyway." He held up the twenty-dollar bill he'd just won. "Who's up for a drink by the pool? I'm buying!"

"Oh, uh, I'd love to," I said. "But we're going to drive Lauren back to her hotel. Rain check?"

Saul wasn't the only one who gave me an odd look. Bernadette was smirking at me, too, over the rim of her to-go cup, as if to say, *Sure, driving the kid back to her hotel.* That's *all you're doing.* Only Jerome acted halfway normal, waving as he walked into the hotel and calling, "Okay! Well, see you later, then."

It was Kellyjean, of course, who had to wiggle two fingers at Will and me and squeal, "Oh, y'all are just *so cute* together! No wonder the entire Internet is calling the two of you literature's new hottest couple."

CHAPTER TWENTY-EIGHT

D o you want to explain to me what that was all about?"
Will asked after I returned to the car from walking Lauren all the way back to her room.

"Oh," I said, as I fastened my seat belt. "I hardly know where to start."

A very sleepy-looking Cassidy—apparently the girls were sharing one room, their mothers another—hadn't looked too appreciative about my waking her by knocking on the door (of course Lauren had lost her key).

"Oh, *there* you are. We were starting to wonder," she said when she saw Lauren. Her eyes—much smaller-looking now that she'd peeled off the faux lashes—bulged a little when she saw me. "Ms. Wright! What are *you* doing here?"

"Just dropping off a package." I gave Lauren a little shove that sent her stumbling through the doorway of her hotel room and into a surprised-looking Cassidy's waiting arms. "See you in the morning, girls."

"Please don't break up Kitty 'n' Rex, Jo," Lauren begged. "They're the OTP!"

"Break up Kitty and Rex?" Cassidy stared at me. "What's she talking about?"

"Nothing," I said. "Good night, girls!"

Down in Will's car, I explained, "There's this rumor going around that last year at Novel Con a male author was hitting on female fans. Some people think it might have been Garrett." Or you, I thought, but didn't add aloud. And that person was me.

But not anymore.

Will's dark eyebrows practically leaped off his face, he raised them so high. "Are you serious? I never heard anything like that. If I had, we never would have invited him here."

"Well, that's the thing about rumors," I said. "Until they're confirmed, how are you supposed to know whether or not they're true? I think after what we just witnessed, though, we can pretty much assume Garrett isn't one of the good guys."

"I suppose." Will squinted through the windshield at a group of hotel guests who were stumbling past us into the Marriot's lobby, tired and happy after a night of carousing. "But that actually wasn't what I was asking about. I was wondering if you could explain what Kellyjean was talking about back there when she said the entire Internet is calling us literature's hottest new couple."

Whiskers! I pulled down the passenger-side sun visor to check my reflection in the mirror, just so I could have time to collect my thoughts. "Oh, that?"

"Yes, that." I didn't dare glance in Will's direction, but I was relieved to hear that there was a note of amusement in his voice. "Any idea what she meant?"

I saw that most of my eyeliner and lipstick had vanished, so I reached into my bag. "Oh, it's nothing. Someone posted those photographs that kid took of us earlier today at the signing, and a few people think we look good together." Try tens of thousands of people. Or more.

Will watched as I fiddled with my makeup. "That's it?"

"Of course that's it." Done fixing my face, I risked a glance at him. "Why, what did you think? You think *I* posted it?"

"No." He looked taken aback. "Why would I think that?"

"I don't know. You seem kind of accusatory."

"I'm not being accusatory. I just think if my name is being bandied about with yours, I have a right to know."

"Well, *my* name is being bandied about with *yours*, but I'm not getting all hot under the collar about it."

"You *seem* bloody hot under the collar about it," he said.

"I'm not," I said, slamming the sun visor back into place. "I'm just hungry. I barely got anything to eat at that thing tonight, what with Garrett pulling that stunt of his, and the fact that all they served was shellfish. Why did you choose a restaurant that only serves shellfish? Shellfish is all well and good, but it hardly sticks to your ribs like a good plate of pasta."

Will looked annoyed. "Do you want pasta right now? Is that what you're telling me?"

"Yes. Yes, I do want pasta right now."

"Well, I'm sorry to disappoint you, but this is a small island in the Florida Keys, not New York City. It's after ten o'clock at night, and there isn't any place that's still open that serves pasta. The only place you're going to get it is at my house."

"Fine," I said, folding my arms across my chest and leaning back against the cloudlike seat. "Take me to your house, then."

"My house?" The corners of Will's mouth twitched, though he was trying his best, I could tell, to continue to look annoyed. "Do you want me to make pasta for you at my house?"

"Yes," I said. "I do."

Which was how we ended up at his house—though we didn't eat pasta.

Oh, Will put a big pot of water on for it. He said he had a delicious recipe for homemade macaroni and cheese—it was the comfort meal he'd always made for Chloe when she'd been a kid, he said.

He took off his jacket and stood at his amazing kitchen's granite-topped island, shredding cheddar cheese, while I sipped white wine and petted Susie the springer spaniel, listening to the soft, gentle rain that had begun to fall outside. Will had left all the glass doors open, so the cool sea breeze and the smell of the rain mingled with the scent of the sizzling roux.

"The trick," Will was saying, looking happier and more relaxed than I'd ever seen him, "is to add pepper, because no one likes a bland macaroni and cheese."

"That's true," I said. Susie was resting her head on my knee. I'd never been much of a dog person, but Chloe's dog seemed gentle and sweet, like her owner. "So can I ask you a question?"

He laid down the chunk of cheese he'd been holding, his gaze wary. "Uh-oh."

I grinned. "Why 'uh-oh'?"

"It's never good when someone asks if they can ask a question."

"You're right about that. What I want to know is, why am I getting a ten-thousand-dollar stipend, and the rest of the authors at the festival are only getting fifteen hundred?"

He turned on the faucet and rinsed his cheesy hands, taking his time before replying. "To be honest, I didn't think you'd come for less."

I nearly choked on my wine. "You've *got* to be kidding me. Ten thousand dollars? I hope you donated the money yourself."

"I did." He'd switched off the faucet, dried his hands, and now walked around the island to stand in front of me. Susie wagged her tail, perhaps smelling cheese and thinking a treat was coming her way. But she was going to be disappointed. All the treats coming from Will were for me. "I told you I'd heard how upset you were with me. And I needed to make sure you'd come so that I could apologize to you properly." He leaned against the counter, trapping me within his arms. "And in person."

I frowned at him, though inside, my heart was racing at his close proximity. He smelled of soap and the rain outside and the cheddar cheese he'd grated. "You know I can't keep that money."

His lips were just inches from mine. "Why not?"

"Because there's a conflict of interest."

"And what is that?"

I set down my wineglass and pulled his face to mine. *"This."*

The Moment by Will Price

"Come on, Johnny," my sister said from her seat on the edge of my bed. "Please. You have to eat."

But I couldn't. Without Melanie, food had no flavor.

"Don't do this to yourself," Zoey pleaded. "I loved Melanie, too, but you've got to let her go. It's over now."

"Never." I knew it wasn't Zoey's fault, but I couldn't help it. "It'll never be over! Melanie was everything to me—everything a guy could want in a girl. And now she's gone, and you expect me to eat? What's the point? What's the point of even being alive?"

I slapped the bowl of mush out of Zoey's hand, sending it flying. I heard the ceramic smash to bits on the floor a few yards away.

But when I turned my head to look at the broken shards—like the broken shards of my life—I saw there was a woman standing in the doorway. She had a veiled hat over her head, and a suitcase in her hand.

Slowly, she lifted the veil to reveal a pair of sparkling blue eyes and ruby-red lips.

"Well, I must say, Johnny." She smiled at me. "You sure do know how to make a lady feel welcome."

"Melanie!"

A moment later, she was in my arms. "Oh, Johnny! Johnny!" she cried, kissing my mouth, my cheeks, my ears, as tears rained down from her eyes. "They told me you were dead. But I knew it wasn't true. I just knew it. It took forever for me to find you, but now that I have, I'll never leave you again—never!"

"You better not," I said.

And then I kissed her. And this time when I held her, I knew it would be forever.

SUNDAY, JANUARY 5

CHAPTER TWENTY-NINE

I opened my eyes and squinted at the morning light filtering into the room. At first I couldn't figure out where I was. This wasn't the morning light that filled my Manhattan apartment. For one thing, I had blackout curtains, and I always remembered to close them before I went to sleep.

And for another, the air smelled different—heavy and wet, like the ocean. Plus, there were unfamiliar sounds, a sort of clanking—which wouldn't have been unusual in Manhattan on garbage day. But farther off, there was a rhythmic whooshing.

What was making the whooshing? And whose satiny-soft gray sheets were these? And whose aggressively masculine digital alarm clock was that on the nightstand that said it was 8:05 in the morning? Who even had a digital alarm clock anymore, when everyone else had cell phones with alarms they could set to tell them to—

I sat straight up in bed, clutching the satiny-soft gray top sheet around me, since I'd realized I was naked. I was naked, sunlight was pouring in through floor-to-ceiling glass windows all around me, and I was in Will Price's bed.

The whooshing sound was ocean waves, washing up against the shore of Will's private island, and the clanking sound, I realized, as soon as I'd pulled on my clothes from the night before and stumbled into his kitchen, was Will, wearing only a pair of boxers, cooking breakfast.

"Oh, hullo," he said cheerfully, when he saw me standing in the doorway. "You didn't have to get up. I was going to bring you breakfast in bed. Coffee?"

I leaned in the doorway, trying to figure out if what I was seeing was real or still some part of a hallucinogenic dream I was having from the night before. Had Kellyjean put something other than essential oils in the diffuser in my room?

Then I realized how tender the skin along my face—and other places—felt from where Will had raked it with his lips. Beard burn.

Oh, no. This was real, all right.

Besides, Chloe's dog, Susie, was panting at Will's feet as he cooked, hoping for a bite of dropped bacon or something. I would never hallucinate a dog. Or sore lips. Or sore other parts. Wonderfully sore. Deliciously sore.

"Do you like your eggs scrambled or fried?" he asked. "I assume you like eggs. You seem to like everything else. There isn't one thing I haven't seen you put in your mouth—"

"Okay!" I sprang from the door and made a beeline for the Jura. "I will take you up on that coffee. Want one?"

"I've had two already. I'm an early riser. You?"

"No. Not at all. Not a morning person."

"That's a shame. And we're so compatible in every other way."

I snorted. "Where do you keep the—"

He caught me around the waist as I was reaching for a coffee cup, pulled me to that strong, broad chest against which I'd cried out so many times the night before in pure joy, and planted a hard, confident kiss on my mouth.

And every bone in my body melted, just as it had last night.

"Hello," he said, grinning as the bacon on the eight-burner Viking range behind him sizzled.

"Hi." I couldn't keep from grinning back. "I think your bacon's burning."

"Let it. I like it crispy."

"Well, I don't. What, exactly, is all this?"

"What's what?"

"This?" I gestured at the breakfast tray he'd been making for me, set with a yellow cloth napkin and a vase full of bougainvillea he'd clearly snipped from the vines out by the pool. I recognized the explosive pink. "Is this all because you still feel guilty about what you said to that reporter about my books?"

"Well," he said. "No. This is because I think you're very good in bed, and I'm hoping that if I keep you well fed, you'll continue to have sex with me."

"Interesting. What about *The Moment*, then?"

He raised an eyebrow. "*The Moment*?"

"Yes." I hopped up onto the kitchen counter. "I found a copy last night when I was on my way to the bathroom—you do seem to have an awful lot of copies of your own books in this house. Have you ever considered donating some of them?—so I finished it."

Now he raised both eyebrows. "And?"

"And I can't believe you finally gave one of your books a happy ending."

He switched off the burner beneath the bacon, then regarded me seriously. "I didn't intend to. I wanted to kill Johnny. He deserved to die."

"Did he? I don't think so. What did he do that was so wrong?"

"He killed the thing that Melanie loved most in all the world."

"No," I said. I realized we weren't actually discussing Melanie and Johnny anymore. "He only thought he did. And he didn't mean to. And he was very sorry for it, and he tried to make it up to her as best he could. Maybe that's why, in the end, you let him live."

"Maybe." Will gave me a piece of bacon. It was hot, but it was delicious.

"And in the end, Melanie forgave Johnny."

"Yes, but only after it was revealed that not only was her husband alive, he was also an abusive brute."

"True. But Johnny was the one who helped her see that. She escaped him all on her own."

"She did." Will began tracing a line with his finger down my collarbone and toward the opening of my jumpsuit, sending delighted shivers down my spine.

"Do you really think my eyes are like twin blue ponds, fathoms deep?"

"Yes, but they're not the parts of you I'm most interested in. Do you remember when you screamed at me in front of everyone I know for not allowing my characters to have happy endings?"

I scoffed. "Of course I remember it. It was yesterday. And I didn't scream at you."

"I don't know what other word to call it. In any case, that's when I began to realize that you were quite unlike any other woman I'd ever met, and that I was, in fact, more than simply physically attracted to you. I'd have felt resentful about it if you hadn't been right—and if you didn't have such a nice arse."

He then illustrated his affection for this part of my body by cupping his hands around it and scooping me up by it.

It took a long time to make—and eat—breakfast, because we kept stopping for kisses—and other things. It was revolting (not the breakfast. Naturally, he was an amazing cook), but the way we couldn't keep our hands off each other. I wanted to throw up at how juvenile we were behaving. Which eventually reminded me:

"When is your sister coming home from her sleepover?" I asked, a few hours later.

"That's an odd thing to be thinking of at this particular moment." We were back in bed after having showered together. We'd both made sure we were squeaky clean on all areas of our bodies. "And why would it be so terrible? Chloe loves you."

"I know. But I mean, I wouldn't want her to walk in on us. That would be awkward."

"Oh, she won't be home for hours," he said, with a casual glance at the aggressively masculine digital clock. "She's got the—" He broke off with a curse and sprang away from me.

"What?" I sat up in alarm. "What is it?"

"The festival." Will began tearing around his bedroom, throwing on clothes—and tossing my own clothes at me. "I forgot. *We've got to get to the book festival!"*

CHAPTER THIRTY

LITTLE BRIDGE BOOK FESTIVAL ITINERARY FOR:
JO WRIGHT

~~~~~~

Sunday, January 5, 10:00 a.m.–12:00 p.m.

- Farewell Brunch and Reading -

With Clive Dean, Jerome Jarvis, Victoria Maynard,
Garrett Newcombe, Jo Wright, and Bernadette Zhang

Moderated by: ~~Molly Hartwell~~ Will Price
Library Auditorium

*M*eeeeee-*OW!*
"What is that *ungodly* noise?" Will asked as we ran up
the library steps.

"My ringtone." I'd only just remembered to turn my phone
back on.

"What sort of ringtone is that? It sounds like a cat being boiled alive."

"I will have you know that that is an official Kitty Katz ringtone made just for members of the Kitty Katz mobile fan club, and only a very select few own it."

Will's tone was dry. "I can see why."

Meeeeee-OW!

"Stop being rude." I put one hand on his broad shoulder to steady myself as I peered down at the screen of my phone and slipped my foot back into my mule, from which it had become loose, at the same time. "Twelve unread texts! Will, I think we're in trouble."

Will was squinting down at his own phone. "Twelve? I've got twenty-two. What could be happening in there?"

When we got inside the lobby, we saw that only a few people were still milling around outside the auditorium, where a brunch of coffee, tea, and "authentic Cuban breakfast foods," like guava pastries and cheese toast, were being served from the library's café.

"Aw," I said. "It's so brave of the library to allow patrons to eat inside their brand-new facility."

"That was a bone of contention during the festival planning," Will said. "Let me tell you—"

"Jo! *There* you are!"

Bernadette came clacking toward me, looking relieved. She was dressed, as usual, in the height of urban chic, this time in pleather leggings, high-heeled booties, and a hip-length cheetah-print shirt. "Why haven't you been answering your phone? I've been trying to reach you for—" Then she saw Will. "*Oh.*"

"Sorry we're late." I wasn't going to get into it with her, especially in front of Will, though I could tell from her ear-to-ear smile that she wanted me to. "Have things started already?"

"Uh, yeah." Bernadette could not seem to stop smiling. "I mean, the author bus never came, so we all had to walk over here from the hotel, but—"

"I'm so sorry about that," Will said. He was blushing as pink as the bougainvillea he'd put in the vase on my breakfast tray. "It's all my fault."

"I'll say it is." Bernadette, still smiling, was giving us both the once-over. "Jo, aren't those the same clothes you were wearing last night?"

Now I was the one blushing. "Shut up, Bernadette."

"No, I mean, you look good, but most of the people in there were at the party last night, so everyone is going to know. Plus, you have beard burn all over your neck."

My hands flew instinctively to my throat. "You can *see* it?" I cried in horror.

Will began to look less embarrassed and more fascinated by our conversation. "What's beard burn?"

"Do you have any moisturizer?" I asked Bernadette.

"I can look in my bag, but what you really need is—"

The doors to the auditorium burst open, releasing a buzz of sound—the room was clearly packed with eager audience members—as well as Frannie, who came hurrying out, dressed all in black and looking impatient, as usual.

"Any sign of them, Bernadette?" she asked. Then her gaze fell on Will and me. Her eyes widened. "Oh! *There* you are."

I felt as mortified as if Frannie had been my own mother. "I'm so sorry, Frannie," I said. "We just lost track of—"

"What did you do to her neck?" she demanded, glaring at Will while she threw a protective arm around me.

"Nothing!" Will looked defensive. "We just kissed! And, er—"

"It's fine." I didn't think Will needed to get into any more detail. "Bernadette has some lotion."

"Oh, here. That's not going to work." Frannie strode forward, undoing the purple scarf she was wearing around her throat. "You can cover it with this. And at least this way it won't look *so* much like you're wearing the exact same outfit as last night." She tied the scarf, scented with her usual perfume—Chanel No. 5—around my neck, giving Will the stink eye the whole time. "Did you have to be quite so inconsiderate?"

"I still don't understand what I did that was so wrong." Will looked bewildered.

Frannie shook her head, disgusted. "The least you could have done was shaved. Or grown a proper beard."

"What's going on in there?" I asked as Frannie gave the scarf a final flourishing touch.

"Well, there's no moderator, since Molly's at home with her baby, and Will was so late." Frannie gave Will one final dirty look. "So Saul took over. Bernadette read from her latest, *Crown of Stars and Mist,* to the delight of everyone—"

"Aw." I smiled at Bernadette. "I'm so sorry I missed it."

Bernadette shrugged. "I know. I was awesome."

"And Saul just read from his latest book, *Hell Hound*," Frannie went on, "to the delight of only his most devoted fans, since he chose to read from the chapter where the hell-hound gnaws off his owner's leg and eats it."

"Can't say I'm sorry to have missed that," Will quipped.

"It's too soon for you to joke, young man." Frannie shot him a narrow-eyed stare. "You're still in my bad graces. Let's see, what else? Oh, yes. Jerome read one of his latest poems, which was highly moving and probably the best thing any of us is going to hear all day, and now Kellyjean is about to read from the newest installment of her Salem Prairie series, which I'm sure will be edifying for all of us, especially the children in the audience, since it will probably feature graphic sex." Frannie looked at Will and then me and then back again. "Wolf sex. Not the kind you two have clearly been having all night."

"All right, Fran," Bernadette said with a laugh, as she took Frannie by the shoulder and began to steer her back toward the auditorium doors. "You've had your fun with them for now. Why don't we leave them alone?"

"Because," Frannie said, "they so deserve it."

The minute their backs were turned, Will reached out to take my hand. "Hey," he said, giving my fingers a squeeze. "I'm sorry about whatever it is I did to you."

I smiled and returned the squeeze. "It's okay. I liked it."

Just as Bernadette was about to open the doors to the auditorium, Will called to her, "Hey. What about Garrett?"

She glanced back at us, looking bemused. "Garrett? Didn't you hear?"

"No." Will's grip on my hand tightened. "What about him?"

"Garrett's not here. He's been banned from the island."

Will dropped my hand. *"What?"*

Frannie turned around, her face alight with joy. No one loved author gossip more than Frannie Coleman. "The sheriff came to the inn at breakfast and charged Garrett with culpable negligence, then permanently banned him from Little Bridge Island! Right now Garrett is on a flight back to New York."

"Yeah, and not only that," Bernadette added, "but Garret has to pay restitution for the search-and-rescue mission for his body—sixty-thousand dollars!"

"Sixty-thousand dollars!" I could hardly believe my ears. I'm not certain Will believed his, either.

But he didn't look too unhappy about the turn of events.

"Well," he said, taking my hand again. "All's well that ends well, I suppose."

"Yes," I said. "For everyone but Garrett."

"Don't worry," Bernadette said. "Saul told everyone in the audience that Garrett was back from the spirit world—only he couldn't make it here this morning, due to a family emergency. Which it's definitely going to be when Garrett gets home, because we found out: Garrett is married."

"He's *what?*" I was flabbergasted.

"Oh, yeah." Bernadette smirked. "Only I would guess probably not for much longer after word of all this gets out."

Then she opened the auditorium doors and, with Frannie, slipped inside.

Will pulled on my hand as I attempted to follow them. "Hey."

I looked up at him questioningly.

"Speaking of flights," he said, "what time is yours?"

"Oh." This was the conversation I'd been hoping to avoid. "Later today. We'd better go in."

"What time later today?"

"I don't know. I hate itineraries. Hadn't we better go in?"

He was grinning. "I know you hate itineraries. You've made that pretty clear by being late to every single event I've organized this entire weekend, including this one."

"Hey, I resent that! You're the one who wanted to—"

"I know, all right? I was just wondering if you wanted to think about possibly changing your flight? Not to spend time with me." He held up his hand in a "stop" gesture. "I swear I'm not the crazy stalker type who's going to ask you to move in with me after one night. I mean to look at houses for your dad. It's high season here, which means there are a lot of places for sale, and it might not be the worst idea for you to take a little time to look around. You're here anyway."

I bit my lip. He wasn't wrong. "I'll think about it," I said.

"Good." He opened the doors to the auditorium, and we went in—quietly, because it was dark, and everyone's attention was focused on Kellyjean, who had taken the stage in another one of her floaty maxi dresses, this one dark blue shot through with gold thread that shimmered under the stage lights.

"Thank you for that lovely introduction, Saul, I mean,

Clive," she was saying, as Will and I hurried to take the only two empty seats left in the house, near the front, in the section reserved for the day's speakers.

Once we were seated and I had a chance to look around, I spied Lauren in the audience with her mother and friends, and, in the aisle, Chloe with her fellow dance team members, still doing duty as ushers. She noticed my glance and waved. I waved back at her.

"Y'all, I know I'm supposed to read something from my newest book today," Kellyjean was going on, up at the podium onstage, "but I was so moved by Jerome's poem, I thought I would do something a little different, and read a poem of my own."

Oh, no. I saw Jerome drop his face into his hands. I didn't blame him. This was not going to be pretty.

Apparently Kellyjean realized what some of us were thinking, since she hurried to add, "I know, I know. I'm a fiction writer and not a poet. There *is* a difference, for those of you who don't know. But I've just been so moved by how magical and warm my stay here on this island has been, I *had* to write about it, and that writing just came out in the form of a poem. Has that ever happened to any of the rest of y'all?"

She looked out over the audience, many members of whom were murmuring in assent. I couldn't help nodding. I wasn't sure about magical, but my stay on Little Bridge had definitely been warm. Hot, even. I pressed my shoulder against Will's, feeling what I told myself was only a companionable burst of dopamine toward him, nothing more. He pressed back against me, grinning.

"Anyway, this is what I came up with," Kellyjean said, unfolding a piece of paper. I recognized it as Lazy Parrot Inn stationery. "Don't be too hard on me, now, when you hear it."

The audience laughed gently. And then Kellyjean began to read:

The Green Flash

There we were, all of us,
The ritual had begun.
Standing there, patiently,
Our eyes upon the sun.
Some of us wished for riches,
Some of us wished for fame,
But I knew my friend had wished for love
When that green flash came.
And who of us can argue?
Who of us can blame?
Those who believed the magic
Of that emerald flame.
I believe in wishes,
I believe in love,
I believe that falling stars
Are signs from God above.
So when I saw that sunset,
As green as green can be,
I wished my friend's wish would come true,
And that wish has come to be.

When she finished reading, Kellyjean looked right at me—
frozen with my shoulder pressed against Will's, and my eyes
filled with tears—and smiled. "I wrote that poem for a friend
of mine," she said. "I'm just so happy that she's found what it
is she was looking for after all this time. Thank y'all so much
for having us here to your pretty little island."

There was a moment of silence as the audience absorbed
what they'd just heard. Then they burst into thunderous applause, many jumping to their feet . . . including Will.

"You know," he said to me enthusiastically, as he clapped,
"that was really quite good. A little amateurish, but quite
a hit with the audience, which is what you want in a book
festival. What do you think?"

I rose to my feet as well, applauding. "I think I'll take your
advice," I said, "and change my flight. Maybe I will stay for a
few days."

He glanced at me in surprise. "Really? To look at houses?"

"To look at houses," I said. "And . . . maybe some other
things."

He smiled at me happily.

And I smiled back.

SIX MONTHS LATER

From #1 internationally bestselling author Jo Wright
comes the most highly anticipated release of the year:

Kitty Katz, Kitten-Sitter #27

SU-PURR STAR!

Kitty Katz has graduated from middle
school and started high school!

Kitty Katz and Felicity Feline have been best friends fur-
ever, and have always dreamed of being Broadway stars. That
dream takes a step closer to coming true when the two of
them are cast in their high school's musical production of

Hello, Doggie!

But as re-purr-sals go on, Kitty isn't sure a life on the stage is
for her, especially as she begins to have feelings for her costar,
Raul Wolf. Once her rival in all things academic and extra-
purr-icular, Raul has always seemed aloof and stuck up—until
Kitty gets to know him better, and realizes that things—
and wolves—aren't always what they seem on the surface.

Could this be the end for Kitty and longtime beau Rex
Canine? And what happens when the star of the show, Susie
Spaniel, develops fleas and can't make opening night?

Looks like it might take a SU-PURR
STAR to step in and save the day!

Purr-raise for *Kitty Katz: Su-purr Star*

"Once again, Kitty saves the day—for all of us." —*USA Today*

"The best furry tail yet from Jo Wright." —*Kirkus Reviews*

"Five stars. Raul Wolf is my new book boyfriend." —Lauren

"One star. Spoiler alert: Rex + Kitty break up. Thanks
for ruining my childhood, Jo Wright!!!!!!" —Cassidy

"Purrfect." —Reese Witherspoon

Look for Kitty Katz, Kitten Sitter #27: Su-purr Star *everywhere
books are sold, coming soon to a store near you!*

To: JoWright@jowrites.com; WillPrice@willprice.com
Fr: Molly.Hartwell@lbilibrary.org
Re: Little Bridge Island Book Festival

Dear Ms. Wright,

It's that time of year! I'm writing in the hope that you will once again join us for Little Bridge Island's annual book festival. You were such a huge hit at last year's event, we couldn't possibly hold the next festival without you!

The 2nd Annual Little Bridge Island Book Festival will begin Friday, January 8, and finish on Sunday, January 10.

We're able to offer you first-class airfare to Little Bridge Island, a luxury suite at the Lazy Parrot Inn, and a $1,500 stipend in exchange for you being a panelist. We'd love for you to do a signing, as well as read from your new book, *Kitty Katz, Kitten Sitter #27: Su-purr Star!* and discuss your upcoming Netflix series, *Kitty Katz: Kitten Sitter*, the reboot.

Please let me know your thoughts. Once again, the festival just wouldn't be the same without you, and I know I'm not the only one who'd miss you if you couldn't attend!

Best,

Molly Hartwell

Children's Librarian, Norman J. Tifton Public Library

Will Price

Little Bridge Island Book Festival Board Chair

To: Molly.Hartwell@lbilibrary.org; WillPrice@willprice.com

Fr: JoWright@jowrites.com

Subject: Little Bridge Book Festival

Dear Molly and Will,

Thank you so much for the kind invitation to next year's book festival. I wouldn't miss it for the world!

Please don't worry about a stipend for me, however. You can donate it back to the program. And I don't need a hotel room, either. I can stay with my father at his new house in Little Bridge.

Thanks again for the invitation! Looking forward to seeing you soon.

Best,

Jo

To: JoWright@jowrites.com
Fr: WillPrice@willprice.com
Subject: Re: Re: Little Bridge Book Festival

Staying at your dad's, are you? We'll see about that!

To: WillPrice@willprice.com
Fr: JoWright@jowrites.com
Subject: Re: Re: Little Bridge Book Festival

ACKNOWLEDGMENTS

Thank you so much for reading this book! I hope you enjoyed it.

The first thing people asked me when they heard I was writing a rom-com about two authors at a book festival was: "Oh, are you going to write about authors you know?"

The answer is no! None of the authors portrayed in this book are based on anyone I know. Although Key West, where I live most of the time, does have an annual literary seminar, the book festival in this novel is not based on the Key West Literary Seminar, and I most certainly do not have a literary nemesis.

I do, however, have many amazing people in my life that I would love to thank for their help and support while I was writing this book. They include my agent, Laura Langlie, and everyone at HarperCollins/William Morrow, especially my editor, Carrie Feron, and assistant editor Asanté Simons.

Special thanks as well to friends and readers Beth Ader, Nancy Bender, Jennifer Brown, Gwen Esbenson, Michele

Jaffee, Rachel Vail, and to my amazing media managers, Janey Lee and Heidi Shon.

Thanks also to the many, many readers I've met at book festivals and signings around the world. Thank you for supporting your favorite authors. We so appreciate you. And please—keep reading!

And last but not least, thank you to my husband, Benjamin, for feeding me not just while I was writing this book, but every day for the past thirty plus years.

About the author

2 Meet Meg Cabot

About the book

3 Author's Note

Insights,
Interviews
& More...

Meet Meg Cabot

Lisa DeTullio Russell

Meg Cabot's many books for both adults and teens have included numerous #1 *New York Times* bestsellers, with over twenty-five million copies sold worldwide. Her Princess Diaries series was made into two hit films by Disney. Meg currently lives in Key West, Florida, with her husband and various cats. ◡

Author's Note

Writing *No Words* was an exciting challenge for me, because it wasn't simply a romantic comedy—it also contained a book within a book. Not only that, but it was set at a book festival, with separate itineraries for each of the main characters, and many of the secondary characters as well.

Because Jo, the main character, had what I'd call a "laissez-faire" attitude about getting to her scheduled events on time. (Unlike me. I'm much more of a "Bernadette" about timeliness when I'm attending an event, but I know lots of authors who are more like Jo. I admire them for being so laid back.)

One way I attempted to keep all of these narrative threads straight was by creating separate documents for them. Here, for example, is Jo's itinerary, even though she never looked at it. I certainly did, so I could keep track of where she was going when, and what she needed to be doing: ▸

Author's Note *(continued)*

LITTLE BRIDGE BOOK FESTIVAL

"Building Bridges Between Authors and Readers"

~~~~~~~~~~~~~~~~~~~~~~~~~~~~~~~~~~~~~

LITTLE BRIDGE BOOK FESTIVAL ITINERARY FOR:
JO WRIGHT

~~~~~~~~~~~~~~~~~~~~~~~~~~~~~~~~~~~~~

Hotel Accommodations: The Lazy Parrot Inn

Unless otherwise noted, all panels, signings
and speaking events are located at:

Norman J. Tifton Public Library
1311 Truman Avenue
Little Bridge Island, FL 33041

(*Indicates events limited to donors, board
members, presenters and their guests only.)

~~~~~~~~~~~~~~~~~~~~~~~~~~~~~~~~~~~~~

Friday, January 3, 6:00 PM–9:00 PM
*Welcome Cocktail Meet-and-Greet and Dinner

~~~~~~~~~~~~~~~~~~~~~~~~~~~~~~~~~~~~~

The board of the Little Bridge Book Festival
welcomes you to Little Bridge in the home of
one of our most prestigious donors.

~~~~~~
Saturday, January 4, 9:10 AM–10:00 AM
Speaking Panel
~~~~~~

"From *Little Women* to *Teenage Assassins in Space*,
How Young Adult Literature Focused on
the Female Point of View Has Developed
and Changed Through the Years"
Jo Wright & Bernadette Zhang in Conversation

(Moderated by Molly Hartwell)

Library Auditorium

~~~~~~
Saturday, January 4, 1:00 PM–2:00 PM
Book Signing
~~~~~~

With Saul Coleman (writing as Clive Dean), Jerome Jarvis,
Kellyjean Murphy (writing as Victoria Maynard),
Garrett Newcombe, Will Price,
Jo Wright, and Bernadette Zhang

Library Parking Lot.
Tents will be provided for your comfort. ▶

Author's Note *(continued)*

~~~~~~~~~~~~~~~~~~~~~~~~~~~~~~~~~~~~

Saturday, January 4, 1:00 PM–3:00 PM
Conch Chowder Luncheon

~~~~~~~~~~~~~~~~~~~~~~~~~~~~~~~~~~~~

Traditional Florida Keys conch chowder
provided for all festival attendees
dockside at The Mermaid Café.

~~~~~~~~~~~~~~~~~~~~~~~~~~~~~~~~~~~~

Saturday, January 4, 2:30 PM–4:30 PM
*Sailing aboard *The Moment*

~~~~~~~~~~~~~~~~~~~~~~~~~~~~~~~~~~~~

Author Will Price invites fellow authors
for a picnic lunch and sail around Little Bridge
Island aboard his 60' catamaran, *The Moment*.

~~~~~~~~~~~~~~~~~~~~~~~~~~~~~~~~~~~~

Saturday, January 4, 8:00 PM–11:00 PM
Building Bridges Dinner

~~~~~~~~~~~~~~~~~~~~~~~~~~~~~~~~~~~~

Please join all festival attendees for a night
of fine dining and drinking by the sea
at Cracked on the Pier.

Sunday, January 5, 10:00AM–12:00PM
Farewell Brunch and Reading

~~~~~~

With Saul Coleman (writing as Clive Dean), Jerome Jarvis,
Kellyjean Murphy (writing as Victoria Maynard),
Garrett Newcombe, Will Price,
Jo Wright, and Bernadette Zhang

(Moderated by Molly Hartwell)

Library Auditorium

Departure

*   *   *

To keep track of the narrative thread in Will's book *The Moment*, which gives Jo some insight into Will's feelings for her, and that he just might be a changed man after his "betrayal" of her, I also wrote enough chapters of that story to have a clear idea of what exactly transpires. Originally, all of these chapters appeared in *No Words.*

But unlike Will and Jo, I do *not* suffer from a lack of words. These chapters were quite lengthy, and I felt they might be distracting readers from what was really important—the love story between Will and Jo! So I cut them down significantly.

But they're all available on the Little Bridge Island series page ▶

Author's Note *(continued)*

on megcabot.com if you find you want more of Johnny and Melanie's story!

Thanks again for reading *No Words*, and remember, if you see a shooting star or the green flash—make a wish! ∾

D iscover great authors, exclusive offers, and more at hc.com.